Rainbird

D0380810

BEHIND HIM, VERY FAINTLY, HE HEARD A FOOTSTEP ON THE FLOOR . . .

Spock's reflexes were quick. Even as he turned, his mind groped at the anomaly, the sense that there *couldn't* have been anyone in his quarters when he came in, dim though the lighting was, for his acute hearing would have picked up breathing, the creak of boot leather, the thousand soft subsensory rustlings that the clothed human body makes . . .

And there was, in fact, no one behind him at all.

Look for STAR TREK Fiction from Pocket Books

STAR TREK: The Original Series

STAR TREK: The Next Generation

Most Pocket Books are available at special quantity discounts for bulk purchases for sales promotions, premiums or fund raising. Special books or book excerpts can also be created to fit specific needs.

For details write the office of the Vice President of Special Markets, Pocket Books, 1230 Avenue of the Americas, New York, New York 10020.

STAR TREK®

GHOST WALKER

BARBARA HAMBLY

POCKET BOOKS

New York   London   Toronto   Sydney   Tokyo   Singapore

This book is a work of fiction. Names, characters, places and incidents are either the product of the author's imagination or are used fictitiously. Any resemblance to actual events or locales or persons, living or dead, is entirely coincidental.

An *Original* Publication of POCKET BOOKS

POCKET BOOKS, a division of Simon & Schuster
1230 Avenue of the Americas, New York, NY 10020

Copyright © 1991 by Paramount Pictures. All Rights Reserved.

STAR TREK is a Registered Trademark of
Paramount Pictures.

This book is published by Pocket Books, a division of
Simon & Schuster, under exclusive license from
Paramount Pictures.

All rights reserved, including the right to reproduce
this book or portions thereof in any form whatsoever.
For information address Pocket Books, 1230 Avenue
of the Americas, New York, NY 10020

ISBN: 0-671-64398-3

First Pocket Books printing February 1991

10 9 8 7 6 5 4 3 2 1

POCKET and colophon are registered trademarks of
Simon & Schuster.

Printed in the U.S.A.

For Mel

Who wears a red shirt
but survives it anyway

It is a common mistake to assume that small size, physical weakness, lack of obvious weapons or an appearance of either stupidity or juvenile "innocence" denotes harmlessness in alien species.

Neary, *First Contact*

The appearance of weakness is the weapon most to be feared. When a warrior smiles in tender amusement, then his muscles are slack.

Analects of a Warrior,
translated from the Klingon

Excepting only mechanical failure by essential life-support systems, an Intruder Alert—the presence or suspected presence on a Starfleet vessel of an unauthorized alien life-form—is to be given highest priority of all ship emergencies.

Starfleet Officers Manual

Historian's Note:

This adventure takes place during the fourth year of the starship *Enterprise*'s original five-year mission.

GHOST WALKER

Chapter One

It was in the Moon of the Blue Berries, in the third year of the twelfth cycle of the Treecat star in the thousand and forty-second turning of the Wheel of the Universe, when the Hungries first began to appear and disappear in the Bindigo Hills. At first they seemed to be like children or like the giant running-apes, not knowing anything but doing no harm; then they began to catch animals and make them disappear, and tried to catch people as well, but the people ran away and hid in the warrens. Later the Hungries began to kill people, and roasted and ate their flesh. Then the hunters of the Bindigo Warren and the other warrens near where the Hungries appeared began to slay them, as they hunted the Flaygrubs and Hootings.

Only in the fifth year of the twelfth cycle did Kailin Arxoras, patriarch [n.b. designation unclear] of the Bindigo Warren and *memmietieffos* [concept unclear—untranslatable from Midgwin language*] draw close enough to the Hungries to walk in their dreams as they slept, and to realize that they were, after their own fashion, people too.

From *Songs of the Midgwins,* translated and introduced by Dr. H. H. Gordon, Oxford University Press.

*See Enchar T'Krau Shorak, "Telepathy Among the Midgwins," *Journal of Intercultural Contacts* v. 93–3, and Neary, R. Jr., "Communications Problems with Non-Verbal Alien Languages," *JIC* v. 30–9.

"CUTE LITTLE CRITTERS, aren't they?" Dr. Leonard McCoy, hands on hips, surveyed the silent crowd of rotund, shovel-headed Midgwins gradually forming in the pale twilight at the end of the box canyon where the landing party had materialized. Now and then a Midgwin would raise its head on an extensible neck, adding another foot and a half to its insignificant height, to look with luminous gray eyes over the heads of its fellows. But mostly they just gazed. Every pair of bony, three-fingered hands held a flower; wreaths of flowers circled many pairs of narrow little shoulders or rested on the long, webby manes of their hair, and against the gathering twilight the pale blossoms seemed to float disembodied, the fragile honey scent of them unbearably poignant against the faintly musty odor of the Midgwins themselves.

"Don't let them hear you say that, Bones," Captain James Kirk reproved his ship's surgeon softly. "They killed a dozen of our scouts and contact personnel before we convinced them that there was a difference between us and the Klingons."

McCoy looked indignant at the possibility of being mistaken for a Klingon. Behind him, Dr. Helen Gordon laughed softly and said, "I expect we all look alike to them."

"We do." A man's quiet voice spoke from the shadows of the fat-trunked, almost leafless barrel plants that huddled thick among the canyon's stones. "But not in the way you think."

Kirk turned quickly, startled, and annoyed with himself. Though the planetary contact team had reassured him repeatedly that the landing party would be in no danger and must be kept to the absolute minimum, he was slightly on edge without the safety margin of Security personnel. He should, he knew, have heard these newcomers arriving at the landing site.

They stepped from the encircling blue gloom into the open: two Vulcans and an Argellian in hard-worn khaki coveralls, led by half a dozen Midgwins, the foremost of whom was so old that his smooth, purple-brown skin had faded to a dusty gray under the whitish ridges of the whorled scar tattoos. His eyes had faded too. They were glacier-gray, wise and sad, and the skin around them, and over his hard little beak, was white, as were the silky strands of mane that hung down over his knobby shoulders. Alone among the Midgwins, he carried nothing in his hands, though he walked with their rolling two-legged stride instead of—as the others occasionally did—assisting himself now and then with one long arm touching the ground.

The male Vulcan, a small, neat little man whom Kirk knew to be the anthropsychologist Dr. Shorak, stepped out ahead of the white-faced Midgwin and presented Kirk, McCoy, Gordon, and the other two members of the Federation contact team with two flowers each. "Hold one in either hand," he advised softly. "It is said that you cannot lift a hand in anger if it holds a flower."

"If I stick one behind the wrong ear, will someone proposition me?" McCoy inquired, sniffing at the tiny, intoxicatingly sweet blossom.

Dr. Gordon smiled teasingly. "If they don't, I will," she promised, and Kirk hid a grin. Unlike Dr. Mei Chu and Dr. Nomias Gzin, the other two representatives of the Federation Xenological Institute, Helen had not kept to herself in the two weeks they'd been on the *Enterprise.* She had instead fallen easily into comradeship, not only with Kirk, but with many of the crew. It was becoming difficult for Kirk to remember what it had been like without her big-boned, awkward presence among them in the rec rooms or the labs—without the sound of that soft husky alto, and the knowledge that she'd be somewhere around when he came off-shift.

Shorak said, "This is Kailin Arxoras, patriarch of the Bindigo Warren and . . ." He hesitated fractionally, then decided against giving whatever other title he would have given. Instead he took Kirk's hand lightly but firmly in his, deftly tucking one of his own flowers out of the way between skeletal fingers, as Kirk saw the Midgwins do, and reached out to Arxoras with the other. "Would you permit him to—to see into you? It is not like the mind meld—it is a surface affair only, to reassure him of your good intentions. If you permit it, would you close your eyes, think of nothing, and count backward from twenty?"

Kirk hesitated as the instinctive caution of years of dealing with unknown factors balked within him. "And how will he reassure me of his good intentions?"

Shorak gave the matter momentary consideration. After an eighteen-month stint in the bush, he was heavily bearded, his long black hair braided back into a short queue. His face, darkened slightly by exposure to the honey-colored rays of the star Elcidar Beta, was grotesquely thin, and under the worn khaki his joints had the disquietingly knobby look of borderline starvation, though he seemed healthy and alert. Other than that he was perfectly neat, sleeves rolled down, trouser legs tucked into boot tops, every tab affixed, which was more than could be said of his wife, Dr. L'jian—a xenoanthropologist of awesome credentials and comprehensively rumpled appearance—and Thetas the Argellian, under whose rolled-up sleeves Kirk could glimpse the whorled marks of Midgwin tattoos. Both L'jian and Thetas had Shorak's look of unnatural thinness, and with it his incongruous air of health. Kirk noticed, too, that unlike his Vulcan Science officer and every other Vulcan Kirk had ever met, Shorak showed no hesitation about physical contact with relative strangers. He logged the anomaly in his mind and saw the half-suspicious puzzlement that narrowed Bones McCoy's eyes.

"I am not sure you would comprehend it if he did," the Vulcan answered him after a moment. "Due to the nature of the local predators, the Midgwins have evolved communications which are largely telepathic, and few humans have the capacity to interpret or even receive them. It is not imperative that you permit this."

For a moment Kirk balanced his natural suspicion of unknown—and formerly hostile—aliens with mind-probing powers against his natural inclination to demonstrate goodwill, and his innate faith that if goodwill were shown, in a significant—if not overwhelming—majority of cases, it would be returned. But what actually won out was his curiosity.

"All right," he said, and closed his eyes.

The Vulcan's dry, twiglike fingers closed on his.

Twenty, nineteen, eighteen . . .

To say that he felt nothing would not be entirely accurate, but at the time he had absolutely no way to describe what it was he did feel. The closest was perhaps the psychic equivalent of standing with shut eyes while a horse sniffed at his cheek.

. . . three, two, one.

He opened his eyes, and blinked. Arxoras looked up at him with that sad gray gaze and said haltingly, "T'ank 'o, Kep-i-tan," the two soft tongues shaping words as best they could around the hardness of the beak. It was difficult to understand, but with careful listening, Kirk could make out the words. "They have made a bright warrior their patriarch, this warren floating in darkness like a flendag nest in a stream." And releasing Shorak's fingers, the old Midgwin reached out to gently stroke the back of Kirk's hand. "I share to others what I learn of you?" With a graceful gesture he indicated the other

Midgwins grouped behind him, squatting on their haunches, watching with those enormous eyes.

Curiously, now that he was a little used to them, Kirk had begun to distinguish their various expressions. The crowds of them still squatting around McCoy, Helen, and Doctors Chu and Nomias in the scuffed circle of crowding stones at the end of the canyon were watching their alien visitors with a look of childlike absorption in their deeply folded, curiously juvenile faces, but these grouped around the three researchers were evidently not so uncritical. Several of them were old, if the fading of color from skin and hair was an indication of age; the folds of loose skin around the protruding beaks were deep and baggy. All were tattooed to one extent or another. But in the eyes of some he could see skepticism, wariness, hostility, at variance with the odd, old man/child physiognomy.

"You may share," Kirk said, and turning his head, caught a worried glint in Shorak's eye.

In turn, Shorak presented the others of the new contact team and Bones McCoy to the patriarch's psychic scrutiny. "A speaker who will teach us the speech of the Hungries," Arxoras said of Helen, touching her hand where Shorak, still acting as link, held it. "A flower that has felt sun for the first time." And, studying McCoy for a long time, he said softly, "A healer living in pain." McCoy turned his face away.

"I shall be glad of the presence of a relief team," Shorak of Vulcan said later. Full dark had fallen. They were sitting outside the door of what Thetas the Argellian solemnly referred to as the Elcidar Beta III Xenological Research Institute, a mud and wattle hut less than three meters in diameter a quarter of a mile from the outskirts of the village. A small campfire burned in the center of a ring of flat river stones and desiccated chunks of the soapy, soft-textured local wood;

and the low, flickering orange light highlighted more strongly than ever the thinness of the researchers' faces, the boniness of the Vulcan's gesturing hands. He went on, "The civilization here, though almost completely lacking in instrumentality, is enormously complex."

"This?" McCoy's eyebrow went up and he struggled unsuccessfully to keep an incredulous chuckle out of his voice. Up the straggling path through the hard, wiry bush jungle of thorn thickets, rocks, and barrel trees the first of the Midgwin houses could just be made out in the gathering gloom, lumpish excrescences of mud that stuck to the towering rocks, the squat trees, and to each other, straggling in all directions up and down the canyon and along the stream. Oddly enough, even downstream from the village, the water was clear, though there wasn't a great deal of it. Through the soft, dust-smelling haze of evening the piping voices of the Midgwins sounded no louder than the chirping of cicadas in the night.

Thetas the Argellian nodded—Dr. Thetas Farnakos Sredji Akunas, whose work on societal structures was standard reading in every anthro class from here to the Barrier, Kirk reminded himself. The photographs Kirk had seen of him had showed a plump little man with very bright black eyes in the smooth Argellian face; only by the eyes had he been recognizable. Kirk had seen McCoy taking surreptitious tricorder readings of all three of the researchers—and had seen him double- and triple-check them. As if oblivious to all of this, the Argellian went on, "The rules of social interchanges—the hierarchies of respect—the philosophical education—to say nothing of their songs and legends—all of them are among the most refined I've ever encountered." He craned his head a little to see through the tangled jungles toward the center of the village. "It's truly a delight to work with . . ."

Kirk got to his feet and followed the little man's gaze back toward the lumpish shapes of the mud huts among the thorn trees. Rose-amber moonlight drenched the scene, dyeing the towering rocks golden and outlining every thorn, every twig of the jungle in numberless shades of orange, cinnabar, and peach. Dimly he saw shadows moving in the moonlight, more and more of them, and became aware that the Midgwins were gathering in force. The intermittent chirps of the verbal part of their language had blended now into a soft, thrumming murmur, like a cat's purr; he thought he could see long lines of the Midgwins forming, setting into thick, ridgy, concentric rings, like the rocks themselves, shoulder to shoulder, hands linked, eyes shut.

"What are they doing?" he asked softly, turning back to the little anthropologist.

"It is the Consciousness Web," Thetas replied. "They do it, not every night, but at least three nights out of five. Each opens his or her or its mind to the others, to feel their troubles, to reassure one another of caring and love, to heal sickness and hurts."

"So they believe," Shorak put in austerely—if he hadn't been a Vulcan, he would have squirmed. The shift of L'jian's eyes was equally uncomfortable.

"Have you ever done it?" Helen inquired, folding her long arms around her drawn-up knees. As Kirk sat down again at her side, his elbow brushed her shoulder, and he was acutely conscious of her touch.

"It can be quite dangerous." There was a distinct frost in the Vulcan's voice. "Any psychoemotional melding . . ."

"I've tried." The Argellian's dark glance slipped teasingly sidelong at his disapproving colleague. "My cold *did* go away." He looked back at Helen. "It's an unnerving sensation to have that much of your consciousness scrutinized and not be able to do anything about it."

"Aren't there mental techniques to protect certain areas of the mind from that kind of invasion?" Kirk asked, recalling, uncomfortably, the twenty-four hours of displaced consciousness he had experienced not too long ago with the strange, godlike alien entity Sargon, the few moments of shared awareness. "As a Vulcan, surely you would have some kind of shielding."

Thetas's next remark about wearing a chastity belt on one's wedding night was cut off by Shorak saying, "Indeed, both my wife and I have had frequent occasion to utilize such technique." He was, Kirk noticed, as brusque and evasive about the topic of mind-sharing and mental disciplines as Spock was, as guarded about the dark shadow-side of Vulcan culture, and Kirk was aware of L'jian's tilted eyebrow as she exchanged a glance of speculation with her husband about where an Outworlder would have acquired such knowledge in the first place.

Shorak nodded to Doctors Chu and Nomias and said, "We can instruct you in those techniques, if you have not been so prepared at the Institute—they are quite similar to certain Vulcan mind exercises. In a civilization where they are accustomed to reading one another's dreams, you might find the disciplines of mental closure useful."

Shrill and sudden, a Midgwin voice cut sharply through the milky stillness of the night. Kirk's glance snapped back toward the village, recognizing the sound of trouble, his every instinct on the alert.

One of the Midgwin patriarchs had sprung up on a stone—or maybe it was somebody's hut, they weren't much bigger—in the center of the dreaming rings of the Consciousness Web. There must have been thirty or forty circles of them by this time, thousands strong, podlike leathery bodies jammed together. Their eyes were open, Kirk could see, a spiral galaxy of dimly glowing stars.

The elder gestured, the sweep of his bony arms filled with tension and fury; even at this distance Kirk could see that his head was flat to his shoulders, his beak tightened to the semblance of an angry bird as he cawed and piped. The huge, three-fingered hand jabbed out again and again toward the shabby hut of the Research Institute, a cutting gesture eloquent of rage.

"What's he saying?"

Shorak, who had risen also and stood, arms folded, head down, listening, did not reply. Helen, who had studied the Midgwin speech in preparation for this mission, got to her feet and said softly, "He's angry. He says the Hungries will spread death upon everything they touch."

"In a pig's eye," McCoy muttered, his mouth twisting. "By the look of them, these people are starving *themselves* to death—their population's outrunning their food supply, if they're gatherers like you say, Helen. I haven't seen anything resembling organized crops . . ."

"There aren't any," Thetas replied softly. "But I do not think that is what the Ghost Walker means."

"The Ghost Walker?" Kirk nodded back toward the speaker, swaying furiously on his rock. He was big for a Midgwin, his shiny, reddish-dark skin just beginning to lose its color around the eyes, his coarse black mane hanging down over the ridgy folds of his back. Tattoos covered his arms and shoulders like a macramé cloak.

"Yarblis Geshkerroth the Ghost Walker," Shorak said quietly, coming over to Kirk's side. "Do not underestimate him. He is said to be responsible for most of the disappearances of the Klingon scout parties during the fighting here five years ago."

Kirk raised an eyebrow and turned his gaze back toward the fire, impressed that any of the pudgy, harmless little race would be able to take on Klingon armed scouts. "I thought you said they understood the difference between us and the Klingons."

"What makes you think *we* understand the difference between us and the Klingons?" Thetas inquired, bending forward to rearrange the fire. "Yarblis's contention is that there isn't any."

"Well, I'll tell you a great big one," McCoy retorted

tartly. "If we were Klingons sitting here, we'd be taking target practice at our flat-headed little friend there instead of discussing the matter in its philosophical light."

"Watch out," Dr. Nomias said, and his short antennae swiveled sharply in the direction of the path. By this time they were all standing, looking back up the twisting path through the brush toward the village. With apelike nimbleness, Yarblis Geshkerroth had swung himself down from his makeshift stone rostrum and was waddling with surprising speed toward the Research Institute. Others had broken away from the circles of the Consciousness Web and were following, Midgwins of all sizes, most swinging themselves along on their hands as well as their short, stumpy legs. They moved easily through the thorn brush, their platy hides making nothing of the barbed spears of the plants; their eyes were a bobbing and luminous sea in the dark.

Almost instinctively, Thetas and Shorak closed their distance to Kirk and Helen; and equally instinctively, Kirk gestured the others back and walked out to meet the delegation alone.

"You . . ." Squatting before Kirk, Yarblis looked far more dangerous than a tubby little alien with wide, glowing eyes should have. Drawn in on himself, the thick wrinkles of his hide clenched to form a protective armor, he was far from comical. One big, three-fingered hand unfurled itself on the end of the bone-thin arm. "Let me walk in," he said, his voice shriller, his English and pronunciation much inferior to Arxoras's. "Let me see in your mind what you mean for humankind." And by humankind, Kirk knew he meant himself and his race.

Kirk hesitated. Sargon, savant of a nameless and long-extinct race, had in their brief time of shared consciousness taught him a certain number of mental shielding techniques; recently, Spock had been teaching him others. Too frequently, starfarers who tangled with telepathic alien races had found themselves enmeshed in cases of possession that would have had any exorcist in Earth's history reaching for his crucifix.

"Let me see!" Yarblis insisted furiously. "You hide from us why you have come!"

Behind him Kirk heard the scrunch of boots on gravel, and from the tail of his eye he saw Shorak coming toward them. Yarblis backed away a little, hissing. "No! Not through this cold one with a soul like a stone egg, who has never let us drink of his dreams. By yourself and for yourself, unveiled by lies."

From the direction of the village there was a stirring among the Midgwins crowding the path. In the gloom, Kirk caught a glimpse of a white mane like a silken flag. Beside him, Shorak said softly, "You don't have to . . ."

Arxoras waddled from the darkness. Flowers were braided into his snowy hair. "Please understand my brother," he said to Kirk, reaching out one hard hand to stroke Yarblis's bony back. At Arxoras's touch, Yarblis relaxed visibly, the taut ridges of his skin loosening, his head rising a little on its neck. By the light of the Institute fire Kirk could see the Ghost Walker's arms were, among the tattoos, blotched with the crinkly scar tissue left by Klingon disruptors.

"He has said that you may be self-deceived—that your belief is that, meaning us well, you can still harm us. He asks to see deeper into your thoughts, to see what you intend for us in this Federation your people speak of. But if this troubles you or causes you fear, do not regard what he says. I trust your people . . ."

Yarblis twisted his head like an owl's on his neck and hissed something at the old Midgwin.

Arxoras blinked calmly at him for a moment, then turned back to Kirk. "I trust you," he repeated.

"You don't have to—" Shorak began softly.

"No." Kirk held out his hands to Yarblis and mentally concentrated his thoughts in the best approximation he could find of the disciplines that Spock and Sargon had taught him. "No, he has a right to know. And we mean only benefits to this world." He slowed and steadied his breathing, wishing briefly he'd made more time to practice meditation than he had . . . An increase in the production of food, he thought. Better ways of living, but only if they chose them freely. Only if they asked for Federation help. Defense against the Klingons, on whose frontiers this undefended, undeveloped world lay. That above all.

The Ghost Walker took his hands.

The shock was horrible. Shared consciousness was always an unnerving thing, more so the further the alien consciousness was from human. Sargon had been civilized, sensitive, intelligent, and, Kirk now realized, trying very hard not to hurt him. There was an animal quality to Yarblis's thoughts, a wild dark blur of pseudomemories, emotions, and snippets of things Kirk knew he was not meant to see: the pungent fragrance of bizarre lust and the horrified shock in a dying Klingon's eyes. He forced his reeling consciousness to hold to the images of other worlds that had entered into the Federation, of world councils asking for new food-production techniques, new learning, new skills. Of the Halkans refusing to sell their dilithium and the *Enterprise* flying silently away.

Yarblis's mind rooted at his, greedy and rough and very angry. Kirk was shaking when the mind link broke.

For a moment he and the Midgwin stood, looking at one another—the man in his gold shirt, his fair hair damp with sweat in spite of the night breeze moving softly in off the veldt. The Midgwin gazed up at him with huge yellow eyes glowing softly in the dark.

"Are you satisfied?" Kirk felt the probe had gone far deeper than he'd wanted it to, far deeper than Arxoras's had, seeing more things about the *Enterprise,* about he himself, than he'd wanted to reveal. But it was a contention he had no way of proving, not even of expressing—certainly not to Shorak, Vulcan reticence being what it was. He wished Spock were there. But evidently no harm had been done . . . "Do you believe now that we are not like the Klingons? That we intend you no harm?"

"Yes," the Midgwin said, his flute voice soft and deadly. "Yes, I believe that you intend us no harm, Jam-es Tiberius Kirk." And turning, he waddled away into the darkness.

"I think you should take Shorak up on his offer of instruction," Kirk said quietly.

The glow of the dying fire, visible away to their right among the thorn trees that surrounded the camp, turned Helen's hazel eyes a greenish amber, like a cat's would be if a cat were ever to think seriously about giving up hunting.

He hesitated a long moment, wanting to bring up the subject and not wanting to, not willing to face what he had known from the first would have to be faced . . .

Oh, what the hell, he thought, and blurted out, "If you're going to stay here."

And the next instant he felt thoroughly ashamed of himself for that kind of blatant fishing. *Helen has her own career,* he thought, as he had thought since that evening when they'd first lain together talking and he'd thought, This is different . . . *First-contact team is an advance for her . . .*

I can't ask her to forego that kind of advancement . . .

His hands tightened around hers.

"I'm sorry," he said. "I shouldn't have . . ."

She glanced across at him, a rueful smile pulling at the corner of her mouth. "Shouldn't have said the Big If?" She moved a little closer to him as they walked, their booted feet as if by instinct finding the narrow, scuffed trail that led along the edge of the thorn forest. She spoke half jokingly, the easiness between them as relaxed, as trusting, as if they'd been lovers for years instead of two weeks. "You don't think it's been itching and eating at me already?"

Behind them, among the stumpy thorns and towering rocks of the plateau rim, the swollen, cantaloupe-colored moon hung like an enormous fruit, outlining the crowding domes of the warren's close-packed mud shelters in amber light. Before them the grasses of the veldt stretched away into distance, the sigh of the tepid breeze a silken music, shifting melodies of flowers and dust. Somewhere a night lizard cried, a heartbreaking alto sweetness. Mr. Spock had noted, back on the ship, that the gravitational pull of the moon here was relatively strong, and Kirk wondered if that had anything to do with the strange sense he had felt ever since his arrival, the sense of bones and blood being more deeply tuned to matters beyond his waking ken.

An unbelievably beautiful world, he thought. A world that seemed to breathe life. As captain of a starship— that strange combination of explorer, strategist, and diplomat—he was well-aware of the implications of that untouched beauty, conscious that those virgin grasses that made such music meant that no agriculture was being practiced here and that the population was balanced on the precarious knife edge of starvation; that the constellations of jeweled stars overhead were maps of Klingon territory.

If Helen stayed here . . .

"I don't want to make things harder for you than they are."

"Sure you do." She grinned, and stopping, turned to kiss him with a gentle passion on the lips. Then she sighed and shook her head, her big, bony hands curiously light in his grip. "Dammit, Jim . . . the universe is so big. It's so easy to lose things. All those roads leading away, and there isn't one of them that doesn't have a one-way sign on it."

"The *Enterprise* will be back in six months." He put his arm around Helen's waist, solid with muscle like the bole of a young tree. The Big If.

"In six months . . ."

She shook her head, the coarse dark abundance of her hair hissing softly against his shoulder.

"It wouldn't be fair." Her husky voice barely broke the deep-breathing sigh of the wind in the grass, the half-heard multivoiced humming of the Midgwin Consciousness Web that seemed to fill the night. "Not fair to the others, to Chu and Nomias, who would hardly be settled into the research and teaching by then; not fair to my replacement, coming in late and having to learn everything in twice the hurry. No." Her voice was nearly inaudible, as if she spoke to herself. "We really have to decide now."

Kirk said nothing. Helen's arm slipped around his waist and they walked a little farther, both automatically keeping a bearing on the tiny glow of the Research Institute's fire—the only fire in the village. Though Shorak had assured them that the major predators—the Hootings and the Flaygrubs—did not approach the warrens at night, Kirk instinctively kept an ear cocked for any sound of danger in the long grass. Glancing back, he could see McCoy and Thetas still sitting by the fire. The two Vulcans, Chu, and Nomias had retreated to the Institute's hut to prepare the few small artifacts to be taken up to the *Enterprise* when the landing party returned for the night. The village Consciousness Web, now over ten thousand strong, still swayed in the darkness, humming, whispering, singing shared dreams and healing songs.

It would be easier, Kirk thought, for Helen to make her decision on the ship, surrounded by the environment, the people, she had come to enjoy . . . easier for her to make the decision to stay there. But much as he wanted her to stay—to become a part of his crew, a part of his life—he wanted her to make her decision clearly, fairly, without doubts. She had to see this planet, these people, this place that was the alternative road—this beautiful world and its curious, secretive, fascinating people, this civilization without artifacts, the work of a lifetime spread out before her like a field of flowers. Arxoras's words came back to Kirk: *A flower that has felt the sun . . .* Was he himself the sun? he wondered. Or was it this place?

"Will the *Enterprise* be back in six months?"

There was a long silence. Then Kirk shook his head. "If everything goes as it should."

"Mmm." Helen nodded wisely, her eyes shadow and silver-glint in the moonlight. "You know, I did notice how much everything always goes as it should on exploration-patrol missions."

Jim had to laugh at the mock gravity of her voice, but he knew she was speaking the truth. In six months, God knew what could happen.

"On a starship, I'd never be more than a cataloger of other people's finds, you know," she went on. "Sending back superficial evaluations for others to follow up. It's not what I want." She turned and put her hands upon his shoulders. They were almost of a height. Her voice was thick, hesitant, the voice of one with little experience in saying how she felt or what she wanted. "But I don't want to lose you."

Slowly, he said, "I won't always be on exploration patrols."

It was the first time he had spoken of what he would do two years from now, when the *Enterprise*'s current mission was done. The first time he had thought of applying for anything other than another five-year stint of the same. Even as he said it, the thought gave him a curious pang, a wrenching hurt, as if he stood at the starting line of a race, electing to remain where he was while everyone else vanished into the distance.

But on starbase duty he would at least be able to see her. To have some kind of life with the woman, to put in the time it took to build a future with someone, to build something that would last beyond a few years.

Helen laughed softly. "Oh, Jim! Even if you were base commander, you'd drive yourself into a nervous breakdown in a year watching starship captains screw up things you'd think you could do better!"

"Oh, thanks a lot!" he groused, laughing too as he gave her a mock shove, because he knew she was right. She shoved back, and they tussled in the dappled moonlight beneath a stand of stumpy, thick-boled trees, giggling like teenagers until their mouths met.

Chapter Two

COMING BACK through the tepid darkness, Kirk heard Thetas's voice and McCoy's, a quiet murmuring beneath the sighing purr of the Consciousness Web in the warren beyond. The *Enterprise*'s doctor and the little Argellian anthropologist sat side by side on a chunk of river rock, the jittering firelight before them glinting on the gold line of service braid on McCoy's sleeves and the streamlined arrowhead of the Starfleet emblem on his breast, seaming Thetas's emaciated face with shadow. Seeing the Argellian reminded Kirk again of the plumpness of the man in his earlier pictures, and he shivered at the thought of Helen growing that thin, that wasted-looking . . .

But no, he thought. It was part of her mission to teach agriculture, to help these people stave off the starvation overtaking the planet.

"What do you mean, resistant to learning farming?" McCoy was saying as Kirk and Helen emerged from the tiny game trail along which they had walked. "They're gatherers, it's the most inefficient way of making a living no matter what planet you're talking about! The food resources of the countryside are just this side of exhaustion! Can't they see they're one good drought away from planetwide catastrophe? You say they cherish life—"

"They cherish life upon their own terms," the Argellian replied, folding his skeletal hands. "Their standards, their intentions, are based upon other things. To them, all things are deeply bound together. They cherish life as a quality . . ."

McCoy sniffed. "Nobody's quality of life has ever been improved by malnutrition. Didn't any of you ever explain Malthus to these people?"

Thetas smiled sadly. "It is difficult to explain any of this to someone who hasn't lived among these people— it's difficult enough for me to try to get some of it across to Shorak and L'jian, who won't participate fully in the Consciousness Web. There isn't an insult scatological enough, poisonous enough, to be the equivalent of calling someone here *mi'ik*—greedy, grabby. The thought of deliberately cultivating food, rather than living day to day upon what Rhea—the Planet Mother Spirit— chooses to send, is absolutely repugnant to the Midgwins on a number of levels."

The deep humming of the crowd, subtle and pervasive as the slow throb of surf, filled the darkness around them. Turning his head, Kirk could just glimpse the backs of the nearest of those concentric circles, up the path in the warren, swaying in the velvety moonlight. Even the children, little pale grublike creatures who hid throughout the daylight hours, curled, dreaming in the circles, bathed in the unvoiced songs, the warm closeness, the profound comfort and content.

Behind them Dr. Chu's voice said something about the new subspace radio they had brought, to replace the old and almost worn-out one the Institute had been using for years. "Do you think we should lay in a supply of emergency rations?"

"They're not stupid," Thetas went on quietly, turning,

like Kirk, from the Institute's low-voiced activity toward the serene stillness of the warren. "They know food is scarce. They know there are far too many warrens, that the warrens are far too large. In the distant past they simply used to let the sick die, the weak succumb to predators. They won't do that now, haven't done that for hundreds of years. Many of them are now saying some kind of compromise should be sought, but the conservatives say that they will not, as they say, make the land their slave, force it—her—to yield beyond what is her will, her free and loving gift. The idea is repulsive to them, the start—according to what Arxoras has told me—of fighting over possessions, of living for things instead of for one another. In a way, it's hard to fault them for this."

"Do they have an alternative solution?" McCoy demanded irritably, poking at the fire with a stick. The yellow spurt of the light showed the cynical anger in his face, the anger of a doctor who sees a man drinking himself to death in spite of every warning.

Thetas shrugged, and smiled again, his wrinkled face and bald head dyed honey-gold in the fire's glow against the squatty screen of barrel trees behind him. "For the most part they say things are not so bad yet, and may not grow any worse." And, when McCoy made a gesture of impotent disgust, added, "How many years did the people of your planet, and of my own, even the well-meaning ones, say the same in the face of the Malthusian alternative?"

"And unfortunately," Kirk put in, folding his arms and leaning one broad, gold-clad shoulder against the nearest tree stem, "the concept of ownership and the practice of agriculture are important points of definition in the index of civilization as set out in the Settlement Accords with the Klingons."

"But that's absurd," Helen protested. "What about the Suriaps? And the Organians themselves? Those definitions of civilization were obsolete before the Settlement was signed! What about the Drommian Belters?"

Kirk shrugged. "Revisions to the index have been proposed for years, but the Settlement is still in force. And as long as Midgwis lies in the path of Klingon expansion, you know they're going to push to have the Midgwins declared subsentient and the planet opened for 'development' . . . Going by their track record, the kind of development they tried with the Organians."

"The poor things," Helen said impulsively, and Thetas chuckled with genuine amusement.

"Scarcely that. One of the main Klingon arguments that the Midgwins are animals and not human is the number of their 'researchers'—read 'scouts'—who attempted to investigate this planet who never returned."

"I don't know," McCoy returned with a wry grin. "I'd call that a pretty good argument to the contrary, considering the differences in size and firepower. If what you said about our little friend the Ghost Walker is true—"

"But how could he?" Helen asked, her dark brows pulling down over the bridge of her nose. "They don't seem to have much technology. I don't think I've seen a weapon—or a tool of any kind—or even fire, for that matter . . ."

A muted commotion from the Research Institute's doorway cut off her voice. The makeshift curtain—a silvery survival blanket hung in the low door arch—was lifted aside and the others emerged, Shorak and L'jian carrying a few small sample cases, Doctors Chu and Nomias bearing the empty sections of crate in which the new subspace transmitter had been delivered. "Those will make good seats, when we get an annex built for you," said L'jian, shaking back the end of her sloppily braided queue from one thin shoulder. "And you'll find the survival blankets you have brought will have their uses, in spite of the relatively high ambient temperature . . ."

"It will take getting used to," panted Nomias, whose pale blue skin was drenched in sweat despite the brevity of his thin shorts and singlet. Kirk smiled a little as L'jian nodded her agreement, knowing that this area's slow, baking warmth would be as uncomfortably hot to the Andorian as it was chilly to the two Vulcans.

"And you say there is nothing else at all that resembles an artifact?" Chu inquired of Shorak, looking up from her tiny height at the skeletal Vulcan beside her. "No pottery, no food bowls . . ."

"They sometimes pile seeds and fruit upon pads of flap lichen they strip from the rocks," Shorak explained. "Invariably they eat the lichen, however—they do not keep anything."

The little Earthwoman sighed. "I suppose we'll be able to make a case for the braided flower chains, but it will be awkward. The Klingons are sure to say that anyone can braid flowers—but then, anyone can chip an arrow point. And the predators they hunt . . . ?"

"In the single hunt we saw," L'jian said, "they drove the Flaygrub over the edge of a cliff—the spindars of M-428 do that to the galfirdach, and no one would argue that the spindars are sentient."

"Except Horace Frill of Oxford Institute, in that dreadful article he wrote for *Interstellar Studies*, no," Chu agreed thoughtfully, and then turned back to Kirk. "We are satisfied as to the conditions here on this planet, Captain, both in terms of our physical safety and the safety of the next phase of this mission. Has what you have seen satisfied you?" She spoke formally, as she had always maintained a formal distance from him, but in her tiny crone face her dark eyes were shining, as Kirk had seen Helen's shine as she looked around her at this strange and beautiful world.

He smiled. "Yes," he said. "I have a few concerns, but nothing that Dr. Shorak has not also expressed. I'll report to Starfleet that I find no exceptional or immediate dangers here; that contact phase can proceed. Tomorrow—"

"If you please," Chu said, again with a formal inclination of her head, "my colleague and I have accepted Dr. Shorak's invitation to spend the night here—our first night upon the planet. We can return briefly to the ship tomorrow before it leaves orbit." The joy of it, the eagerness, was palpable in her voice. "Helen . . . ?"

Kirk turned, to look at the woman who had suddenly fallen so silent at his side.

He thought, *I may never see her again after tomorrow* . . . His past had taught him to be philosophical about good-byes, and that people always did turn up again.

But he knew, too, that when they turned up again, it was seldom the same.

Helen said slowly, "I . . . I think I'll spend the night on the ship." She did not look at Chu—didn't look at Kirk either. Her hazel eyes were lowered, her angular face very still.

Nomias's prim mouth flexed a little, repressing whatever his thoughts were, but Chu came over to the tall woman and took the powerful hand in her own tiny one. In her neat little khaki coveralls and heavy boots, she looked like some strange little wrinkled doll, oddly similar to the Midgwins themselves. Her voice was neutral as she said, "Then you can bring our things with you when you beam down in the morning." Her black eyes, looking up into the downcast hazel ones, were understanding behind their scholarly detachment. *Or not,* she seemed to add, unspoken.

"It will save us a trip back up," she went on chattily, while her wise, dark glance flicked over Kirk, as if evaluating the decision she knew Helen would have to make, while saying nothing that would influence it. And indeed, since the decision was, as Mr. Spock would say, completely irrational, there was nothing much that she could say that Helen hadn't already considered. Instead she continued, "I agree with the good Dr. McCoy on the subject of transporter beams . . . I never did like the thought of having the component atoms of my being disassembled and reassembled like a bagful of puzzle bits."

Helen chuckled softly in spite of herself, and squeezed Dr. Chu's hand. "Thank you."

The old woman smiled, and patted her arm. "Good night. My things are in the corner of my room by the door . . . If you'd check the backs of the drawers for me, I'd appreciate it. Nomias's things are all boxed up beside his bunk. We shall see you in the morning."

Or not. Kirk's thoughts echoed again. He put the words from his mind.

Helen said nothing, only turned and walked up the path toward the warren, passing close to the ropy lines of dreaming Midgwins, toward where the rocks of the box canyon sheltered the transporter coordinates. McCoy was already on his way there, the sample cases he'd taken from L'jian tucked under one arm—the pitifully slim evidence that this "rich and complex" culture, as Thetas had termed it, was in fact culture at all, and not an anthropologist's dream that politicians could exploit. The world, untouched by agriculture, was ideal for colonization. A braided wreath of flowers—a few mud-smeared sticks . . . to be carefully cryostored by the small Anthro department, and eventually passed on, as Helen had said, for others to analyze more fully.

Watching her walk away into the darkness, Kirk felt a pang, knowing in his heart what she would be leaving behind here. Behind him he heard Nomias say to Chu with a slight, superior twist to his high voice, "If you think you're seeing that woman in the morning, you're deceiving yourself."

Chu sniffed as the two of them turned back to the hut, her long white pigtail gleaming like frost-killed grass in the moonlight. "Oh, don't be a fool."

"I'm pleased you feel yourself able to make a favorable report on conditions here," Shorak said quietly, as he and Kirk stood for a moment beside the dying fire. "I will admit to an occasional mistrust of Starfleet's view of certain matters. The Midgwins are not easy to explain."

Up the thorny slope behind them, the warren had sunk into near silence, though, peering through the moonlit blueness of the night, Kirk could see the Midgwins still sitting in their crowded, hand-linked lines. They were no longer swaying, but the peace, the joy of their communion, seemed to lie on the night like the scent of summer grass, healing, caring, enfolding. Cherishing even this prim Vulcan researcher, Kirk thought, with some amusement, whether he admitted it or not, as it would cherish the new research team . . . cherishing everyone, every living soul in the village, in the world, who stood within its spell.

He smiled. "I'm not sure I understand the explanation I've been given. But nowhere in the Federation Charter does it say that we have to understand each other . . . only that we be willing to try." He extended his hand, and Dr. Shorak took it without even the slight hesitation that Spock showed—and Spock's instinctive avoidance of physical contact was far less than most Vulcans'. Evidently, living among the Midgwins had had at least some effect.

The moon was setting as Kirk climbed the thread of path and passed through the silent warren. Everywhere, Midgwins sat in their close-furled spirals of caring peace, their triangular, flat-topped heads gleaming like a pavement of cobblestones in all directions, a sea of life washing up against the low domes of their houses, the high sides of the rocks. So many of them—thousands— in this one small area, he thought, trying to eke a living from wild fruits and grains.

And yet Shorak—and Chu—had refused supplemental food supplies, which, Helen had explained, would have alienated them irreparably from the community. It was grabby, greedy . . . and lacking in faith in Rhea, in the Earth Spirit Mother, who gave her children what they needed when they needed it.

He shook his head. No, he thought. He did not understand.

Ahead of him in the dim starlight that filtered down into the canyon's darkness he made out the shapes of Helen and McCoy. They weren't talking, though Helen had taken one of the sample cases and was holding it folded in her arms. Her head was down, her rumpled coveralls bleached colorless by the filtered light; McCoy, a little apart from her, was looking quietly around him, thinking his own thoughts of this strange and beautiful world.

Bones would know, Kirk guessed, as well as any of them did, what it meant that Helen was returning to the *Enterprise* tonight. Bones would realize what the decision to remain with the ship would mean to her.

If that's the decision she comes to.

She raised her head at the crunch of the stream gravel underfoot as he stepped clear of the shadows of trees and rocks, and she greeted him with a half-apologetic smile; by it, he knew that the jury on that one was still out.

He wanted her to stay. And, he reflected, half amused at his own reactions, he wanted to know *now* what her decision was to be—wanted to feel safe. He knew already he was in for a long night of wondering whether he'd have this woman at his side for the next two years—with luck, the next sixty—or not.

But like Chu, he knew there was nothing he could say.

Still, there was a feeling of relief in his chest as he flipped open his communicator and said, "Three to beam up, Scotty."

The final setting of the moon had softened its shadows. A diffuse fill of starlight touched what had been pockets of velvet blackness and glimmered on the strange, low-growing plants that clogged the canyon walls, the spicy sweetness of their blossoms drenching the dusty air. And in the shadows of the rocks, Kirk saw, suddenly, the shape of a solitary Midgwin, its stumpy, podlike body barely distinguishable from a plant or a stone itself. In the same moment that he wondered what any Midgwin was doing absenting itself voluntarily from the comfort and healing of the Consciousness Web, he recognized by the dim starshine the ropy network of tattooing and the ugly blotch of disruptor scars, and read the malevolent hatred in Yarblis Geshkerroth's fishlike yellow eyes.

Then the cold glitter of the transporter beam enveloped him, breaking his atoms into electricity, his mind into a flashing stream of neurons leaping across the dark.

Chapter Three

SOMETHING WAS WRONG.

Mr. Spock's hand shot to the Emergency Quarantine button almost without his conscious thought. The band of amber lights sprang into being like a coronet around the transporter room's ceiling, and blast doors slipped down into place with an oiled pneumatic hiss almost before the three gold figures in the light of the beams solidified into human shape. Assistant Transport Chief Oba looked over at him in surprise; Captain Kirk, stepping swiftly down from the transport disk after one quick glance at the flashing lights, asked, "What is it, Mr. Spock?"

But after that first second—and indeed, even during the flare of the impulse itself—the Vulcan himself could not have said. "I'm not sure, Captain." There was no apology, no uncertainty, in his deep, slightly rough voice, and even as he spoke he looked around the brightly lit chamber, searching, analyzing . . . McCoy had stepped off his transport disk with his usual celerity, as if he feared—which he half did, in spite of Transport Chief Kyle's repeated reassurances—that the beams would

29

come on again and snatch him back into electrostatic limbo. Dr. Helen Gordon remained for a moment where she had appeared, holding a duraplast sample box cradled in her arms and regarding the captain worriedly.

"My impression was that something else materialized with the transporter beams."

Kirk's eyes narrowed and he scanned the room again. "But you didn't see anything?"

"Negative, Captain," Spock replied formally. "A subliminal impression only."

"Mr. Oba?"

The communicator in the console crackled on; the voice of the night officer on the bridge came on. "Mr. Spock? We've got a reading of Emergency Quarantine down there . . ."

Kirk touched the switch on the console's front and turned to the small black eye of the in-ship visual receptor high in the wall. "We have a possible alert situation here, but nothing serious at the moment." He turned back to the transport assistant.

Oba shook his head. "Looked kosher to me until Mr. Spock hit the panic button." His long, slender, ebony fingers were already keying in a playback sequence. All of them, including Helen now, were grouped around the console as a readout single-framed through.

"I always said you can't trust those things," McCoy growled with a glance back at the transport disks, cold silver circles on the red floor of the chamber itself.

"I sympathize with your objections, Doctor," Spock replied, mechanically punching in a visual replay of the transport sequence, "but the *Enterprise* does not carry rope ladders long enough to reach from the planet's surface up to our current orbit."

"Oh, come on, Mr. Spock," Dr. Gordon teased with a shaky grin, "you couldn't bring the ship in a little closer to the planet?"

"Not even to oblige Dr. McCoy." Spock studied the slow-motion sequence as it replayed on the console's small screen: the preliminary glitter of the matter beams, the gradual taking-shape of those shimmering, cutout forms, swiftly solidifying as the atoms reassembled. Then he played it through again, studying the spaces behind and around the materializing forms, while Captain Kirk, who had been watching the screen over his shoulder, prowled cautiously to every corner of the small room and up onto the transport platform itself, hazel eyes half shut, turning his head this way and that as if listening, scenting for some anomaly.

"I see nothing abnormal on the visuals."

The captain came back to the little group around the console, touched the communications switch. "Lieutenant Dawe? Can we have an intensive life-readings scan of the transporter room at a submicron level? Feed it through to us here."

The transporter rooms, the designers of the starships had known, were the ship's weak point on missions of exploration. They, and the shuttlecraft hangar, were equipped not only with the capability for almost instantaneous quarantine, but with the finest and most accurate of the ship's internal scanners. In the early days of warp-drive exploration, there had been far too many cases of hideous stowaways in the form of viruses, larvae, and unknown parasites that, multiplying, growing, or cloning in the ventilator ducts or electrical conduits, could easily wipe out a ship's crew before they could be destroyed, sometimes before they were even detected.

But, studying the readouts fed to them by the ship's computer, with McCoy looking over his shoulder, Spock could detect no anomaly within the room itself, no evidence of any life-form whatsoever unaccounted for. And indeed, even that first, fleeting impression that there was something else in the room was fading. He could not recall exactly what it was that he had sensed, only that he had sensed something wrong and had reacted instantaneously to prevent its possible spread.

"Most curious," he said after a half hour's examination and reexamination of the readouts revealed nothing. He looked across the little room at the captain, who was still pacing slowly along its metallic walls, touching them every now and then and looking up at the lighting and ventilator ducts, as if searching for some means of possible egress. "Captain . . ."

He paused, for the captain had shut his eyes, his eyebrows pulled slightly together, listening—scenting, Spock would almost have said—for something, some clue, as to what might have been heard or seen. But at the sound of Spock's voice, those eyes opened quickly. "Yes, Mr. Spock?"

"Have you a hypothesis from information learned on the planet?"

The captain hesitated for a long moment; then his glance shifted. "I don't . . . I'm not sure. No." He shook his head, and said more strongly, "No."

"Dr. Gordon? You have studied the native life-forms of Elcidar Beta Three."

Dr. Gordon, who had remained quietly to one side during most of the examination, shook her head. Mr. Spock had not been unaware of Dr. Gordon's increasing intimacy with the captain; he had, indeed, not been surprised in the slightest when the captain had gone over to the researcher's table in the mess room the first night out of the Institute.

Three years of interested observation had made Spock familiar with James Kirk's reactions to the female of the human or humanoid species, and though he himself felt no physical attraction to any of these women, these days he could usually pinpoint which female of a group would appeal to the captain's gallantry. Dr. Gordon had few of the physical characteristics typical of the captain's choices—she was six or seven centimeters taller than the tallest representative of the romantic sampling so far that Spock knew about, nearly the captain's own height, her eyebrows darker and thicker and her chin squarer. At first glance Spock had been deeply curious about the nonphysical factors at work, though of course he was not about to pursue such information verbally among other males of the human species, like Dr. McCoy or Mr. Scott.

Within a very few days he had come to understand how he himself could find this woman appealing, had he permitted his human side to overcome the Vulcan training inculcated into him by his father's people—not to mention his own unspoken determination to be completely Vulcan in his soul, even if he could not be so in his chromosomes. Dr. Gordon had a fine intelligence and a clear-thinking logic, a high degree of abstract aesthetics, and a quick-witted, if sometimes regrettably frivolous, verbal facility. But Spock surmised on the strength of previous observations that these were only secondary factors in the captain's initial interest. Nevertheless, he had, in three years, only once seen the captain so seriously involved with a woman. It had taken the captain a long time to recover from the loss of Edith Keeler—in some ways, Spock suspected that he never would recover. His Vulcan logic deplored an involvement which was, to say the least, an invitation to inefficiency—but some rebellious human corner of his soul applauded Kirk's judgment.

Not, he reminded himself austerely, that it was any of his business.

Dr. Gordon said now, "There are some very small, very quick predators listed in the Midgwis initial reports, and something called a sheefla, which is supposedly very hard to see. But according to Shorak, sheefla avoid the villages, especially when the Consciousness Web is in operation."

"And either of the smaller predators would have left a

physical residue on the walls if it had gotten into the vents," Dr. McCoy added, walking over to where the captain still stood, his clear-cut, boyish features stained honey-gold by the amber warning lights as he looked up at the steel-blocked vent shafts nearest the transport chamber itself. "And there's no trace of that in the microscans."

"And in any case," Dr. Gordon added, "they couldn't have moved swiftly enough to beat the blast doors down. And there's no sign of them on the playbacks."

"No," the captain said slowly, and looked back at McCoy and Spock as if seeing them for the first time. "No, I suspect it was some kind of electromagnetic surge effect from the transporter itself, like a static backfire . . . Isn't that possible, Mr. Oba?"

Oba nodded. "Now and then I've heard about the beams throwing off a 'ghost' . . . I've never seen it, though. I'll ask Mr. Scott."

"Do," the captain said. "I recall reading something about it in the 23.5 issue of *Starship*." He crossed between them to the console and touched a switch. "All systems check out here, Mr. Dawe. False alarm. Deactivate quarantine." His fingers flicked through the four-digit security code. A moment later the blast doors hissed open and the amber lights went out.

As always, Spock felt the slightest flinch of uneasiness as they did so, wondering if he had truly investigated all possible contingencies. Preoccupied with this, he was for a moment barely conscious of Dr. Gordon stepping a pace toward the captain as Kirk strode with his usual briskness through the opened doors. But his ears were quick, and he heard, as probably few others in the room did, the soft breath of her uncertain voice whisper, "Jim . . ."

The captain was already turning back in the doorway, silhouetted against the crisp white lighting of the corridor outside. For a moment Spock thought he was going to speak—either to himself or to Dr. Gordon, who stood at his side.

But shaking his head, the captain thought better of it. He only said, "Good night, gentlemen . . . Helen." And was gone.

"Are you all right?"

The small guest stateroom was dim—it was possible to cut even the very low safety lights for sleeping, but few people did—and the lights of Deck 5's corridors that streamed in from behind Lieutenant Uhura as she stood in the doorway weren't much brighter at this hour of the night. But by then the Communications officer could see that Helen had packed to leave, small bundles of personal possessions lying in a neat row along the wall opposite the bed.

A backpack. A small duffel. A pair of good rock-climbing boots. A carrier of books on wafer—Uhura knew from earlier visits to Helen's cabin that they were mostly classics of interstellar field anthropology and all preliminary reports on Midgwis and its inhabitants.

Helen herself, clothed in pajamas of thin white lawn with her shaggy, coffee-colored tail of hair spread out over her shoulders, sat cross-legged on the rust-colored coverlet of the narrow bed, a look somewhere between relief, pleasure, and disappointment in her eyes.

She had, Uhura realized, been half expecting the captain.

And half dreading the interview.

"I'll be fine."

"We'll all *be* 'fine' in twenty years," Uhura said with a smile. "How *are* you?"

And Helen laughed with a soft, ironic amusement as Uhura perched herself on the other end of the bed. She gestured toward the packed bundles along the wall. "The others said they'd spend the night on the planet. I said I'd be down in the morning."

Uhura said nothing, understanding from her own experiences that last, desperate push against a decision that has to be made. The tall anthropologist sighed, a deep hurtful gust that seemed to come from the core of her bones, and folded her long arms around herself. "God, this stinks," Helen said without rancor, as if she knew that Uhura would know exactly what she meant.

"You want some coffee?" Uhura asked—for Helen looked chilled with the inner cold that had nothing to do with the *Enterprise's* excellently controlled climate.

Helen nodded. The VIP guest cabins were all equipped with food slots; as Uhura crossed the room to punch in the order, she remarked, "Well, that's too bad, because all you're going to get is what comes out of this."

It surprised Helen into laughing, as Uhura had hoped it would. "Oh, come on! Yeoman Brunowski would commit seppuku if he heard you imply he couldn't get a decent adjustment for coffee out of his remixers."

Uhura took the blue-gray velfoam cup from the slot and turned back toward the bed. "They can warp space-time and unravel molecular structure, but even with the kind of fine tuning you can get with a starship's computer, they still can't *really* get coffee right except with real beans. Will you?" she added quietly. "Be down in the morning?"

Helen looked up at her with a lopsided twist to her mouth and eyes that shined suddenly with moisture in the dim glow of the reading lamp beside the bunk. "I don't know," she said helplessly. And when Uhura sat down beside her again, folding up her long legs under the red-and-black caftan she wore when off duty, Helen added, "I don't think so."

Uhura sighed, and there was a moment's silence. Then she said, "I checked for you. You're way overqualified, but once we get to Starbase Nine, you can enlist as ensign and work as Anthro/Geo assistant to Lieutenant Bergdahl . . ." She paused as Helen winced.

"That's the only position open? With Bergdahl?"

"I'm afraid so. And that's only because Emiko's willing to transfer to Input. It's a tight area."

"And I expect Emiko's only looking for a way to get out of working with Bergdahl," Helen added glumly. It was a conclusion Uhura had come to already.

"He's a damn good researcher," Helen went on, "but he's never going to forget that I've got my doctorate, and he doesn't . . . and he's *never* going to forget that I came on as the 'captain's woman.'" There was sudden bitterness in her voice. Uhura made a noise of protest, fractionally too late—she knew Helen was right, about the sour and prissy Anthro/Geo chief at least, and possibly about others onboard besides; Helen's eyes were defensive as she said, "You know that's what they'll say."

"Only for a little while. And only the people who always say things like that. And everybody," Uhura added wisely, "knows who those are. Technically you'll both be working under Spock. You won't have to see old Birddog half the time . . ."

"But the other half I will." She set the coffee aside—it was just as flavorless as always, despite the cutting edge of remixer technology—and shook back the loose tangle of her dark hair. "Dammit, Uhura, I can't avoid the man I'm going to be assistant to, no matter how many holes he picks in my work. And I'm coming on this ship to work, to do a job . . . to salvage what I can of my career after I . . ." She visibly bit back the words *blow it to be with the man I love* . . .

Uhura said nothing. There was not much, she reflected, that one *could* say under the circumstances.

"Dammit . . ." Helen whispered again.

"You do have six months," Uhura began hesitantly.

The younger woman looked back at her with weary irony in her eyes. "Do you really think the *Enterprise* is coming back to Midgwis in six months? That there won't be some emergency, some unexpected mission, that gets it transferred forty sectors away? That's what starships *do*, Uhura. They're the knights of the fleet, not the pawns. How many times has the *Enterprise* been able to return on a regular basis to a planet it visited? Jim isn't his own master, any more than . . ."

She bit off her words again, and Uhura finished for her, "Any more than I am?"

Helen's cheeks reddened in the ocher glow of the lamp.

Uhura's lips framed a wry smile. "Why do you think we get to be such close friends in Starfleet? We're all we've got . . . if anyone's got anything, that is. And you don't. You never do."

"No," Helen sighed. "No, you never do." She pushed back her hair again, stared out into the shadows of the tiny room. It seemed to remind her of something, for she glanced over at Uhura again and asked, "Did you check on who I'd be rooming with if I signed on?"

"I tried," Uhura said guardedly. "But that's something you can't really know in advance. The computer's usually pretty good about match-ups, but with a mid-voyage transfer it's catch-as-catch-can. I know Zink's roommate just transferred—"

"Zink's roommates *always* transfer, according to what Giacomo from Computers told me. Zink never shuts up."

She was silent for a time, rubbing her big hands together as if with cold, her knees drawn up under her chin. The VIP guest quarters were better soundproofed than most of the ship; here there was not even the faint murmur of voices passing in the corridor. Only the soft, subliminal throb of the ventilators, and the distant hum, more felt than heard, within the walls themselves, the resonances of engines and pumps, the heartbeat of the ship itself.

At length Helen said softly, "But the thing is, I don't want to lose him. To lose . . . I don't know. These six months, this year, or two years . . ." She got to her feet, an impulsive move like a big lioness's, and paced the confines of the room, her bare feet making no sound upon the floor. "Time can be so precious, and it disappears so fast. I don't want to look back when I'm fifty and say, 'I found a man I loved like I've loved no one else, but we both had other commitments.'"

Uhura's lips tightened suddenly, and she looked aside.

"All my life I've studied, and learned, and trained myself to add to the knowledge of the universe, to learn how to work with other species . . . but never with people of my own species. And my work is mostly done alone. And I want . . ." Helen shook her head, her voice faltering like a cracked beam under sudden weight.

"And the captain?" Uhura asked.

"This isn't easy for him either." Helen paused, and drew a deep breath. "I won't always be a third-class assistant to Uriah Heep, you know. Some kind of compromise is possible if we're together. If we're not . . ." She shook her head. "We have nothing. There!" She grinned shakily, though her eyes glinted with tears again. "Now I've talked myself into it."

Uhura got to her feet with one smooth motion, strode over to Helen and hugged her firmly. "I want to say, 'Don't do anything you'll be sorry for later,'" she said gently. "But what I'm really thinking is, I'm glad you'll be with us for a while longer. Welcome aboard."

Helen squeezed her hand, a powerful grip like a man's. "Thank you," she whispered, and Uhura could sense the tears perilously near the surface. "Thank you for coming."

She would cry, Uhura thought, when she was alone.

So she bade her good night, and walked away down the corridor in the dim lighting of the late-night shift, for everyone in this sector worked the day watch, and everyone—or nearly everyone—would be asleep. She had said, "Don't do anything you'll be sorry for later," but either way she knew Helen would be sorry. It was the nature of choice. But she knew from her own experience that nothing was so hurtful as a decision unmade. When Helen cried, they would be tears of regret for the road not taken, but the pain would be less desperate, less awful, than indecision would be.

Uhura wrapped her caftan more closely around her, hugging herself as if with cold, though the mild coolness of the *Enterprise*'s corridors never varied. She remembered her own decisions, the roads untaken that would have led her anywhere but here.

It was something one couldn't afford to think about too much. Infinite diversity, infinite combinations, Mr. Spock would say . . . But unless you picked one of those infinite roads at the crossing of the ways, you would never walk on any. And in space the distances were so great, and the times so long. She could only hope that Helen would be happy in the choice she had made.

And Captain Kirk . . .

She turned down the corridor that led to the turbolift up to the junior officers' quarters on Deck 4, and stopped.

In three years she had walked these corridors in the muted lights of the late-night watch hundreds of times, even when, as now, they lay before her completely empty, silent but for the almost soundless throb of the engines far below. Even returning from rec-room showings of the gruesome horror films to which Mr. Sulu was addicted, she had never felt nervous or uneasy with the empty dimness . . . For all her lively imagination, Uhura's practical mind did not work that way.

But now she felt it, the creeping chill of irrational dread.

She fell back a pace, telling herself not to be silly, but her hands were cold. Her eyes searched the shadows, quartering the corridor ahead of her with quick efficiency, searching for anomalous shadow, for movement, for a break in the familiar pattern that would have caused her senses to shrink like this, would have caused the alarm bells to go off in the back of her brain.

There was nothing. Only a darkness not noticeably darker than it had ever been before, a stillness that seemed to wait for her, to watch her with dreadful intentness from some point along the right-hand wall between where she stood now and the turbolift's shut doors.

Uhura stood for several moments looking down that empty corridor, feeling the slow growing of a creeping cold over her, fighting desperately against the terrible sense that something was coming toward her, something moving slowly, gropingly, uncertainly along the wall . . . Something that reached out toward her, and tried to form the syllables of her name.

There is nothing there. She fell back another pace and told herself this two or three times more . . .

Then suddenly she turned and walked quickly back the way she had come. There was only one turbolift from Deck 5 to the smaller decks of the primary hull above this point, but she followed the corridor around to one of the lifts going down to the ship's central lounge on the deck below. As she emerged from the turbolift and threaded her way between the tables and couches of the brightly lighted room, waving a greeting to her various acquaintances of the small late-night shift taking their breaks at its white plastic tables over remixer coffee and various other delicacies fabricated from the recycled raw elements in the lowest holds, she cursed herself inwardly, calling herself a fool . . .

At the far end of the lounge, which sprawled enormously across the center of Deck 6, she got back into the main turbolift that led up, eventually, to the bridge and tried to sound casual as she said, "Deck Four." She felt obscurely embarrassed, as if the turbolift computer would recognize her voice and ask her why she'd made such a pointless detour.

As she hurried down the long, dimly lit corridor from the turbolift to her room, she kept glancing back over her shoulder, though she knew there was nothing there to see.

Chapter Four

"HELEN!" At the sound of the transporter-room door opening, Chief Engineer Montgomery Scott slid out from under the main console's access hatch and stood up with a smile. On the few occasions on which he'd visited the rec rooms—mostly at mealtimes—in the past few weeks he'd had a couple of long conversations with Dr. Gordon, and she was one of the few people onboard who shared his taste for bagpipe music. Then, too, as one of the older members of the crew his instincts as a matchmaker were strong. His pleased expression wavered a moment as he saw that she carried packs and duffels, but she smiled at him and shook her head.

"Chu and Nomias," she explained.

Scotty beamed. "Then you're staying?"

She nodded. But looking at her again, the Engineering chief saw the marks of sleeplessness on her face: the smudgy look under the eyes, the lines around the mouth. It had been a hard choice for her, he realized, though privately he couldn't understand how anyone would deliberate for even a moment between joining the crew of the *Enterprise* and spending who knew how many years on a godforsaken backwater planet whose inhabitants not only had not invented the wheel but had no intention of doing so. But still, it *was* the job she'd prepared for.

She smiled, and forced cheer into her voice. "I'm putting in for provisional fleet status today; my papers should be waiting for me by the time we reach Starbase Nine. I'll be in Anthro/Geo with Bergdahl."

"Garh," muttered Scotty in alarmed distaste. "Never let that whey-faced laddie catch you takin' a glass of wine, then, if you don't want to hear about it for the next three months." As he spoke he took the two heaviest duffels from her and carried them to the transporter disks, Helen following behind with the rest of the assorted packs. "What did the captain say when you told him?"

She hesitated awkwardly on the steps of the transport chamber itself. "I haven't told him yet," she admitted. "I didn't decide myself until late last night."

Scotty's eyes twinkled. "Then he should be down here himself any minute"—he smiled—"thinkin' he's going to see you off."

Her self-conscious blush belied the quick shake of her head, but he'd seen the way she'd looked around the room when she first came in, half expecting to see him there. "Is there some problem here?" she asked quickly, gesturing toward the console where Transport Chief Kyle's red-coveralled legs still protruded through the open access panel.

Scotty shook his head, all considerations and speculations of his captain and his captain's romances dropping from his thoughts in the face of the larger consideration at hand. "Nothing that we've been able to find," he said.

"You mean something that caused the feedback ghost we got last night?"

"Aye. And feedback's likely all it was." Scott shrugged. "It happens now and then, if there's some bit of dust or foreign matter in the transporter room that picks up a sympathetic resonation. You'll get an energy jump, but it's nowhere near strong enough to be of danger to anyone. Just a bit of a sparkle. Mr. Spock's not the first man who's pulled down a quarantine on the strength of it."

He walked back over to the console and hunkered down to check the readings on the micro-fine ion scanner. It registered zero. There was not so much as an atom of foreign material inside the console's sealed circuits, not even the occasional film of water vapor that would sometimes leak through the vent filters . . . nothing. Pleasing to know, of course, but it did leave an unanswered question.

He straightened up again, and shook his head. "It used to happen more often, before they began using filex shields on the wiring. I remember a shipwide intruder alert that kept us orbiting Lyra Omicron Six for twenty-four hours while we went over this ship with flea combs, and nary a thing did we find except the head librarian's cache of chocolate bonbons. But you have to be careful."

Helen smiled, ducking her head a little. There was a small silence.

"We've a few minutes till beam-down time," said Scott after a moment. "We can open a channel to the planet, if you'd like to tell them you won't be joining them after all."

"I'll speak to them from the bridge, when Jim . . . when the captain makes contact. I suppose," she added with a half-smile, "that I'll have to learn to call him Captain if I become part of the crew. Thank you." She glanced at the chronometer on the wall. "It's 0700 hours . . . he'll be on the bridge now, won't he?"

"Aye . . ." Scott nodded and saw her shake her head a little, as if putting aside some thought or disappointment, or telling herself not to be silly.

She smiled. "I'll speak to him there, then."

And she was gone, leaving Scotty to return to the puzzle of the ghost that shouldn't have been there.

On the bridge the usual quietly efficient commotion was under way as the *Enterprise* prepared to leave orbit. Helen caught a sidelong glance from Uhura as she walked over to the captain's chair, where Kirk was listening to Mr. Spock's summation of conditions between the star Elcidar Beta and Starbase Nine. Helen waited until he was done, then took a step closer and said, "Captain?"

He turned his head, and Helen flinched a little with startled shock. She had guessed that James Kirk would get little sleep last night, but never that it would have done this . . . His face looked strained and oddly gray, and it flashed through her mind that if concern about what her decision was to be—about what it would mean to him in terms of their commitments to one another—could do this to him . . .

But of course it couldn't, she thought. It was laughable vanity on her part to even consider that it might.

Something else was bothering him, something serious. It was in his voice as he said, "Yes . . . Helen?"

She kept it short. "I'm here to request transfer to the *Enterprise* . . . admission on a provisional basis into Starfleet."

Something changed in his eyes. Her peripheral vision picked up the quick motion of Mr. Spock's eyebrow, the slight tension of Sulu's shoulders, and Chekov's, as they stopped themselves from looking around from the Navigation console and grinning congratulations at her . . . But the captain only nodded, and began, "Do you have a—" and cut himself off quickly. But just for an instant he looked as if he were groping for a response, trying to sort out what his next step was to be.

He's surprised, Helen thought with the same sense of shock she would have experienced if he had suddenly dashed a pitcher of cold water into her face. *He didn't really think I'd do it.*

How could he not have? After all we said on the planet . . .

Everything in her seemed to turn cold; as if life support and gravity had suddenly glitched.

He recovered quickly from his surprise, and manufactured a smile. "Lieutenant Uhura, transmit a subspace request for processing to Starbase Nine. It can be ready by the time we reach there."

"Aye, Captain." Helen could hear the pleasure in the Communications chief's warm contralto voice. But looking back at Kirk, baffled, hurt, and shaken to her bones, she could see the veiled uncertainty in his eyes.

She stared into the polite, slightly wary blankness of his eyes, and thought, *I've said I'll be in the fleet, I can't turn around immediately and say no I won't* . . .

Before she could speak, Uhura broke in on them again, saying, "Communication coming in from the research party, Captain. Shall I put it on the visuals?"

He turned away a little too gratefully. "Pipe it in, Lieutenant."

And there, on the main screen, was the place that would have been her home, the people who would have been her family, for the next three years at least, years that would now be spent on this ship . . . with Jim . . . Jim who had reacted with that blank-faced surprise to what they had spoken of last night . . .

Long morning shadows splashed a hot blue on the dusty ground around the Research Institute's insignificant, lumpy bulk. In the sulfurous light of the planet's surface, everything seemed strange, burning. The short trunks of the barrel trees loomed in a golden screen behind the hut, and beyond that, the dark tangle of thorns, the gentle, amber meadow stretching away down the hillside . . . the meadow along whose edge she and Kirk had walked last night— *Stop thinking about that!*

Around the extinguished firepit before the door were heaped the packs she'd taken down to the transporter room half an hour previously, and standing beside them were the people who would have been her colleagues: Thetas, like a small and quick-moving gnome, with his great, dark Argellian eyes and the whorls of scar tattoos spread like a jungle over his arms and back; Shorak, prim and scholarly with his carefully trimmed beard, and L'jian impatiently pushing a metal comb into her wild hair; Nomias, with his supercilious smile, and Chu, wrinkled and tiny and kind.

At the corner of the screen, at a respectful distance, a small group of Midgwins stood, great fishlike eyes watching and blinking inscrutably. Among them Helen recognized the old patriarch Arxoras, his long white hair a thin cloak over his skinny shoulders, a white flower in either hand.

"Dr. Shorak, Dr. Chu," James Kirk said, and Helen felt her chest get cold and heavy with dread, wondering what he really felt, and wishing she were sure of herself, one way or the other.

It had all seemed so clear at two o'clock that morning . . .

"Dr. Gordon has decided to turn down the mission on Midgwis, and has opted instead to return with the *Enterprise* to Starbase Nine." Any of the researchers could have done that, if for whatever reason—from prevailing climate to personal health to an inauspicious astrological conjunction—he or she decided not to participate in the mission that they had all trained for. But Helen read the downturned flick of Nomias's mobile blue lips, and the slight slump of Chu's shoulders as she realized her younger colleague had made the choice, taken the road that ran in the direction she herself had long ago chosen not to travel.

Kirk went on, "We will make arrangements from Starbase Nine for a replacement to be selected and sent from your list of alternates; one should be out here by the earliest possible transport."

"Leaving us one short—" Nomias began, and Shorak cut him off.

"Thank you, Captain. Dr. Gordon . . ."

Helen stepped forward, into the narrow range of the small visual pickup unit, part of the new transmitter that the *Enterprise* had brought out to them with the additional research team.

"We respect you for your choice," the Vulcan said, "and for the courage it took to follow an alternate course at this late date." With a nod he stepped back; Vulcans, once away from the elaborate formalities required by their own hierarchical culture, tended to speak baldly to the point.

But Chu said, "I wish you every happiness—and you, Captain. Thank you for a most pleasant voyage."

Kirk inclined his head, and the screen went dark. Standing beside him, Helen watched his profile from the corner of her eye. His face was unreadable. Then she saw his glance slide to her, studying her sidelong, inscrutably considering, and she thought, *It was a sham. Jesus, it was a sham . . .*

She felt sick to the core of her being. With a formal, "Captain," she inclined her head to him, and quietly left the bridge.

Behind her she heard him telling Mr. Sulu to set a course for Starbase 9 at warp factor 4.

Captain Kirk remained on the bridge when the shift ended, deep in the study of the reports on yesterday's transporter ghost. Lieutenant Uhura, after checking the guest VIP staterooms, ran Dr. Gordon to earth in sickbay, in a small lab where Nurse Christine Chapel had stayed on after hours to run an analysis of herbs brought up from the planet's surface.

Uhura heard Helen's voice as she came down the corridor, and stepped through the door. It slipped shut

49

after her, just as Chapel turned on her high lab stool to regard Helen with deep compassion in her blue eyes. Helen had spent a lot of rec-room time with Uhura and Chapel, working jigsaw puzzles and talking—inconsequential talk, most of it, but it overlay a growing core of friendship. Upon the workbench before the thin-featured blond nurse a row of a half-dozen graduated cylinders was arranged, each filled with a clear liquid; a pile of flimsiplast hardcopy lay before her, annotated in Dr. McCoy's nearly illegible script.

"You can still go back, you know," Chapel pointed out gently.

Helen, who had been pacing the room, only shook her head. She still wore her many-pocketed khaki researcher's coverall, her dark hair bound up in a leather thong and a bronze pin. She looked over at Uhura, her hazel-green eyes puzzled, and said, "You were there. Was it just my imagination? I didn't expect him to fall into my arms weeping with delight, but . . . he looked surprised. Not even floored, not knocked for a loop—certainly not relieved. Just a little surprised. You know him . . ."

"I'm not sure any woman really does," said Uhura, bringing up a second lab stool and perching one flank on it as Chapel turned back to her procedure, adjusting the temperature control on one of the cylinders.

In practice, neither Chapel nor Dr. McCoy was ever off shift. Though they had more unstructured time than anyone else on the *Enterprise,* in fact they were like the senior officers, always on call. Uhura had known she'd be able to find Christine here—if she hadn't been working on one of Dr. McCoy's ongoing procedures she'd have been working on the paper she was writing for the *Journal of Alien Pathologies*—and had known that Helen would probably be with her. She had passed Dr. McCoy's office and had seen him, too, still hard at work. On a mission of exploration, no medical officer could afford to simply rely on existing information or practices. In dealing with a constant bombardment of alien microbes, unknown conditions, and shifting biosystems, awareness of new possibilities could literally be the difference between life and death for every person in the crew.

Uhura leaned an elbow on the workbench and added quietly, "I would have said, 'except you.'"

"That's odd . . ." Chapel paused in the act of jotting a note of the numbers which had flickered to life on the small screen at the rear of the bench.

"What?" Helen came over and Uhura turned, both distracted for the moment from the puzzle of Captain Kirk's behavior by the uncertainty in Chapel's voice.

"Well . . ." Christine consulted Dr. McCoy's notes again. "The odd thing is that there's nothing odd. I mean, these are just ordinary homeopathic herbs. There's nothing in them to account for some of the medical effects Dr. McCoy—and Dr. L'jian—observed down on Midgwis."

"He mentioned he was puzzled by the tricorder readings he got," Helen said thoughtfully. "I know he kept taking them."

Chapel punched up a reading on the second of the series of vials, and the third, jotting notes on her stylopad as she spoke. "He said they were all badly deficient in ten or twelve essential vitamins . . ."

"They looked like they were just this side of starvation," Helen said frankly. "It . . . it scared me, a little."

"At that level of starvation, they should have virtually nothing left of their immune systems—and according to the readings, they don't! Like the Midgwins themselves. In L'jian's analysis of ancient bones, she says the Midgwins are severely malnourished in comparison to what they were even fifty years ago."

Uhura frowned; even she sensed the anomaly, and Helen said, "That was mentioned in the preliminary reports. But everyone down there seemed fine."

"Exactly." Chapel looked up from her note making.

"It's got Dr. McCoy stonewalled. According to Thetas, there have been a series of plagues, the sort you start having once a planet's food resources are bottoming out. But each of those plagues stopped, cut itself short after a dozen casualties. Dr. Shorak attributes this to some kind of herbal medicine, but I can't find anything in any of the herbs we've tested to justify that contention. In your reading, in your prep work on the planet, did you find anything that might account for it?"

Helen thought back for a moment, then shook her head. "There's been almost nothing written about Midgwis, you see," she said. "The early reports described the Midgwins as nonsentient—certainly not the dominant life-form of the planet, which is the Bargumps. The Midgwins just colonize whatever land the Bargumps aren't breeding in and stay out of their way. It wasn't until five years ago that anyone guessed they had a culture at all, and not until the Organian Peace Treaty two years ago that the Federation was willing to fund research to keep the Klingons from going in and strip-mining the place like they did Marcipor Two. They still don't know whether the Marcipex were a sentient race or not—no one ever will, now. But they've found artifacts . . . That's why the mission on Elcidar Beta is so important, why the finds there will be so . . ."

She broke off suddenly, and Uhura, seeing the flinch of pain of those dark brows, remembered the strange, gold-lit landscape she'd seen in the viewscreen, the alien beauty of the place.

Chapel must have seen it, too, for she asked quietly, "Have you talked to him?"

Helen did not reply.

"He hasn't left the bridge all day," Uhura said.

"I know," said Helen softly. "I thought he'd come to the rec room, like he used to when he took a lunch break, even a brief one . . ." She shook her head again.

"I'm not very good at this, you know. It sounds

stupid," she added. "At the age of twenty-four you'd have thought I'd have had at least some kind of experience, but . . . I worked damn hard for my scholarships, and studied hard once I got them. Oh, yeah, I had boyfriends, but they never seemed anywhere near as important to me as studying."

She shrugged, and looked away from Chapel's worried, compassionate gaze. "So I don't really know if he's reacting strangely or not. If he's avoiding me, or if this is just something men *do.*"

"It's something *some* men do," Uhura said quietly. "But I would have sworn, not the captain. He's never been deliberately insensitive . . ." She frowned, remembering back to the captain's preoccupation all day on the bridge, to his repeated checking and rechecking of the ship's internal systems reports. "To tell you the truth, my impression is that he's had something on his mind since he came back up from Midgwis."

"That could be," Chapel said thoughtfully.

"And as a relatively minor member of the crew," Helen finished, with a lopsided smile, "it's none of my affair what it is." There was relief in her face, but Uhura guessed it was an uneasy relief, a hope against hope that she hadn't seen what she knew perfectly well she had.

"Minor member hell," Uhura said firmly. "At the moment you're the only one onboard who's done extensive research about Midgwis. If it was something on the planet that worried the captain . . ."

"Nurse Chapel . . ." The lab door slid abruptly open again, framing the spare, blue-smocked figure of Dr. McCoy. He nodded a greeting to Uhura and Helen—people were always coming in and out of sickbay and none of it ever seemed to throw Chapel's work offstride—and turned back to his assistant. "Did you by any chance leave the door of the small med lab unsecured?"

Chapel shook her head. "No . . . those samples need

to settle out in a controlled environment if we're going to get any kind of an accurate reading on them."

"And you didn't mention the changed door code to anyone?"

"No. You only changed it the day before yesterday, and it isn't as if anyone but you and me ever goes in there."

"No," agreed McCoy quietly. "Come in here for a moment." When Helen and Uhura glanced at each other and made to go he added, "You ladies might as well see this, too. The experiment's shot to hell anyway."

The small med lab was situated almost 180 degrees around the curved central corridor of sickbay, in a position corresponding to that of McCoy's private lab on the other side of the central ring. It lacked the elaborate facilities of the main med lab or the biochem lab, and was generally used for long-term experiments that needed to be left in a sterile environment out of everyone's way. "This was just a routine precipitation analysis of blood and fluid samples we picked up at Persis Nova," McCoy explained as he stood aside to let the three women precede him into the bare-walled little room. "Aside from the fact that the information's necessary to a preliminary report on another planet in the disputed border zone with the Klingons, there was certainly nothing unusual about them."

"Good heavens!" Uhura exclaimed, drawing back and looking around the small room in dismay. "Why on earth . . . ?"

Every vessel, every beaker, every test tube on the long table and the shelf behind it had been overset; even the petri dishes full of soft, ashy, dried precipitates and powders were surrounded by scattered dunes of their contents, as if an impatient hand had knocked them sharply back and forth. Distilled water pooled on the floor, and the more viscous solutions lay in colored puddles on the table, or clung in half-congealed blobs around the vessels that had contained them. The dim, sweetish pungency of organic decay filled the air, making Uhura wrinkle her nose with disgust.

"Look over here." McCoy gestured to the end of the table where the blood precipitates had been.

Chapel frowned, puzzled and a little alarmed. "What . . . ?"

"It's as if someone tried to write in it," Uhura said slowly. "To write with their finger, look." Her own slender hand traced the drawn-out smears pulled from the sides of every sticky, purplish puddle, jagged, childish tracks that wavered and went nowhere.

"Why would anyone have done something like that?" Chapel asked, baffled.

"And how would they have gotten in?" Uhura demanded, looking up at the join of ceiling and walls where the narrow vent shafts opened. "The ventilator grille's only ten centimeters square . . ."

Helen, too, was looking at the small metal square above the door, gauging the distance between it and the table with a calculating eye. She turned her head to meet McCoy's speculative gaze.

"A projection out of the vent, maybe?"

"A tentacle or a pseudopod?" he added thoughtfully. Behind them Uhura and Chapel traded a nervous glance, for picking up an intruder, an alien stowaway, was the nightmare of every man or woman who had ever traveled the spaceways, and the source of a thousand tales, authentic and apocryphal, with which the junior crew regaled one another in the rec rooms after hours.

"It would account for a certain amount of clumsiness across that distance . . . but I could swear those marks were made by a finger." Cautiously, he brought the lab's single tall-legged stool up under the vent and, taking a small magnifier and a tiny flashlight from one of the table drawers, stood on the seat. He shined the light down the vent shaft as far as he could—which was only as far as the filter twenty centimeters or so in—and sniffed the soft flow of cool air coming out, then examined the neat mesh of the grille, first visually and then with a tricorder Chapel handed silently up to him.

"Nothing," he said after a time. "No deposits or smudges of any kind, not even of the precipitate solutions. No scratches, no marks, no sign that the vent cover was removed." Bracing one hand carefully on the wall beside him, he climbed down and looked around him again at the disrupted lab. Then he walked to the communications panel beside the door, punched in the number of the captain's personal page and said, "This is McCoy, Jim. We've had a problem in sickbay. I think you'd better get down here."

Chapter Five

"AND AN INTERNAL SCAN of the ship shows nothing?" The captain glanced beside him at Mr. Spock as they emerged, last of the group of Science and Security personnel that had for the past hour been going over the small lab with every analytical tool on the ship.

Spock paused, looking back over his shoulder at the bright, small, evenly lit room, with its tumbled beakers and its liquids pooled untidily on the floor. It had not been hermetically sealed, true, but something about the situation disquieted him.

"Negative, Captain. Both the scan run immediately after the quarantine alert, and the scan just completed, account for every life-form aboard the ship, including the plants in Botanic, the rec room, and Mr. Sulu's quarters."

"I wouldn't put it past one of Sulu's babies to have gotten loose and stuck a tentacle out that vent," McCoy muttered, folding his arms and regarding the disordered lab dourly. More security officers came around the curve of the corridor in which they stood—the main offices of the Security section were just a few corridors away.

"That thing with the gold flowers he picked up on Iolos Six . . ."

"The *aetavis spengleris* would have very little interest in anything with the protein chains characteristic of the Persis Nova life-forms connected with your experiments," Spock remarked quellingly. "Its affection for you, Doctor, was based solely upon body temperature . . . most plants being entirely lacking in aesthetic judgment."

"I could tell that by the way it went after you," McCoy retorted. Spock merely raised a dismissive eyebrow and turned back to Kirk as Dr. Gordon came around the curve of the corridors and into view from the direction of Nurse Chapel's duty station.

Spock, though well aware that it was no more his business than had been any of the captain's other numerous affairs, was interested to note the diffidence with which Dr. Gordon approached the captain—the way she stopped for an instant when she first saw him and then approached with an uncertainty that amounted almost to hesitation, as if she feared a rebuff. That morning on the bridge he had seen her disappointment when Kirk had made no acknowledgment of her decision to remain on board the *Enterprise*—a decision that had lowered Spock's opinion of her powers of logic. He personally regarded it as irrational of her to expect congratulation on the forsaking—or at best the postponement—of her career, even from the man for whose sake the decision had been made.

But why Dr. Gordon would have felt—or feared— rebuff was, to Spock, a mystery.

"I've been over all the preliminary research reports on the life-forms of Midgwis," she said in her gruff, rather abrupt way. "There's nothing that would have been able to get into the locked lab, nothing that would even have been able to get onto the ship undetected . . ."

"That you know about," Kirk said softly.

Helen hesitated. A short ways down the corridor, Security Chief DeSalle had opened another outlet of the vent shafting and was checking the square metal duct with infrascope and magnifier for marks or smears in the fine film of moisture that collected on the filters. Back in the lab itself, Nurse Chapel was holding a reflector for the ship's photographer to get shots of the puddles of liquid from every conceivable angle and in every conceivable lighting and perspective, for analysis both by computer and by DeSalle himself.

The captain went on, "You said yourself the reports are preliminary. Your—" He stopped whatever his next remark would have been, reconsidered, then said, "The research teams made only a cursory survey of the planet. Even Shorak and his party saw only a small portion of the world, never truly appreciated . . ." He paused, a frown appearing suddenly between his fair brows, as if he were picking his words carefully, sorting through a tangle of ideas for what he wanted to express. "My impression was that even their observations were . . . frequently at fault."

McCoy looked around sharply, as if startled; Spock raised one eyebrow for amplification, but Kirk shook his head, not able or not willing to say more.

"We have not, of course, eliminated the possibility that the intruder entered the lab in a perfectly normal fashion through the door," Spock pointed out after a moment. "Nor the possibility that the intruder was a member of the crew . . ."

"Why would anyone have wanted to disrupt that experiment?" McCoy demanded, and Spock regarded him with mild surprise.

"I am not an expert on the vagaries of human motivation, Doctor. I am merely saying that in our quest for the apparently impossible, we should not overlook the obvious. It is a fairly easy matter to disrupt a simple security latch on a door of that kind."

"No," Kirk said quietly. His gaze moved, not restlessly, but with a kind of narrowed deliberation from the door of the violated lab along the curving, light blue walls, taking in the vent grilles, the doors, the small access hatches and conduits that led into the mazes of the ship's walls and tunnels. DeSalle and his assistant were packing up their findings, shaking their heads uneasily; everything having been photographed, McCoy and Chapel were beginning to pick up the fallen beakers and vacuum the spills. "No, there's something. I knew it in the transporter room. I felt it."

"Computer analysis reveals nothing amiss—" Spock began.

"I would say that merely reveals the limitations of the computer."

Back in his quarters Mr. Spock, with his customary deliberation, activated his computer screen and scanned again through the results of the security investigation of the small med lab, the results of the shipwide life-form scan that had accompanied that investigation, and the results of the earlier scan during the quarantine emergency. He punched through a request for the latest results from the analysis lab, where he knew DeSalle would still be working, despite the late hour, on what little he'd found. But as he had himself earlier informed Captain Kirk, there were no anomalies.

Still, he was uneasy. He knew the captain had an acutely developed awareness of subliminal cues, a hair-trigger sensitivity to almost-indetectable breaks in patterns that humans tended to refer to as a "sixth sense," though it was in fact merely a more efficient usage of the existing five.

And he trusted the captain's judgment implicitly. In dozens of tricky and dangerous planetary missions, and in hundreds of chess games, he had seen James Kirk's wits and instincts in action, and knew that the captain had something that he himself lacked: the conviction that hard data had limitations, and the ability to spot those limitations.

Something was troubling the captain. He'd known it that morning on the bridge, seen it in the stress lines of his face, the marks of sleeplessness and strain. He suspected now that Kirk had lain awake most of the night, quite possibly going over these same scan results on his own viewscreen, trying to find some flaw, some telltale clue to tell him that his own instincts were correct—that against all evidence to the contrary, they did have an intruder on board.

And, like Spock, he must have found nothing, for there was nothing to find.

For a long time Spock sat gazing at the computer screen in the warm dimness of his room—the *Enterprise* was a vessel designed principally for an Earth-human crew, though at maximum setting the temperature controls for his private quarters could approximate Vulcan's pleasant heat. After some moments he reached forward and keyed in another sequence, and played through, frame by frame, the video of all the events in the transporter room the previous night. He saw himself hit the quarantine button, but oddly enough, there was not even the characteristic glittery flicker of a feedback ghost that everyone assumed he must have seen.

There was nothing at all.

Nothing except his memory of that momentary, fleeting conviction that there was something in the transporter room that should not have been there.

Then behind him, very faintly, he heard a footstep on the floor.

Spock's reflexes were quick. Even as he turned, his mind groped at the anomaly, the sense that there *couldn't* have been anyone in his quarters when he came in, dim though the lighting was, for his acute hearing would have picked up breathing, the creak of boot leather, the thousand soft, subsensory rustlings that the clothed human body makes . . .

And there was, in fact, no one behind him at all.

For some moments Mr. Spock sat, half turned around in his chair, looking back into the small, somewhat featureless room behind him. Even officers' staterooms on a starship were not large, and offered very little in the way of either architectural interest or places of concealment. Despite his subsequent return to speaking terms with his father, Spock's departure from his family on Vulcan had, for all its exquisite politeness, been stormy enough that he cherished few souvenirs to remind him of the world that had always considered him a half-caste and an outsider. A shelf held a few geological curiosities he had picked up on various worlds; three terminals on his desk permitted him access to as many programs or scientific journals as he wished to peruse at any one time. One could have bounced a coin off the Spartan bunk, had one wished to utilize so illogical a method of testing the taut neatness of its coverlet.

There was nowhere in the room that anyone or anything could hide, and no corner of it not immediately visible from the chair before the desk.

Nevertheless Mr. Spock got to his feet and, in a manner reminiscent of Captain Kirk's recent behavior, walked slowly around the little room, looking, listening, almost scenting, for further anomalies, further clues to account for what he had heard or thought he had heard.

There was, of course, nothing. Dismissing the matter as some chance refraction of sound, but filing the incident for possible later reference in his mind, Mr. Spock stripped, showered, meditated, and retired to bed.

"Jim?" As the door slipped closed behind Helen, the light from the hall—dimmed, as they were in this part of the officers' quarters, for the *Enterprise's* artificial night —caught on the eyes of the man sitting at the little desk, and just for a moment she paused. He'd turned quickly to look at her as she came in, and for that instant his eyes had had a wariness, an almost animal quality that turned them into the eyes of a stranger.

But then the shadows hid him, and his voice was Jim Kirk's voice. "Helen." He got to his feet, came to her and took her in his arms.

"Jim, wait a minute!" With her hands against his broad shoulders she held him off; for an instant his grip tightened greedily around her waist, dragging at her, and she felt, fleetingly, a strength that would not listen, that would not let go.

But the next moment his hold slacked a little and he drew back, regarding her, his face with its strange new lines of worry and stress inscrutable in the dimness.

"Jim, what's the matter?" Her voice shook a little, for even in his arms, where she had wanted to seek what comfort she could all day, she felt a kind of strangeness, as if he were holding off from her, holding something back. His head tilted a little, the single night lamp in the sleeping cubicle beyond catching a gleaming edge on his fair hair. He said nothing.

"We said . . . the truth," she went on, stumbling over her words, cursing herself for not knowing how to say what she wanted to say without inadvertently destroying what lay between them. "Please tell me the truth."

"The truth about what?" His voice was stiff, mechanical, unfamiliar. She had thought at one time she'd been able to read its every variation, its every gradation . . .

She had thought she'd known him. What should she do now? Pretend there was nothing wrong and hope it sorts itself out?

"The truth about me," she stammered slowly. "The truth about . . . about us. This morning on the bridge, when I said I was staying with the ship, you just . . . you just said, 'All right, fine—' " She cut herself off, fumbling for what to say, trying not to sound like a clinging vine petulantly reminding him of fancied promises, and whining because he hadn't paid her sufficient attention. But there *was* something wrong. She couldn't say what, couldn't say how she knew it. She felt burningly conscious of his hands, resting on her sides.

Still he said nothing, and she went on quickly, "But you were—surprised, or you looked surprised . . . Does it bother you that I decided to stay? I can still go back . . ." Her whole soul cringed from the thought of what she knew Nomias would say.

His silence—the silence that felt to her so calculating —unnerved her. "Jim, talk to me! Tell me what's going on with you! I know you love your ship, I know you need your career, I'm not asking you . . ." Her voice tailed off despairingly. Looking across at his face, she could see little of it, for his back was to the dim desk light, but she could almost hear the wheels of his thoughts spinning, calculating, piecing together this explanation or that. Under her hands she could feel the tension in his pectorals, the uncertainty as he hesitated over what would be best to say.

At length he said, "Helen, I . . . You're saying that I didn't react as you expected this morning. But how did you expect me to react?"

"I'm not saying that!" she pleaded, exasperated and tired and desperately confused. "I'm just asking how you *did* react!"

Another long pause. Then, slowly, still picking his way carefully, as if piecing together bits of sentences from previous conversations, "This is something that's never happened to me before. I am . . . new to this . . ."

He hesitated again, then went on quickly, "Helen, can we speak of this another time?"

64

"I'm sorry!" Remorse stabbed her. "I shouldn't have sprung this on you now. You did see—or sense—something in the transporter room, didn't you? The same thing Mr. Spock sensed?"

"Yes." He almost pounced on the words. "Yes, there is—something aboard the ship. I know it. I feel it. Give me a few days, Helen. We will . . . we will talk of this. We will sort this out. But not now."

"All right." It was better than nothing, she thought—it probably didn't have anything to do with her at all . . .

She turned to go, but his arms tightened suddenly around her, dragging her to him. More surprised than anything, she yielded.

She had wanted him all day, wanted the day to end just as it was ending . . .

But what she had wanted was not his body, but reassurance, and in spite of his words, she felt only deeper and deeper confusion, not knowing if it was appropriate to go or to remain, to protest her own needs or to yield to his. Never had she felt so much that, as a man, he was a species utterly alien to herself, and more than anything else, as he dragged her to the bed, she wanted to ask Uhura what she ought to do . . .

The crashing noise jarred Spock awake to darkness, disorienting and profound. For a moment he lay listening, the silence around him thick and waiting, wondering what it was that he had heard.

Logically, he should not have heard anything, he thought. Though the soundproofing of crew quarters was an expensive luxury, at least some measure of it was necessary on a five-year mission, and all crew members —even the real convivials like Mr. Scott and Bray in Maintenance—observed the noise regulations fairly strictly. Most of the time even Mr. Spock's hypersensitive hearing could not distinguish words, though he could usually hear voices through the doors of any room he passed and occasionally through the walls of his own quarters.

But as he lay listening, he heard nothing, for it was the deep of the *Enterprise's* artificial night.

Engine noise? he wondered. But the subsonic, throbbing hum of machines and systems, the veins and nerves of the ship's metallic flesh that made a background tapestry to all his other perceptions of the ship, sounded normal. Still, he thought that what he had heard had been a ship noise, not human . . .

Then he heard it again. Somewhere close . . . For some reason, he did not think it was in the room with him, though logically he could not have heard it so clearly had it not been.

Someone hammering on a bulkhead?

The noise was impossible to identify beyond that it was a pounding: dull, heavy, furious. There was something in its rhythm that made him think it was sentient, not mechanical; a scream of frustration, of hopelessness, by that which cannot make a sound.

The room felt cold. A timer was set to reduce the high temperature at night, in mimicry of Vulcan's desert climate which still ruled his physiology, but for some reason there was a bitterness to this chill, a malevolent clamminess. Spock drew the coverlet over him more closely, but it did not help—after a moment he threw it back, switched on the bedside light and walked to the door.

In the corridor outside he could not hear the pounding at all.

It was possible, he thought, considering the dimly illuminated line of the shut doors of other officers' quarters stretching out before him around the curve of Deck 5, that certain sounds could carry within the walls themselves, if the harmonics were correct—and indeed, that might account for whatever soft, almost stealthy noise it was that had disturbed his thoughts earlier in the evening. But that could very well have been some sound in the corridor itself—his Vulcan hearing frequently picked up footfalls and voices of the people in the passageway that ran by his door.

When Spock entered his room again, the pounding had ceased. It was warmer than he had thought it had been when he'd first awakened; cold as the Vulcan nights, but without that icy frigidness. He turned on the main lights and by their prosaic white glare walked around the small room again, examining the ventilators with the half-formed notion that the sound might have carried along an access tunnel or vent shaft.

Finding nothing amiss, he shut off the lights and returned to bed.

But he was still awake an hour later when he heard stumbling steps go by his door, and the muffled sound of a woman crying as she returned to her rooms.

Chapter Six

EVEN BEFORE THE ALERT CAME, it was a queer and curiously disquieting voyage toward Starbase 9.

Very little of the talk filtered up to the senior officers at first, but there was a subcurrent of rumor, especially among those who worked at the farther corners of the ship. Ensigns Brunowski and Miller spoke of hearing a kind of knocking or pounding while working in the main computer room on Deck 8. At least Miller was working; Brunowski, being off-shift from Laundry and Recycling —or Lose and Ruin, as the ship's cleaning and molecular breakdown/reassembly facilities were fondly known by those who liked to wear something other than uniforms while off duty—was keeping his friend company. The sound seemed to be coming from somewhere close by, possibly carried in a vent shaft or in the walls themselves, but ceasing before they could get any kind of fix on it. Miller, a protégé of Mr. Scott's seconded to Computers because of a temporary shortage in that area, said that the sound didn't strike him as being mechanically produced; more like someone or something pounding on a wall.

Ensign Gilden in Historical reputedly heard something similar, while working alone in his cubicle on the Deck 11 dorsal; a tapping noise coming, he thought, from somewhere among the maze of metal shelves filled with historical documentation gathered from various planets which he was inputting, though he admitted that he did not go seeking the source of the sounds until after they had ceased. He was one of the several who complained of objects being moved—coffee cups, note tablets, bundles of hardcopy and styluses that were no longer in the places where he was sure he had set them, though a glance at the assistant historian's tiny cubicle was, on the surface, sufficient explanation for the phenomenon of disappearing objects. Nevertheless, as Lieutenant Uhura pointed out one evening in the rec room, Gilden could hardly have survived this long in the fashion that he did without developing a fairly strong sense of where he'd placed things. But hers was a minority opinion, at least at first.

Those were the things that got talked about. There were things that didn't.

Mr. Scott, whose cubbyhole down in the Engineering hull was another place that suddenly seemed to suffer from disappearing or oddly transported objects—the most inexplicable of which was the coffee cup that was missing from his desk, subsequently found on top of a two-meter storage cabinet—mentioned to no one the strange sensation that had overwhelmed him while working alone in the shuttlecraft hangar deck, the certainty that had overcome him that someone was standing nearby. The hangar deck itself was nearly thirty meters long, unlit—being out of immediate use—save for a single line of half-strength lumenpanels across the center of the ceiling and the localized white glow of Scotty's worklights near the open access hatch he was testing. The shuttlecrafts *Herschel* and *Copernicus* were looming masses of shadows at one end, but the area around the hatch itself was clear in all directions for thirty feet or so, and sitting up, startled—for he had not heard the inner doors open—Scott had drawn in breath to speak, assuming whoever was there was one of his assistants.

But there was no one there.

And a prickle went down his spine, a coldness, an irrational dread that brought sweat to his palms. In that first second he fumbled to hold his worklight up, illuminating the space all around him more brightly. "Who's there?" he called out, his heart beating fast.

But no one answered. The only sounds were the distant throb of the engines, the faint humming of the worklight itself, and the occasional muted chirp of test gear cycling through.

Annoyed with himself, Scotty went back to work. But after a few moments the dread, the uneasiness, at being alone in that great echoing space grew so strong that he got up and, taking his worklight with him—an unnecessary precaution that he would never have considered under other circumstances, since the vague illumination provided by the lumenpanels far overhead was sufficient for him to see, and he knew the hangar as well as he knew his own cabin—he crossed to the main switches and lit the entire giant chamber.

He shook his head at himself as he went back to work, all his pragmatic Glaswegian sensibilities offended. But the fact remained—he felt better with the lights on.

At about this time Mr. Spock was called down to the central computer chamber.

"We've heard it three or four times, sir," Miller reported, rubbing a big hand through the stiff brush of his hair. "Kind of a tapping noise sometimes. I've heard it, Giacomo's heard it . . ." He shook his head. Spock was familiar with his work, both as Mr. Scott's assistant in Engineering and as a fill-in for one of the higher-level computer techs, and knew his judgment could be trusted.

"Common sense tells me it's got to be mechanical—

you just don't *have* mice on a starship—but the timing is just enough off that I don't know."

"Fascinating." Spock walked thoughtfully around the central computer core—a shoulder-high monolith two meters long by nearly a meter thick, surrounded by concentric rings of data banks, terminals, program-logic cubes, worktables, wafer scanners, and monitors, and painted a neutral shade of Starfleet blue. His boots thumped hollowly on the raised subfloor which masked the tangle of cables and wires connecting this immense nerve center with every monitor screen, visicom, and reader port on the ship. "Where does the noise appear to be centered? In this room?"

"Not really. The first thing I thought of was that it might be something under the floor—there's about forty centimeters of crawl space down there. But to tell you the truth, sir, it's damn difficult to tell."

Spock nodded. It seemed almost impossible to him that a human's hearing, particularly in terms of direction-finding, could be that poor, but it was also difficult for him to understand how humans stood the overpowering, sickly gaminess of the animal proteins on which they routinely glutted themselves. At least Miller was reporting accurately, and perhaps the odd, adirectional quality of the sound was significant in itself.

"Thank you, Ensign," he said, returning to the worktable where he'd left his small troubleshooting kit to extract a handlight. "I shall be here some time. Dismissed."

He had been at work 1.3 hours, finding nothing, when he heard the noises himself.

The first he knew of anything amiss was the sudden blare of gritty and outlandish music from the room above him—for he was lying in the narrow confines of the space between floor and subfloor, meticulously checking every centimeter of cable and wire with the handlight and an ion beam. The noise made him flinch, and he barely caught himself from banging his head on the underside of the floor above. He recognized one of the more outré forms of what passed on Earth for popular music, and realized that someone—probably Miller—had hooked up a dot player somewhere in the room, though how anyone could work with such racket going on was a source of mystification to him.

A moment later he realized that he had not heard the hollow thump of footfalls crossing the floor above him to switch on the device.

He emerged from the hatch and located the player, a smooth black box the size of his hand tucked into a shelf with the spare backup batteries. He keyed it off and stood looking around him at the vacant room.

He would assuredly have heard, had anyone crossed to that shelf from the door.

With the abrupt cessation of the noise, the silence in the room seemed even more profound. The central computer chamber lay in the core of Deck 8, a nerve center carefully protected in the event of attack or disaster, and though it was surrounded on one side by the recreation and entertainment areas, and on the other by the galley and L&R, such was its shielding that no sound penetrated to it from the corridors and rooms outside. Spock stood, the player cradled lightly in his bony hands, listening, and it seemed that a queer, creeping uneasiness prickled at his skin and, just for an instant, quickened his breath.

It was absurd, of course. He slowed his breath and concentrated on finding the source of that . . . dread? His hearing was acute enough to detect a subsonic note, and there was no such thing in operation—a scent, perhaps? There were gases that instilled anxiety, and the *Enterprise*'s ventilation system was sufficiently selective that one area could have been flooded while adjacent rooms were left clean. But stepping quickly to a reader, he keyed in the code for an air-quality report and found nothing amiss in the screenful of numbers that flashed, a moment later, before his eyes. And there was nothing to account for the sudden sensation of icy cold.

Then, quite near him, he heard the knocking.

Miller was right. There was absolutely nothing mechanical about the sound.

It was, in fact, virtually identical to the tapping he had already heard in his own cabin, seventeen hours after departure from Midgwis. It was less violent, less enraged —why, he wondered, did he persist in anthropomorphizing it with an emotional context? Another subliminal cue to be investigated . . .

And as Miller had said, it was virtually impossible to detect from which direction it came.

Belatedly, Spock realized he was still holding the dot player in his hands. Miller would undoubtedly object to the loss of his entertainment software, but Spock switched the little machine to recording mode, multidirectional; then turned to key into the nearest monitor for readings of every life-form, every energy source, atmosphere, gravity, anything at all, concerning the room in which he stood.

There was absolutely nothing amiss. No anomalies, nothing unaccounted for.

The knocking ceased before the computer had finished giving him its information.

Playing back the dot recording later, Spock found that though the machine had erased Radovic Ja'an's *Shaken to the Bones* album, it had picked up no sound at all.

It was Ensign Reilly who first said the word, "Ghost."

"Gah," Chekov said, sorting out his cards. "Trust an Irishman to go looking for spooks . . ."

"Trust an Irishman to beat you hollow round the

cribbage board, you mean—and who's to say there's no such a thing? It was you Russians who set up the Vorodny Institute . . ."

"Of course. We went about it in the correct way, scientifically."

Reilly snorted. At the other end of the long rec-room table, Uhura and Chapel were engaged in sorting out the pieces of the latest of the Communications officer's collection of jigsaw puzzles. Across the room Yeoman Brunowski, square and dark and sloppy in a red L&R coverall, was playing ragtime piano with a touch surprisingly light and sure; and Ensign Tracy Giacomo was singing one of the more scurrilous of the spaceways ballads, to the great amusement of a handful of the junior crew.

"And precious little you found at it, didn't you?" Reilly retorted, moving his cribbage counter several more places ahead of Chekov's.

"Because there was nothing to find," the Russian replied, glancing up from his disappointing collection of fives and sixes. "Why don't you say we've got a werewolf on the ship and have done with it?"

Sulu, kibbitzing over Uhura's shoulder, laughed. "Can't you picture a werewolf on a planet with four moons that all come full at different times? He'd have a nervous breakdown . . ."

"Or a vampire on a world like Trigonis that has three suns and the biggest silver deposits in the galaxy?" Uhura added, looking up from her puzzle bits with a grin.

"Scoff all you may, you heathens," Reilly said serenely. "It'd be a clever werewolf, or a vampire either, to get into the labs and spill whatever's to be spilled, wouldn't it, Christine?"

"That was just an accident," Uhura said quickly. But when she looked across at her friend for confirmation, the nurse had her eyes fixed on the bright-colored blobs of plastic she was moving about on the tabletop, and her thin cheeks were flushed.

"Once is happenstance, as the Great Man said," Reilly went on goadingly, shaking back the loose lock of brown hair that fell over his forehead, "and twice is coincidence. How many times has it been, Chris?"

Chapel raised her eyes to Uhura's. "Last night," she said quietly, "made four."

"Four!"

In the shocked silence Yeoman Zink's rather strident tones could be heard relating the details of an ex-roommate's love life to several interested third parties; a gust of laughter swirled around the piano, and over by the food slots Lieutenant Bray from Maintenance was griping about the remixer program's idea of chocolate.

"The labs have been locked every time," Chapel went on in a muffled, uneasy voice. "It's never the same lab—just wherever there are liquids. Covering the flasks doesn't help; the covers are pulled off, if the flasks themselves aren't broken." She sorted a straight-edged piece from the tangle before her as if it were of some critical importance, and moved it over to where the other edged pieces were, never raising her eyes to her audience.

"Have you tried staying in the lab and watching?" Reilly asked, leaning forward on his elbows, fascinated by the prospect of a ghost story.

The blond head nodded. "That was the time all the bottles in the doctor's liquor cabinet were opened and spilled." She extracted another edge piece, long fingers working as deftly as they did when they were manipulating bits of experimental paraphernalia, or the implements of life and death. Even in her off-duty clothes—exercise tights and a baggy Starfleet sweatshirt—there was something formal about her, some of that quiet aloofness that frequently made her seem older than her years.

"Last night we set up a recorder in each lab. Three of them worked fine. In the fourth—the lab where the beakers were spilled—it hadn't recorded. It must have jammed, though it worked perfectly well in the morning. It just . . . didn't switch on."

Reilly and Chekov had abandoned their game and come close to listen, though it was to be noted that Reilly kept hold of his cards. Though her chair was close by, half concealed from the table by a grotesque potted plant known to all as the Man-Eating Monster, Helen Gordon did not look up from the small reader screen in the arm of the chair before her, though Uhura was aware that Helen hadn't touched the next-screen key for nearly ten minutes.

Chapel fingered another piece free, and after a judicious moment, fitted it into one to which it was obviously the mate. "The thing is," she went on, "about half those puddles of liquids had been . . . touched. Like someone pulled a finger through the edge of them, trying to drag out liquid and make streaks with it . . . Sometimes the powders that get spilled have been traced in too. And I mean liquids that have blistered ceramic countertops and would take a man's fingertip down to bone in seconds. So in spite of what Mr. Spock says about how easy it is to disrupt a security lock—and it might have been the first time, though we've had all of them upgraded to tens since then—it really doesn't look like it's some member of the crew playing pranks."

Giacomo had finished her song, and amid the chatter and talk near the piano Brunowski could still be heard playing, shifting from ragtime to Vivaldi with a delicacy of touch utterly at odds with his unprepossessing appearance. Miller had joined him on the bench, and a moment later the sweet mournfulness of a harmonica threaded into the melody.

"That still doesn't mean it was a ghost," Chekov said stubbornly. "For one thing, nobody has died . . ."

"Don't be ridiculous, boyo," Reilly retorted. "Since the start of the mission we've lost dozens!"

"What's likelier," Sulu said quietly, "is that it's the intruder." He'd come in from the gym next door, still clothed in his close-fitting black bodysuit; his bare arms and face gleamed with sweat like oiled oak in the gentle light.

"Now who's being ridiculous?" Chekov shot back. "They've run life scans on this ship backward, forward, and upside down, and no trace of an intruder has shown up. And anyway, why would an intruder spend his time breaking into Dr. McCoy's laboratories to spill things?"

Under cover of the general noise, Uhura rose with her usual dancer's grace and circled past the Man-Eating Monster to where Helen still sat silent in her chair. Uhura rested one slender hand on the younger woman's shoulder. Helen looked up with a start.

"What is it?" Uhura asked softly.

Helen did not look well. Her hazel eyes were surrounded by dark rings of fatigue, and the lines of strain from nostril to mouth, around her eyes and back from their corners, were deepening to gullies. She had been quiet, too quiet, and looking down at her now, Uhura could see the puffy flesh that spoke of tears—not tears shed once and forgotten, but of hopeless weeping, again and again, alone in the guest VIP cabin that she would occupy until she officially entered Starfleet at Starbase 9.

"Look, if we had an intruder somewhere on the ship," Chekov was arguing to Chapel, oblivious to the fact that Reilly was surreptitiously changing the position of the markers on the cribbage board, "it has to have shown up somewhere on the readings. Even electrostasis life-forms will read on an ion scan . . ."

"The ones that we know about," Sulu returned.

"And anyway, there are no electrostasis life-forms on Midgwis . . ."

"That we know about," Sulu said again. "I know the captain has sent a subspace message back to the research party there to ask about it . . ."

"It's nothing," Helen replied to Uhura's question, her voice almost inaudible under the general good-natured clamor around them. Her hand played nervously along the edges of the reader screen, and Uhura saw how bitten the cuticles of the nails were, how fidgety their touch. It troubled her to see how Helen had changed from the strong, sure woman who had come onboard with the research party—even from the woman, uncertain of her future but confident that all would be well, who had come onto the bridge and quietly looked up into Kirk's face and said she was requesting a transfer to the *Enterprise*. . . .

Something had happened since then. Something drastic.

Slowly, without looking up at her friend, Helen went on. "I— It's just that I've . . . I've decided not to apply for Starfleet status after all. Once we get to Starbase Nine I'm going to subspace back to Midgwis, and ask if they'll still have me."

Uhura said nothing for a moment. The rec-room doors slipped open and Mr. Spock came in, crossing the room with that curious, graceful aloofness to the chessboard, where he began to set up the pieces for a game. The way Christine Chapel's head turned wasn't lost on Uhura, the hopeful look in her eyes that changed so swiftly to carefully concealed hurt. Mr. Spock frequently neglected to greet anyone when he came into the rec room like that, there being no logical reason to do so, but Uhura knew that Chapel—though Chapel herself was the first person to admit the illogic of it—was wounded by being thus ignored.

Dammit, Uhura thought unhappily, *doesn't she realize she's asking for water from a dry well?*

Then her eyes returned to Helen. "Would you like me to send a message back to them now?" she asked softly.

Helen shook her head. "And anyway we've had no messages from them even in reply to the ones the captain sent." Protocol aside, there was something deliberately distant in her use of Kirk's title, as if, Uhura thought, Helen sought by it to put him from her.

She frowned a little. The messages had troubled her. "No, we haven't," she said slowly. "And that's beginning to worry me. I checked out that new subspace transmitter we left them myself. Nothing should have gone wrong with it."

"They might be busy . . ."

"Too busy to answer a question about a possible intruder on a Starfleet vessel? That's one of the top priorities on any—"

The rec room door slipped open again and Captain Kirk came in. He paused in the doorway and looked around him, as was his habit, and it struck Uhura, looking at that trim, broad-shouldered form in the gold command shirt, that he, too, had the appearance of a man who'd been spending his nights wrestling demons in the dark of his room. Like Helen's, his face was taut and weary, though he hid it better; the smile he manufactured as he crossed the room toward Spock and the chessboard was a strained facsimile of his usual grin. *Not that Spock would consider it any of his business to ask about it,* Uhura thought dourly. She knew for a fact from Christine that the captain was avoiding McCoy and sickbay as he would a pest house.

She saw him catch sight of Helen and pause. But Helen got swiftly to her feet, and before either Uhura or Kirk could speak to her, crossed the room to the doors. They swished open sharply before her. Kirk said, "Helen . . ." but she was gone.

For a long time he stood there, looking at the shut doors, and there was something that disturbed and frightened Uhura greatly in the speculative expression of his narrowed hazel eyes.

Chapter Seven

"ARE YOU SURE we're not going to get in trouble for this?" Ensign Gilden shifted the weight of the box he carried in his arms, and the bulky squares of the fat paper books rustled inside it—a complete set of the Margolian novels, with the original Brodnax covers. At this point in the second watch, the medical labs flanking the long corridor from the dorsal elevator to the emergency bridge in the center of the saucer were usually deserted, and in the low lighting, the shadowy forms of the assistant historian and the Anthro/Geo clerk had a furtive air not materially lessened by the sturdy plastic boxes they carried or by the mechanical cargo runner that hissed along like an overloaded donkey in their wake.

"What we're doing is not illegal," Yeoman Emiko Adams said softly.

"Bribing Ensign Miller to clear out and pressurize a hull section is not illegal?"

"I didn't bribe him," Lieutenant Bergdahl's clerk pointed out reasonably. "And if Brunowski can talk Danny into pressurizing one of the hull sections down on Deck Twenty-three to set up that secret lab of theirs, for

God's sake, the least you're entitled to is to do the same to store objects of antiquarian value."

Gilden ducked his head a little—a thin, depressed-looking young man of medium height, slightly stoop-shouldered in his red Ship Systems shirt. "Well," he said modestly, "I don't know about antiquarian value . . ."

"Of course the original faxes of the bulletins from the Castorian wars have antiquarian value," Adams retorted bracingly, her delicate oval face—with the flat cheekbones and bright black eyes that were, with her diminutive height, her private despair—peeking around one side of the enormous box of Mongese romances, the complete illustrated collection of all the various cycles. "And I don't care *what* the computer jockeys say, copying the stories from the novels—or copying the 'best' of a series, and who's to say that the really trashy ones aren't just as much fun?—or copying 'relevant' articles from the *Earthlog* journals isn't the same as having them to look through, to hold them in your hands."

"Well . . ." said Gilden, who was a little embarrassed by the way his pack-rat instincts had gotten out of hand. "The thing is, it's not like they give us all kinds of room, even for 'temporary storage.' 'Only until input,' they say . . . Do the people who write the regs have any idea how long it *takes* to feed a book into the computer? Even with automatic input scan? And to check the translation? And you always have to go through and check the analysis. And what do they give us? Two rooms partitioned out of the Deck Eleven dorsal observation lounge, and we had to fight for those! They've got a goddamn *bowling alley* down on Deck Twenty-one, and they say, 'Dump the hardcopy after the relevant stuff is input' . . ."

"That bowling alley is full every shift," Adams pointed out. "It's one of the most popular rec rooms on the ship."

"Well, it shouldn't be. People should have better things

to do with their time. And anyway," he added, his sparse eyebrows pulling together. "Even after I'd input the information, I couldn't just let them get rid of this stuff. I know there're copies in the Institute Special Collection, and on Memory Alpha, and in other places. But I just . . . I couldn't."

"Nor should you," Adams said. There was a soft, nostalgic look in her shoe-button eyes, for she was a pack rat too.

Their voices dropped as they passed a bulkhead beyond which other voices could be heard, the voices of Security Chief DeSalle and the ship's photographer, examining the computer analyses of the latest lab-breakage incidents, and Gilden and Adams hurried their steps a little. "And furthermore, it's ridiculous that there's no corridor from the Deck Eight dorsal lift across to the central lift," breathed Gilden as they ducked into the alcove near the biochem lab where the turbolift doors were. "We have to go right past DeSalle's office . . ."

"We could have taken the turbolift straight across from the dorsal."

"Nobody does it at this time of the late shift," Gilden pointed out. "Somebody'd be bound to ask who's running fifteen trips back and forth from the pylon at this time of night. It's all worked through the central computer, and it logs it for Fleet Statistics . . . What do they think we're going to do, raid the food remixers?"

The turbolift doors slipped open—Adams and Gilden had a certain amount of maneuvering to get themselves, their respective burdens, and the high-piled bulk of the cargo runner in at the same time. Adams had to do considerable backing and filling with the little hand toggle that controlled the thing in order to get its burden of ephemeral hardcopy clear of the closing doors. "I mean, what're they gonna do in an emergency? Deck Nine," he added, speaking to the ceiling.

"There's the food conveyor," she pointed out as the turbolift whirred into life. "It goes from the pylon into Deck Eight."

Gilden sniffed disdainfully.

There was no sound in the materials reclamation section on Deck 9, but they heard the soft throbbing of the molecular breakdown units, and beneath that, the subsonic whisper of the engines, like the half-heard beat of the ship's heart. Decks 9 and 10 of the saucer, like the lower decks of the Engineering hull, were the automated stomach upon which the *Enterprise* and its crew traveled, the nameless mechanical processes without which the strategies of the bridge, the genius of the labs, and the wisdom of the computers were pointless ephemera, helpless before the cold black vacuum of entropy and space. There was no night shift here, barely any day shift, save for an occasional patrol to make sure things were functioning as they should; the huge, echoing rooms with their crowding, angular machines, their tangles of cable and pipes, were almost dark. Gilden and Adams moved uneasily along the curved wall of that shadowy corridor, the click of their boot heels and the soft humming of the cargo runner echoing in an oddly comforting manner.

"Here." Adams set down her box in the gloomy, odd-smelling cavern of the organic fabrication room and set to work with a small ganymede driver to extract the bolts of a bulkhead. "Miller pressurized three sections for you, the one below this and the big one above. That should give you plenty of room . . ."

"What a guy," Gilden said admiringly, putting his head through the resultant opening and peering around. It was utterly black—Adams produced a small handlight from her belt and shined it around. The chamber beyond the bulkhead was some three meters wide by five deep, and still held the faint, slightly nasty pungency of the raw carbon-hydrogen-oxygen-nitrogen compounds it had contained—the basic raw elements from which all food and water on the ship were fabricated. It was icily cold there, and the clerk's breath puffed whitely in the dim yellow beam of her light.

"Danny said along with the pressure, he'd run in some heat bled off the power conduits from the molecule shakers. He says it'll warm up a little more."

"That's fine. Cold never hurt paper." Gilden ducked through and set his box of books down, then began to unload the cargo runner. "I'll have to do something to thank him."

Adams shook her head and smiled. "He owes me one," she said. "I helped him and Brunowski move the computer terminal in."

"For what?" Gilden asked, puzzled.

Her grin widened—she lost her look of geisha fragility when she grinned that way, and became all street urchin. "It's not illegal," she reassured him.

Gilden thought about what he knew of Dan Miller and John Brunowski, and said hastily, "I don't think I want to know."

Adams ducked back through the hole in the bulkhead and screwed it shut again after her friend. "Here, you'll need this." She handed him the ganymede. "I mean, they're not stealing anything or smuggling anything or running a still or a gambling game or selling fleet secrets to the Klingons . . . nothing like that."

"Then why do they need a lab-quality computer terminal? Or a food remixer? Or a—"

"Well, it's just that John—" She broke off suddenly and looked sharply around. The huge, silent chamber, curved in the shape of the saucer's hull, all at once seemed deathly cold. "Do you feel . . . ?" she whispered, and Gilden held up his hand for silence. Above his short-clipped beard his face was chalky.

There was something else in the fabrication room with

them. They both knew it, could feel it; the cold had nothing to do with the icy vacuum of space outside. It was somehow personal, aware . . . centered somewhere near them, among the crouching shapes of the molecule shakers, hidden in the gloomy shadows. From where they stood, pressed against the wall, most of the vast room was hidden from them, lost in darkness and in the curve of the walls that took in ninety degrees of the saucer's arc. But for some reason, Adams felt that whatever it was, was near them . . . and moving.

Beside her, Gilden whispered an archaic curse word; her hand automatically sought his. Across seven or eight meters of floor the dark rectangle of the door loomed . . . *If we ran,* Adams thought, *if we ran across the floor . . . what if it didn't open?*

Somewhere among the looming monoliths of the machines a knocking started, a faint tapping sound, ringing hollow, metallic. Adams fumbled with her handlight and flashed it in the direction of the sound, but nothing moved there, no shadow, no stirring. Only that hollow knocking, like something seeking its way . . .

With sudden strength Gilden thrust her forward onto the low platform of the cargo runner, pulled the control from her hand and thumbed the toggle for full speed. In a whining whoosh the little cart bolted toward the door, which slashed open before them, whined shut in the dark behind them as they swooped along the corridor's arc, clinging against the yaw of centrifugal force and heading for the turbolift as fast as the cart's engine could carry them. They didn't get off the runner until they'd reached the lift, springing in and manhandling the runner in after them rather than taking the time to maneuver it with the toggle.

They ran the lift straight across Deck 7 and down to the Deck 11 dorsal lounge—deserted at this time of night—and to hell with who was logging trips. Neither wanted to get out and walk that dimly lit, echoing corridor that ran between the central and dorsal lifts.

They didn't speak until they were back in Gilden's office again, a cramped cubicle partitioned, as he had said, off the dorsal lounge on that deck, and crammed—floor to ceiling around the walls, and shoulder high in most other places—with old books, old sets of magazines, box after box of scrolls, files of letters, cases of notes . . . the original hardcopy of historical records, gathered up from every planet the *Enterprise* visited, from every culture and civilization it discovered or explored, information waiting to be logged, digitalized, input for retrieval and transmission to the central knowledge banks of the Federation on Memory Alpha. Some of it had not been looked at for years—or centuries—even on the planets from which it had been gleaned. In the dim light of the small desk lamp the place had the claustrophobic air of a cavern; Adams huddled nervously on a chair between two mammoth stacks of old books and videotaped adventure serials while Gilden ran hot water out of the food slot that was a legacy from the days before the room had been partitioned off the Deck 11 lounge.

"This is real licorice tea I bought on Starbase Twelve," he said, handing her an unwashed ornamental cup. "The remixers only have camomile and mint and they both taste like lawn clippings."

She gave a whisper of a chuckle, but her hand was trembling as she took it. "Thank you." Gilden still looked very pale in the upside-down reflections of the tiny lamp, and he almost spilled his own teacup when he picked it up.

Their eyes met.

"Do we report it?"

She remembered that dreadful cold, the sense of overwhelming fear—the knowledge that something she could not see, could not detect, had been in that room with them . . . "You want to explain what you were doing down in organic fab at this time of night?"

He hesitated, visibly torn between his sense of duty and what he knew the ship's historian would say about the sequestering of useless hardcopy that had already been input. He thought about all the rest of his precious caches of odd weapons, ritual implements, sets and series of arcane books—scrolls and notebooks and letters from and to people a century dead whom he'd encountered in the historical byways of a hundred worlds—that stacked his tiny personal quarters to the ceiling and crammed every cranny and corner of Historical's meager storage area and the minuscule closets of every friend he could talk into providing them room.

Gently, Adams said, "It won't be there if we send someone to look, you know. Not now."

"No," Gilden said shakily, sipping at his tea. "No, I suppose not." He shivered again, thinking about the knocking he had heard in this office. Thinking about the way things had begun to appear and disappear when he wasn't looking, about the sense he had had, once or twice, that there was something in the room with him . . . about the night he'd come down to this office and had heard, beyond its locked door, movement within. "And if it is when we take the next load down . . . I guess we'll deal with it then. You think you could get Danny to borrow a bigger light for us?"

"Helen . . ." It was Uhura's voice, worried and frightened, a moment after the quick, light flurry of taps on the door. "Helen, it's Uhura."

Lying on her bed in the darkness, Helen made no reply. She did not trust her voice to remain steady, and in any case, what could she have said? In time she heard her friend's soft sandals retreat up the corridor, leaving her alone.

Alone with despair, and desperate confusion of mind. Alone with the memory of both a dream and a nightmare.

The dream . . .

Helen dropped her head to the flat, tidy, regulation Starfleet pillow.

The last evening on Midgwis returned to her, with a clarity so intense that it hurt her chest with physical pain. She could feel the warm strength of his fingers enclosing hers, the firm gentleness of his lips—smell the dry, sweetish scents of the grass and feel the warmth that radiated back upon them from the ground itself. In that honeysuckle moonlight the expression of doubt in his face had been clear as by daylight. If he'd known he was lying, would he have felt doubt? Or was the doubt merely something he'd faked to convince her?

Or had she made it all up?

She rolled over and stared at the ceiling above her, a flat and neutral blue-gray, like everything else in Starfleet. It had that impersonal sameness that she'd always despised about the service, that regulation-issue simplicity of the lowest common denominator that she'd been willing to embrace for his sake.

She shook her head bitterly. How *could* she have been that stupid? To fall in love with Jim Kirk—to *still* love Jim Kirk, or still love the man she thought she'd known . . .

But she realized she hadn't known Jim Kirk at all.

That, she knew, had to be the source of the nightmare.

At the thought of it, she reached over quickly to the bedside lamp, switching it on to surround the narrow bunk in its comforting glow. She'd been sleeping with it on for the past four nights.

Rationally, her waking mind knew what the nightmares had to mean. They were, she told herself in the voice of every psychology teacher she'd ever had, just the reflection of her own horror at finding out that Jim wasn't what she'd thought he'd been. That was all.

That was absolutely all.

But waking in the night—or dreaming of waking here, in her cabin on the *Enterprise*—or worse still, dreaming of waking in Jim's cabin, waking up and looking over at the thing in the bed beside her, the thing she had been making love to, and thinking it was Jim . . .

As a xenoanthropologist, she had never been repelled by the concept of sexual congress with alien species, in spite of years of hackneyed anthro-department jokes. But in the nightmares, it had not been the alienness that repelled her, but some deeper and undefinable horror. And always there would be a moment when it would turn to her with its slow grin, and look at her with eyes that were hazel like Jim's—but not Jim's.

She shuddered, pushing the recollection of the dreams away. A glance at the clock told her it was 2200 hours, and she wondered if the novel she'd picked to read that night would keep her awake, as she'd hoped it would . . . wondered if the nightmares would cease when they got to Starbase 9 and she got off this haunted ship.

Footfalls tapped in the corridor. She heard McCoy's voice, the soft southern accent rising and fading in conversation: ". . . swear I haven't felt like that since the time my Butler cousins and I dared each other to spend the night in what was left of the old Hawks plantation . . ." She wondered if McCoy could give her something to keep her from dreaming, but shrank from the thought of asking him.

Because then he would ask her about the dreams.

And he'd ask her when they'd started.

And she couldn't very well tell him that they had started the night she had gone to Jim's quarters after they'd left Midgwis, the night that, lying in his arms, she'd looked suddenly up into his face and had thought, abruptly, blindingly, and for no reason that she could fathom:

This man isn't Jim Kirk.

Chapter Eight

HE WALKED THE CORRIDORS of the *Enterprise* alone, as he had walked them he did not know how many times.

There was something in the familiarity of the action itself that helped him, grounded his mind and soul. Without the *Enterprise*, he did not think he could have survived.

In that first second in the transporter room, when he had realized there was something wrong, when with the tingle of rematerialization he had felt the brute shock, the wrenching pressure of an alien mind forcing him away from the reassembling atoms of his body, it had only been the fact that he was on the *Enterprise*, in the place that he knew as he knew the nerve endings of his own body, that had let him remember who and what he was.

He was James T. Kirk, and the *Enterprise* was his ship.

He would not be forced out. He would not be displaced.

He would not die.

But in those first few seconds, staring in panicked horror at his own body, seeing it move and speak to the others . . . seeing them respond . . . it had been a very near thing.

How well he remembered it, as he moved silently now down these corridors—moved step by step, forcing himself to supply with his mind the recollection of his own footfalls, the slight jar of now-vanished muscle and bone. He was passing along the observation gallery that overlooked the shuttlecraft hangar, an area known to be deserted at this time of night—an area where he knew he would not meet that other self, that alter ego, that creature that walked the ship now in his body. To his left the long transparent aluminum windows looked out into the bluish darkness of the chasm of the hangar, where the single shuttlecraft always ready for swift emergency egress—the *Copernicus,* he knew, from walking this gallery a dozen times—sat docked, a small, square, dark shape in the gloom.

First had come shock, hideous and disorienting as he realized there was something amiss; then horror as he'd seen himself stepping down from the transport disk, speaking to Spock in a voice of command . . .

And then rage, like a red explosion of heat. Maybe it was the rage that had saved him, yanked back the unraveling elements of his mind to a fiercely personal center.

The rage burned him still.

Whatever it was, he thought, moving along those shadowy hallways in the deeps of the night watch, whatever alien mind had taken possession of his rematerializing body—whatever it intended to do with his ship—he would survive. He would win.

But how he would do it without a physical body, without any means to communicate with his friends, without even the ability to tell them that the man they spoke to, the man whose orders they took, the man who commanded the *Enterprise*—HIS *Enterprise*—was an impostor, he did not know.

And so he walked, alone.

In Engineering on Deck 16 Scotty was lovingly dismantling and cleaning one of the power exchangers at the base of the starboard Jeffries Tube in the support pylon, going over every cable and servo with cleaning solvent and the finest of hairline lasers, and explaining to Miller —crouching on the floor just outside the hatch in a neatly arranged welter of tools, with his head thrust in to listen—exactly where each of the power lines ran from and to, and why.

". . . now, on the destroyers, the Saladin-class cruisers, you'll no' be gettin' this much power to the slave relays off the main drive. The housing's about half a meter wider, and the lines run around it—see?"

Miller wedged himself into the base of the tube at his mentor's side and shined a handlight up into the narrow space. He'd already put in a full day in the computer room to which he'd been seconded, but like Montgomery Scott, he was a man who'd rather tear down an engine than eat his dinner. "So if you needed to shift the azimuth, and the servocams quit on you . . ."

Scotty beamed with delight at having a pupil who thought the same way he did. "Well, I'll tell you a little secret. There's an access tube for the mechanical cable stringers that goes up this side of the housing, but in a pinch a man can get up there and change the angle manually . . ."

Miller turned his head suddenly, slithering his upper body out from the tube and whipping around to scan the wide, red-lit chamber behind him, and Kirk saw fear in the young man's brown eyes. He remained still, close to the great dark mass of the starboard turbine; a few meters away from him, Miller stood flattened to the wall, looking up the corridor toward the shuttlecraft deck, then swiftly back into the main turbine room again.

Scotty moved out of the tube to stand beside him, and

his face, too, broad and homey and dark-browed, was troubled. "What is it, lad?"

"I don't . . ." Miller hesitated. "Nothing," he finished.

"Did you feel it get colder?"

Scotty thought about it for a long time before shaking his head. Kirk moved silently away down the corridor, past the dark maintenance shops, the deserted repair bays and the auxiliary infirmary, seeking silence and safety once again.

It was becoming more and more difficult for him to remember what his arms and hands and feet had felt like, what it had been like to walk, to speak, to breathe. He had to concentrate harder to call them back, to create moment by moment in his mind the electron shadow of every eyelash and fingernail, and the concentration tired him more. Sometime, he knew, he must sleep—and without living tissue to contain that shadow, everything he held together by his will, by his mind, would vanish like smoke in the wind.

After his experience of consciousness shared with the alien ruler Sargon, he had asked Spock about the mechanics of this type of personality autoprogramming. Spock, who had his own unpleasant memories of the experience, had been silent for a time, and then he had talked—for the first time since he had known the Vulcan—about the Vulcan concept of *katra*.

Katra, as far as Kirk understood it, was the inner consciousness, the mental reality of a sentient being— the soul, though being a Vulcan, Spock had spoken in terms of the neuroelectronic patterns of the brain and their interaction with the physical form of the body. There were exercises to consciously strengthen and ground the *katra* against dissolution, he had said.

Later, seeking a means to deal with the stresses of captaining a starship, Kirk had gotten his first officer to teach him some of the Vulcan forms of meditation, and though he did not pretend to comprehend any of the spiritual lore of that ancient and secretive race, after practicing the meditation's outer forms, he began to get a dim inkling of what it might be about.

That, too, he thought, had saved his life now, by at least giving him a rough idea of what he must do.

But he didn't know how much longer he could keep it up.

As it was, he could only cling to what he knew, the memory of his body, and the bone and nerve and artery of the *Enterprise* itself.

Down on Deck 23 all was dimness and silence, save for the deep throb of the molecular reconverters in the main fabrication plants on the deck above. Here among the cargo holds all was silent and still. Along the dark corridor only a streak of light marked the bulkhead panel behind which Yeoman Brunowski tinkered with his arcane schemes, whatever they were; above the faint, slightly metallic smells of dust and grime and machine lubricants in the big cargo holds, the dreamy odor of bittersweet chocolate drifted on the air.

In the clandestine lab itself, a five-by-four-meter bulk-storage compartment in the outer hull which Brunowski had talked his incurably good-natured friend into rigging with "borrowed" pressure, the L&R yeoman himself sat at a makeshift table, a lab-quality terminal before him, with an assortment of archaic knobs and dials breadboarded between it and what looked like one of the molecular remixers from the galley. Jury-rigged wiring snaked up the wall, connecting the whole shebang with the main computer line and the power lines that fed the fabrication facilities on the deck above. Overhead, a roughly wired lumenpanel shed a half-strength yellow glow on the young man's unruly dark curls, always just—and only just—this side of Starfleet's regulations about "clean and neat." His dark eyes held a look of almost maniac concentration as he moved the dials hairline fractions of millimeters, listening to the infinitesimal changes in the remixer's soft hum.

Abruptly the lumenpanel made a faint *sput* and went out.

Brunowski swung around in his chair and sat frozen, staring at the narrow rectangle of the opening in the bulkhead. Kirk stepped back a little, though he knew that his own shape would not be silhouetted in the dim corridor lights. He was aware that he himself had, in some way, caused the makeshift wiring to fault. It was something associated with the energy of his presence, like the strange cold that emanated from him, something that he could not always control, as he could not always control the knocking that seemed to arise near the places where he stood. From a dozen minor disciplinary brushes, he knew Brunowski was a difficult man to frighten, but by the faint amber illumination of the terminal screen, he saw fear now in that shapeless unshaven pudding of a face.

After a long moment, never taking his eyes from the hinged bulkhead, Brunowski groped for the handlight on the table beside him and flicked it on. The reflected glow sparkled on the sudden film of sweat on his forehead, but the beam was steady as it flashed across the opening where Kirk had stood. Slowly, hesitantly, the laundryman got to his feet and approached the place, and Kirk fell back a few paces into the dark of the corridor again.

Behind him the remixer gave a soft cough and the smell of bittersweet chocolate was abruptly replaced by that of sweet-and-sour pork—a Starfleet standard. Brunowski cursed quite surprisingly, and added to himself, "I swear to God this place is haunted."

But like Gilden and Adams, Kirk knew the laundryman would tell no one, no matter how many times he might sense his presence in these lower decks.

It was now late enough that he felt he could venture higher, up the central pylon to the saucer itself.

These nights of endless walking, of moving through the familiar corridors and empty, darkened labs, he had been aware that the other Kirk, the impostor who had taken his place, walked too. He wasn't sure why, for he kept strictly away from any chance of meeting a creature whose mental abilities might very well encompass his destruction should they meet, but he knew that the impostor did walk, prowling the decks and corridors of the ship as he himself did. Perhaps, he thought, seeking for some trace of him, some sign. But the *Enterprise* was large, and offered infinite refuge. Perhaps for some other reason.

But in the deep night watch—the third watch, when only a skeleton crew was awake and the humming of the *Enterprise's* machines was virtually the only sound in all those darkened halls—even the impostor slept. Then, for a time, the ship was his again, and he dared emerge from the cargo holds, the storage bays, the vast, humming, automated recycling plants, to do what he could to get his kingdom back.

Ensign Giacomo was working the Central Computer room on Deck 8 when Kirk got there. She was a thin, pretty, dark-haired girl in the short blue tunic of the Science section, running routine input designed more to keep an operator mildly busy than for any real use. The experience of thousands of spacegoing vessels, both in the early days of the Federation and handed on to it by the Vulcans and other starfaring allies, had taught that the central computer core of any ship must never be left physically unattended, no matter how boring and routine this baby-sitting function might be. It was not something which could be done by another machine. There is human error, but there is also human instinct and human judgment.

Kirk crossed the room to the computer itself. The "ship's computer," he well knew, existed in actuality in three separate banks, here on Deck 8 and in two other places in the Engineering hull, all its essential systems backed and double-backed, all linked to one another by superconductor nerve bundles and thence to monitors, readers, and visicoms in nearly every room in the ship. But here was the computer's heart, its brain, its central plexus . . . here in these curving banks of featureless, pale blue metal, protected at the very heart of the saucer, at the ship's innermost core.

And, after the incident with Redjac on Argelius II, well and truly shielded.

It was impossible to guard against the completely unexpected—and Kirk was a firm believer that somewhere in the galaxy lurked sentient life-forms of configurations and capabilities absolutely unimaginable, and therefore impossible to guard against. But part of the *Enterprise's* mission—the essential part—was to see what needed to be made up as they went along. Thus Mr. Spock had taken the Xeno/Anthro/Bio records and devised a projection probabilities program, and from it had jury-rigged a faint electron-bombardment field over each unit in the interlocking concentric rings of the banks, which, he believed, would prevent the entry into the computer of a sentient mind intent upon using the computer as an electronic brain. The ship was far too dependent upon the proper functioning of the computer —and the computer itself too interconnected in its various program paths—to permit that kind of thing to happen again.

The irony of it was, thought Kirk, with a shadow of his old humor, that in ordering Spock to do so, he had very probably sealed his own death warrant.

And since he had no idea what that alien intruder wanted with his body, and his ship—who knew how many other death warrants besides?

He looked around him at the curving banks of memory, of files, of thought units filling that vast and brightly lit round room, the brain of his ship through which every oxygen level and cabin temperature passed, which controlled everything from the conversion rate of the anti-matter pods to the sizes of uniforms to be fabricated by L&R—analysis, documents, translation, records, automatic logs and times—enough and more than enough memory to house the synapses of a human brain.

Spock had told him—Sargon had told him—that without some kind of physical structure, the electron shadow of his mind—the *katra*—would eventually disperse, dissolve. If it hadn't been for the initial stabilizing matrix of the transporter beams, it probably would have done so already. How long it would take, Kirk did not know, and Spock, as he was whenever the discussion touched the dark and secret ways of Vulcan spirituality, had been uninformative on the subject. But Kirk knew, could feel in his bones—*except,* he reflected dryly, *that I don't* have *bones*—that it would be soon.

Giacomo looked up from her work at the central of the three main terminals, her quick-moving fingers stumbling to a halt as she scanned the silent room. She shivered, rubbing her thin arms; Kirk knew, seeing the expression of her eyes, that if there'd been more lights to turn on, she'd have done so. Her hand moved a little toward the comm-link button and then pulled back as she told herself not to be silly; but he could see her fingers shake. Unconsciously echoing her friend Brunowski down in his illegal recycling lab, she muttered to herself, "I don't care what they say, I swear to God this place is haunted." Kirk moved quietly to the wall at the far end of the room.

And began to knock.

He wasn't entirely sure how he produced the knocking. He only knew that he could, by a kind of controlled flailing with his mind. The first time he had produced the sound, it had been unconscious, the reaction of sheer, blind rage, of helpless horror, when the intruder, the alien, whoever and whatever it was and whatever it wanted, had taken Helen in its arms, had hurt her . . . had hurt her, Kirk understood, in a way that might never be healed.

And there had been nothing he could do.

It was that rage that kept him going now, putting all his strength, all his concentration, into the effort to communicate. It was desperately difficult even to produce sounds, and Morse or any other code was out of the question—he simply hadn't enough control.

Giacomo flinched, dark eyes huge with terror, but she didn't get up and leave her post. Kirk, with what little of his mind he could spare from the agony of his task, admired her guts and wished he didn't have to frighten her. But he had to get Spock back here to investigate once more. He had done so once, and could have taken the Vulcan by the shoulders and knocked his head against the wall when Spock had spent his time patiently and calmly searching for a reasonable explanation.

But there was nothing he could do. He had to communicate somehow, with someone. He had to have help, before it was too late—too late for him, and perhaps too late for them all.

"I dunno, Spock." Dr. McCoy poured two centimeters of bourbon into a water glass and relocked the security medical-stores cabinet in which he kept his liquor—the cabinet in which, Spock recalled, every bottle had been found broken the night they'd put all the liquids in the medical labs into unbreakable containers. He returned to perch on the corner of his desk. "There are more things in heaven and earth than are dreamt of in your philosophy, or contained in your computer either, and if it's an alien, it's the damnedest one I've ever heard of."

Spock, seated primly on a lab stool, pointed out, "There is no evidence that the destruction is not being caused by some member of the *Enterprise* crew. All the readings indicate that there is no life-form unaccounted for on this vessel."

"'Readings' my grandmother's left hind leg. Maybe the first time someone could have broken that door code, but after we put the security locks on them . . ."

"I doubt that with the scientific and technical resources available on the *Enterprise* there is a room on board that could not be entered by someone truly determined, and I fail to see what your grandmother's anatomy has to do with the accuracy of the in-ship scans." The Vulcan folded his long, bony hands around his drawn-up knees. At this late hour sickbay was quiet. When Spock had left the rec room after his chess game with the captain, Nurse Chapel had still been there, engaged in the mystifying ritual of picture reassembly even after Uhura had departed.

The chess game had been unsatisfactory, the captain's mind still clearly preoccupied with Dr. Gordon's irrational behavior, though the captain had made no mention of it, and Spock's Vulcan training made even the notion of asking unthinkable. Spock had been interested, though disquieted, to note how deeply the affair with Dr. Gordon had affected his commanding officer. Whatever turn had been taken upon Midgwis, and subsequent to the anthropologist's decision to remain on board the *Enterprise,* its effects seemed to be adverse upon both parties concerned—the captain's chess playing, though it had not precisely deteriorated, had certainly changed qualitatively, and after a single game the captain had excused himself and departed for bed. He had looked exhausted, as he had since the problems with Dr. Gordon had started; Spock was ashamed to admit, even to himself, the concern he felt for the captain.

Still wakeful, he had made his way down to sickbay and had found McCoy still puzzling over the latest manifestations of the putative intruder which might or might not be aboard.

"It is not the 'how,'" Spock went on, "that interests me so much as the 'why.' The choice of the medical labs as the target has, of course, been obvious from the first . . ."

McCoy's eyebrows scaled up. "I'm glad you think so."

Spock tilted an eyebrow in return. "Surely it is clear even to a human, Doctor, that the medical labs are—or were—the only place where free-standing containers of liquids were to be found unguarded at least one third of the time. Since very little else has been damaged or even disturbed, it is clear that liquids somehow have something to do with the disturbances . . ."

"But it doesn't make any sense!" McCoy leaned his back against the edge of the desk behind him, looked up at the Vulcan in frustration. "Certainly not for a human; not even for an alien, really, since half those liquids were inorganic and would have killed anything that tried to drink them. No, Spock," he sighed, and shook his head. "What this is starting to sound like . . ."

He hesitated, turning the water glass in his hands for a moment and regarding it as if momentarily absorbed in contemplation of the reflected glow of the overhead light in the complex carbohydrate bonds of its amber depths. Then he looked up at Spock again with his sharp blue eyes. "How much have you read of the literature of poltergeist manifestations, Spock?"

"Less than point-five percent of what was available in the Academy library," Spock replied with his customary accuracy. "Of the tapes available in the library section of the *Enterprise's* computer—"

"And you haven't noticed a similarity?"

Spock was silent, instinctively unwilling to open a subject that Vulcans seldom discussed with other Vulcans.

"The knocking, the objects moved around without people seeing them, the—"

"I am familiar with the poltergeist effect," the Science officer replied slowly. "The Vulcan word for it is *eschak.*"

McCoy blinked. "I didn't think Vulcans had anything so irrational as ghosts."

"Eschak—poltergeists—random and destructive psychokinetic effects—are, as you quite well know, Doctor, unconnected with the chain-jangling headless horsemen you humans take such delight in frightening yourselves with. They are, as you point out, irrational, perhaps one reason that they are so much more common in your world than in mine . . ."

"Don't tell me," McCoy moaned, "that even your ghosts are too logical to haunt houses."

"I would not tell you anything for which I have so little data," Spock responded politely. "Nevertheless . . ." He frowned, dark eyes focusing upon some middle distance of contemplation. Contrary to what most humans believed, Vulcans were not entirely creatures of rationality —their notorious logic was, in fact, a necessary defense against the other side of the Vulcan nature. Due to more widespread use of meditation and other spiritual techniques, cases of *eschak* were indeed few—no more than one or two per century, and even fewer now—but those that had been substantiated made human poltergeist manifestations appear laughably ineffectual.

"Nevertheless," Spock went on, "in most such cases, both in your world and mine, the manifestations are associated with a human focus, usually a young boy or girl, or someone in a deeply disturbed frame of mind."

Their eyes met.

After a long moment McCoy said, "What's going on with her, Spock? And with Jim? Seeing the two of them in the rec room tonight . . ."

"It is certainly not my place," Spock replied, "to

investigate—or to discuss—the captain's romantic entanglements."

"Dammit, Spock, you know as well as I do that this isn't just a romantic entanglement! Jim is damn serious about the woman . . ."

Dryly, the Vulcan said, "You would know more about such matters than I, Doctor. But it appears that Dr. Gordon is in some state of strong emotional turmoil, which seems to date from her trip to the surface of Midgwis; and no manifestations of the poltergeist effect were reported before that time—certainly not before Dr. Gordon's appearance on the ship. One could theorize—"

With a sharp whistle, the intercom on the desk came to life. McCoy reached out and slapped the switch. "McCoy here . . ."

Uhura's voice came on, breathless and shaken. "Doctor, I'm down in Helen's room—visiting officers' quarters. Can you get here right away?"

Chapter Nine

SHE WAS WALKING in the observation lounge on Deck 12 with Jim. It was very late in the second watch; they had already been to his room, and in the warm aftermath of loving, he had spoken to her of his ship, and she had said, "Will you show it to me?" He'd chuckled, "What, now?" and, deep asleep now, Helen still felt in her dream the touch of his lips on her bare shoulder, still smiled at the way the hanging forelock of his rumpled blond hair dangled in his eyes. But she saw the delight in his face.

The observation lounge, like all the dorsal lounges in the pylon, was a single long, narrow room with an emergency gangway at one end and the turbolift shaft at the other, a double line of chairs running down its center, and a food slot programmed for the more popular combinations of starch and grease. At this time of the shift the long room was empty, and only dimly illuminated. The stars outside seemed very close.

If she stood near the heavy, structural-weight plex of the windows, Helen could see the underside of the primary hull spreading like a weightless parachute of pale gray rhodium overhead, the long, sturdy pod of the Engineering hull stretching beneath. But below that pod dropped infinity, literally infinity, pitch-black and deep beyond conceptions of deep. In it the stars, hideously distant, did not twinkle or sparkle, but burned with a chill skeletal light that made the shadowy structure of the great nacelles and their slender pylons seem strangely fragile.

And over all that silver surface shone pinpricks of light, tiny reminders of the warmth of life which temporarily baffles even the entropy of infinity, the individuated joy of humanity capable of briefly conquering that all-encompassing dark.

It was only her second time on a spacegoing craft at all. The passenger liner that had taken her from Mars, in whose colonial domes she had grown up, out to Delta Cygnus to the university, had not boasted observation ports. She was interested to note that in spite of the life-support systems, the pylon's observation decks and lounges—and the Historical Section that had been commandeered from one of them—were noticeably colder than the inner areas of the ship. The wall that separated them from eternity was icy to the touch.

She looked over at Jim's face and saw the dreams there, reflected by starlight in his eyes.

"It's the freedom out there that you want, isn't it?" she said softly. "Not the ship itself, but where the ship is going."

He thought about it a long time before replying. There was something in the dim intimacy of the empty lounge that, for all its echoing length, was like the warm confines of the cabin they had just left. In a way, it was as if they still lay twined together like animals in an underground den. Helen could think of no man to whom it would even occur to her to speak like this—to ask the why, to inquire about the heart spring that few people even like to admit that they have . . .

But somehow, with Jim, it was easy.

Slowly, as if it were a matter difficult to put into words,

he said, "I—I don't really know. It isn't freedom, really. If it was freedom, I think I'd have become one of the free-traders, the planet-hoppers—God knows, if it's freedom you want, you don't go through Starfleet to get it. And I don't think it's power, exactly. I may have absolute power over 430 people, but when you think about it, that's not very much. It's—it's as if the words for it have been forgotten. Longing . . ." He shook his head, fair brows descending over the bridge of his straight, well-shaped nose.

"I used to think I was crazy," he went on softly, speaking as if to himself. Speaking, Helen thought, as he had spoken to no one for years—perhaps never. "Just to go to these places, to see them . . . to be where no one has imagined being before, at least no one I've ever known, have ever heard of." His arm around her waist had tightened a little, iron-strong, and yet there was no desire now in his grip—for desire had been sated—but only a kind of gratitude that someone was there. It occurred to her that, like the aloof Mr. Spock, for all his womanizing, this man had been essentially alone much of his life.

"It sounds so silly when you pick it apart," he said after a time. "But when it's inside you, calling you on . . ."

"Yours goes out," Helen said softly, speaking of whatever it was—that longing that had no name. "Mine goes deep. To see how things fit together, and what's going on underneath. It does sound silly, to say I've spent my life studying how things work, but . . . I had to. I couldn't not. But for the life of me, I can't explain why."

"If we could explain why," he'd said with a rueful half grin, "we'd talk ourselves out of it, and be the poorer."

He'd drawn her closer to him then, and they had kissed, not in passion, but taking pleasure in the affection; and from thinking that the captain of the *Enterprise* would be a good man with whom to have a teeth-rattling affair, Helen found herself thinking that Jim Kirk was a man she would want to know for a long, long time . . .

She turned in her sleep, troubled, trying to surface from the gluey darkness of her dreams.

There was something wrong.

Her flailing hand brushed the switch of the bedside lamp—it was on, as was the small reader by the bed on which page 215 of a murder mystery called *The Shirt Off His Back* still glowed with amber letters on darkness.

But she couldn't wake up.

She sank back down, this time to nightmare.

It was the nightmare that had become terrifyingly familiar, the nightmare of Jim's arms around her, of Jim's lips crushing hers, rough and brutal and impersonal—the nightmare of her own confusion and indecision. She had never felt this frightening sense of being taken by an utter stranger. *But this is Jim!* she kept saying, desperately, to herself.

But looking up into his eyes, she had known it wasn't Jim.

She didn't know who it was.

Or what.

Then she was lying asleep in her bed—or maybe it was Jim's bed, for in her dream she couldn't tell. In her dream she could see by the faint glow of the nightlight that someone was lying beside her, an indistinct mound beneath the rumpled sheets, a faint sheen of light—maybe—on the blond hair . . .

Terrified, she tried to wake up before he turned toward her with the face that wasn't Jim's face. That wasn't human at all. She was trying to wake up, trying to get enough air into her lungs to scream and wake herself up, but there wasn't any air . . .

Let me out of this! Let me out before he turns to me . . .

The covers stirred, moved.

She managed to open her eyes.

She still couldn't breathe.

Her head was throbbing. The room—her own room, and not Jim's quarters, in which she'd been dreaming she'd lain—was nearly dark, but for the glow of the night lamp and the orange reflection of the reader. She tried to inhale but couldn't, her lungs sucking, her sinuses full of some strange, metallic smell. Panic flooded her, panic that she might still be dreaming . . .

She looked at the bed beside her and saw it empty of the thing in her dreams. But the buzzing cloudiness filled her head, like sleep or something close to it, disorienting and terrifying. She fought her way clear of the coverlet and rolled numbly to the floor, dragged herself to her feet, fumbling, clouded, not really sure whether she was still asleep or not. But whatever was happening, she thought numbly, there was something wrong, something very wrong, and she had to get out of the room.

Reeling like a drunkard, she made it to the door. Her fingers groped at the opener switch.

Nothing happened.

Panic flooded her, panic beside which the panic terror of the dream vanished like a leaf whirled away by a stream. There was something in the air of the room, something that weighed and burned her lungs, filled her head with dull humming and wrapped her limbs in lead. *The ship!* she thought, terrified. *The life-support systems have gone—there's an emergency—the intruder—there is an intruder—it's shut down the life-support systems!* She remembered someone had shown her the emergency manual switch to the door, but couldn't recall where it was or how to use it. Her vision was graying out as she stumbled to the tiny desk, pounded desperately on the comm switch. But of course if all the life-support systems were gone, everyone else would be dead too . . .

Dead—she was dying . . .

"Uhura . . ." she gasped, her throat on fire and the

words a harsh guttural croak, not knowing whether the intercom was working or not. "Uhura!"

"Methoamyline gas." Mr. Spock held up the long, narrow cylinder for the captain and McCoy to see. The thumb-sized gauge at the top read almost empty. "It had been placed in the ventilation duct in Dr. Gordon's quarters; the outflow duct had been closed and the door pad disconnected."

Kirk held out his hand, his eyes blank and hard.

"I could have told you it was methoamyline," McCoy growled, glancing back at the high diagnostic bed where Helen lay, her dark, level brows black and startling against the gray waxiness of her face. "She's lucky she woke up long enough to call for help . . . and luckier still the person she called was awake to do something about it."

"I—I don't quite know what woke me." Lieutenant Uhura frowned, wrapped the heavy black folds of her robe more closely about her. "I just—I'd been worried about her." Her dark eyes slipped sidelong at Captain Kirk, but he stared straight before him, unresponsive. "Then I—I thought I heard something falling. That's what waked me." She shrugged. "And when I opened my eyes and looked around, the comm light was flashing . . ."

"The methoamyline was one of the spare breathing tanks left over from when we transported the Denovian consular party to Giermos, of course," Kirk said quietly. "It wasn't being kept under any particular guard . . ." He hesitated, and passed his hand suddenly across his eyes. Behind the hardness of furious anger in them Spock could see exhaustion, the ragged look of a man living on his last reserves. He was keeping it concealed, as a commander must, Spock thought, but the harsh lights of sickbay showed up cruelly the new lines on Kirk's face, the hollows under the cheekbones where he had visibly lost weight.

Slowly, he walked back to the bed, and stood looking down at the woman there. The slow rhythm of her breathing was soundless, echoed in the faint pulsing of the diagnostic screen above her. Even in unconsciousness so deep it bordered on coma, there was a slight pucker to her brows, as if she still struggled with some haunting, abyssal dream.

"I thought she—" Kirk began uncertainly, and stopped. Then, "I wonder why she didn't try to call me?"

Spock caught the slight compression of Uhura's bronze lips, and the look of both puzzlement and irony in her eyes, and remembered how Helen had fled the rec room earlier that evening upon Kirk's entrance. It was, of course, absolutely none of his business what was going on, and indeed, from a Vulcan standpoint, in appallingly bad taste even to notice so blatant a display of emotions. But had a biochemical or technical problem presented this many fascinating anomalies, he would have been tinkering day and night with the follow-up of those contradictory clues.

He wondered if there were a way of consulting privately with Uhura on the subject, once the present problem of the intruder, with its new and alarming ramifications, was solved.

Since Uhura said nothing, Nurse Chapel, who stood on the other side of the bed, replied tactfully, "She was in a panic, Captain. She'd often call up Uhura to talk during the off-shifts, as she couldn't call you."

"Oh," Kirk said, a little blankly, his brows pinching together as if with thought or pain. "I—I see . . ."

"Do you?" McCoy growled as he led the way from the intensive care ward down the corridor to his office, leaving Chapel and Uhura by Helen's bed. The door slid soundlessly shut behind them. "Well, what *I* see, Jim, is that you look as bad as she does. What the hell is the

112

matter with you? You've been avoiding this place like the plague . . ."

"And I'll continue to avoid it as long as there's a threat to my ship." Kirk paced a few strides, then turned back with a fidgety restlessness, like a caged tiger, to face them.

"And there *is* a threat, gentlemen," he went on in a taut, quiet voice. "I've known it—I've felt it—since we left Midgwis. I've sensed it, hiding somewhere in the corridors, somewhere in the walls. And now it's turned lethal."

"And has attacked the only person on board who has done any kind of extensive research on the fauna and inhabitants of Midgwis itself," Spock concluded thoughtfully. "Which indicates that it is intelligent and, to some degree, informed. And yet the lack of any kind of physical readings . . ."

"The galaxy is a big place, Mr. Spock," Kirk replied softly. "None of you—none of us—has any idea of the true capabilities of the Midgwins."

"Then you don't consider it an accident," the Vulcan said, "that we have had no reply to our efforts at subspace contact with the researchers on Midgwis itself?"

"No." The captain shook his head. "It's becoming more and more obvious that communications were deliberately cut—and that someone is trying to keep us in the dark about something on Midgwis itself. We're turning back, gentlemen."

Spock raised one eyebrow—Kirk walked to the comm link on the wall of McCoy's office, keyed the bridge. "Ms. Fontana . . ."

"Yes, Captain," came the night navigator's voice.

"Lay in a course for Midgwis. Lieutenant Mahase, notify Starbase Nine that we have changed our course and are returning to Midgwis due to a potential threat to vessel's safety, and possibly to Federation security. That is all."

"You're making it sound like a conspiracy," McCoy said doubtfully.

"I agree with the captain," Spock put in, walking to the table where McCoy had laid down the empty methoamyline cylinder and examining the gauges once again. "Indeed, it may explain in part our extreme difficulty in locating the intruder by conventional scans. However, it does not necessarily have to be a conspiracy of the Midgwins. The Klingons have every reason to wish to sabotage the mission there, and have been known to buy or extort the services of fleet personnel before. The manifestations—"

"No," Kirk said sharply. "No, it is—something from the planet. And it must be destroyed, as quickly as possible now, since it will almost certainly try to prevent us from returning to Midgwis."

Spock's left eyebrow tilted still farther at this sudden dogmatic certainty; McCoy perched on one corner of his desk and said, "Fine—but just how do you go about destroying something that doesn't leave physical readings on an in-ship scan? Something that can go through walls, apparently at will?"

"There was research done at Columbia University in the late twentieth century on the effects of proton waves upon electronic kyrillian fields," Kirk responded, resuming his pacing. "You're the expert on *katra,* Spock—you should be able to put together some kind of disruptor that should disperse our little friend."

Spock was shocked silent for a moment, as if Kirk had casually mentioned in company some confidence about his sex life, and for just an instant he was startled to find that the pang of that casual betrayal of trust went so deep.

But the man was the captain, and, he reminded himself, under considerable stress. Stiffly, he replied, "Indeed, a kind of proton-acceleration field can be devised. But I would be much more inclined to attempt to communicate with the intruder before destroying it out of hand."

"No!" Kirk insisted again. "That would be dangerous —perhaps fatal." And, when Spock looked at him blankly, he went on in a calmer voice, "It's a disembodied intelligence, Spock; a bioelectrical shadow. It could . . . possess anyone who came near enough to let it. If you, or you, Doctor"—he swung around, his eyes suddenly, burningly intent—"or anyone, in fact, hears, or sees, or . . . or senses . . . any kind of manifestation, any appearance of this—this poltergeist effect—flee it *immediately*. The risk is too great, especially for you, Spock."

"Indeed." Spock remained standing beside the workbench, long fingers resting idly on the gauges on the cylinder, his straight, dark lashes veiling his eyes. On the wall behind him the lighted readouts of the observation monitor showed Dr. Gordon's bio readings inching slowly back toward normal as the poisons were cleared from her blood. Dimly, his Vulcan hearing picked up the voices of Nurse Chapel and Lieutenant Uhura in the corridor, exchanging low-voiced words—then the retreating click of Chapel's boot heels as she went into the lab, and the soft pat of Uhura's Morocco leather slippers vanishing down the corridor. He turned back to the captain, troubled by his growing sense of wrongness, of something amiss.

"I find it curious, however," he went on, "that when Mr. DeSalle fingerprinted this cylinder, it was found to have been wiped clean. This argues for a degree of sophistication in our intruder—if, in fact, the attempted murderer and the intruder are one and the same."

As she approached the door of her cabin, Lieutenant Uhura slowed her steps. Two or three times, coming or going from Helen's quarters or the rec room late in the second watch, when the corridors were nearly deserted, she had felt again that strange fear that had come over her the night after they'd left Midgwis, the eerie sense of being watched by something that knew her name. She had mentioned this to no one, aware that rumors were already buzzing around the ship, but some of the things she'd overheard in the rec room troubled her more than she liked to admit.

And now this.

It was turning lethal, the captain had said. She wondered if what she had felt that first night had been only her imagination, or whether she'd had a closer call than she cared to think about.

She had dreamed about it, she thought, hurrying her steps toward her door; dreamed about it just before she woke up, dreamed about cold, about someone calling her . . .

But why would it call her, if waking her up would save Helen?

She shook her head. Probably too many of Reilly's rec room ghost stories, she thought. The thumping sound that she had the dim impression had waked her had undoubtedly been due to that.

But it hadn't. The door slid open, and though a week ago she would simply have walked over to her bed and gotten in, the uneasiness of the last several days caused her to switch on the light while still standing on the threshold.

And she saw immediately that the small Martian bronze that usually stood on her tiny, metal, Starfleet regulation dresser lay on the floor in a corner. It must have been its fall that had waked her in time to see the flashing light of Helen's call.

Behind her in the corridor, the small amber lights of a Yellow Alert began to flash. The alert light over the comm link in her room was flashing also, and though she was virtually certain she knew what she was going to hear, she reached out and touched the open-announce button. Yellows you had to key in to find out what the trouble was—it wasn't a roll-you-out-of-bed emergency, but definitely something for everyone who was awake to know.

As she'd expected, the voice of Lieutenant Mahase, her night replacement, was speaking. ". . . on board. Exercise all precaution; avoid being alone." In spite of herself, she smiled at the recollection of Mahase's outrageous rec room parodies of the standard announcements about exercising precautions and avoiding being alone under any circumstances. "Intruder Alert—it has been confirmed that an alien intruder is on board. Exercise . . ."

She removed her fingers from the switch, then looked back at the little bronze, lying on the floor. Dubious, almost afraid to touch the thing, she walked over and picked it up, then looked from it to the dresser where it had stood. Uhura was meticulously neat—living in a three-by-five-meter stateroom for three years, you had to be—but there were only so many places to put things, and the top of the dresser was one of them. A few perfume bottles, the tiny amber gleam of the Alert lights flicking on and off in the depths of the glass; her jewelry box; the small, cased disk of a favorite movie; a note tablet and stylus . . . The place the Martian bronze had occupied was clearly delineated by the things that had stood around it. It was nearly ten inches from the nearest edge.

There was no way it could have fallen by itself.

Chapter Ten

BACK IN THE CHAMBER of the captain of the Hungries, Yarblis Geshkerroth sank slowly onto the bitter hardness of the bunk and lowered his head to his hands. *"His" head,* he thought ironically, *"his" hands,* and held the hands out to look at them. Little and white and weak, fragile enough to crush in his beak, had he still had a beak.

Yet with finicking little stubs like these, the Hungries had made machines, machines that made machines, which in their turn had created this, this monster thing, this half-living city, this iron Bargump that carried them all in her sterile belly through the screaming black void of nothingness they called Space.

Loneliness ate him like a cancer. He wondered how much longer he could last.

Longer than the captain of the Hungries, the man Kirk, he thought, with sudden, vicious desperation. At least longer than he.

Touching him in the village, he had felt the alien captain's strength. But never had he guessed the man would have such strength to hold his soul together in this

fashion. Not for so long. Only barely could he remember
how long it had been.

Dear Rhea, he thought desperately, *let me last . . . let
me last until it is accomplished.*

But Rhea—the sweet life that informed every tree,
every stream, every glade and covert in which he had
grown up, the breathing spirit whose name and nature he
knew deep within his heart—was far away. Having all
the brain of this James Kirk at his disposal, being able to
see the memories in his mind as easily as he saw the
memories of his siblings in the Consciousness Web, he
knew in a sense how far away the world, the Mother
Spirit that had surrounded him, was, though he could
barely grasp it with his heart.

Farther than a Midgwin could walk, if he had begun
walking at the dawn of the world, through all the years of
ancestors, till now . . . and he could not even walk that,
because there was no earth here, no rock, no water. No
Rhea, no family, no Consciousness Web, no love. Only
nothingness, and the cold metal of the vessel, and the
hysterically precise measurements that the Hungries
occupied themselves with to the point that they could
not think without thinking *centimeters, microns, seconds,
years . .*

How easily they slipped in and took over, first the
language of the mind, then its perceptions, then its inner
heart.

No wonder they all became grabby, thinking that
because they knew how many of a thing existed, they
could then apportion it, so many to me, so many to my
sibling . . . only they did not think of others as their
siblings. Only as "them."

No wonder they became Hungries, hungry with a
hunger that could never be filled no matter how much
they had.

And all the evil, all the craziness, all the tight greediness he had read in their dreams, in their minds, in their memories—greediness that they did not even recognize as wrong, which they seemed to think the right and natural order of things—greediness that would now spread among the Midgwins, cause his people to seek it, because it masqueraded as good—stemmed from that.

Counting. Hunger-of-the-soul. Mine and yours.

If Arxoras could be deceived by them, Arxoras who was wise and good with his many summers of experience, how much more would others less experienced be deceived?

Yarblis staggered to his feet, turned to the mirror above the dressing table which held the things the captain's memories marked as "his." He had never occupied an alien body for this long. The Hungries he had ousted from their bodies when they materialized in a golden cloud of glitter—the Hungries that Shorak and the others had called Klingons, and claimed were not the same as themselves or James Kirk and his party—he had taken when they arrived in the world, and had kept only long enough to kill the others of the party before returning to his own body. He had never before realized the terrible stresses of the alien flesh, and how those stresses marked the body he occupied: his inability to sleep in this new body, his loathing distaste for the slimy food that his mind told him he had to eat to keep from being conspicuous . . .

And like a darkness in which all things else must grope, the hideous, devouring loneliness of separation from the Consciousness Web.

That above all.

He stood now looking at the face of James Kirk. It was more lined than it had been, grayer, the discolored flesh around the eyes making them seem pale and glittery. The physician had begun to notice. The man Spock, the cold Counter of Everything, had noticed more.

Like the woman Helen, he would have to be disposed of before he, Yarblis, could accomplish his plan with the ship, the plan that would save the world from the Hungries forever.

He had not thought that—

Abruptly the door note sounded, its mechanical quality unbearable for all its softness. Yarblis swung around, fighting the grate of irritation that these things caused, with all their implications about the way these people lived; calling back to his mind everything about James Kirk, everything that *was* James Kirk. *He* was James Kirk now . . .

"Come," he said.

It was Spock.

"Captain . . ." The Science officer—Kirk's mind identified him as Science officer and all that it meant—inclined his head. Spock was like the researchers Shorak and L'jian, who would never enter the Consciousness Web, whose souls were like stone eggs and whose dreams he had never quite been able to read. He would have liked to read Spock's dreams, but the concentration required merely to remain in Kirk's body precluded anything else, and, robbed of the usual mental links, it was difficult sometimes to read the verbal and physical cues of a species alien to himself.

"What is it, Spock?"

Spock considered for a moment, an uncharacteristic uncertainty in his hawk features. Then he said, "Perhaps I should be asking that of you, Captain. I did not wish to speak of it before Dr. McCoy, but it is my impression that you know more about this intruder than you have said. Certainly you seemed to be expecting an intruder long before the manifestations began to be reported by the crew."

He frowned, tilting his head a little and regarding the captain with those dark, calm eyes. His experiences with

121

the Klingon-Hungries had given Yarblis a little experience in reading these elongated, oddly featureless faces, with their tiny eyes and minimal folds—he had long since grown used to having them around him.

"I did not speak of it, as I was not entirely certain that it was that which was preying on your mind." Spock spoke diffidently, as if skirting another matter, and Yarblis remembered/knew from Kirk's memories that this Vulcan, this stone-egg-soul, would have regarded mention of the affair with Helen as bad taste and none of his business. Though Yarblis knew Kirk was Spock's friend (though friendship could not truly exist without the Consciousness Web), he himself disliked the Vulcan and everything he stood for: the cold self-containment, the precision that negated all the freedom of soul for which he, Yarblis, strove, the obsession with counting things, with rules.

He shrugged—a gesture within Kirk's repertoire—and said, "If I'd spoken of it, would you—or anyone—have believed me? We went over this ship top to bottom —your precious readings didn't show us a thing. But I knew there was something in that transporter room. And I think you did too."

"Indeed, I had a momentary impression of there being another life-form there," Spock said doubtfully. Yarblis, his back to the dimness of the room, his face to the lights in the hall, was aware of how narrowly Spock was regarding him, aware of the intonations of worry and uncertainty in the deep, rough-textured voice.

But the Vulcan (another piece of knowledge from Kirk, though Yarblis was not entirely certain how to interpret all those things that went with that label on these particular family of Hungry) merely went on, "Did anything take place on the planet that would have led you to your conclusions about the intruder? I have been meaning to speak to Dr. Gordon about it . . ."

Yarblis realized he had put the metal gourd of poisoned air in her room just in time. And now he would have to make sure of her, before she regained consciousness enough to speak.

"Only my impressions gained from encounters with the Midgwins themselves." What Kirk knew, or thought, of his people, Yarblis knew to be so simplistic and distorted as to be almost unrecognizable. What Helen knew, he could only guess from memories of what she had told her mate. The others would know nothing, but he realized he had spoken from knowledge that there was no way he could have had. There were so many things to know, so many things to sort—it was not like the brief masquerades before.

He went on, carefully, "Some of the things Thetas and the others told me on the planet about the abilities of these people . . . Be careful, Spock. I'm telling you again, this thing must be destroyed, and as quickly as possible. Don't get near it. Don't let it get near anyone."

"Indeed not, Captain," Spock replied formally, though Yarblis could see he was not pleased about that. There was an awkward silence, in which Yarblis was aware that the Vulcan was watching him, as if waiting for something. What it was, he could not be sure, not knowing the physical cues of these people, but whatever it was, he did not get it. In time, walled behind his formal manner, Spock went on, "I have double-checked the shielding on the computer, as the poltergeist effect has been reported itself a number of times in the Central Computer room or its vicinity."

"Good," Yarblis agreed, though it was less than completely clear to him why Spock seemed to consider this important. This "central computer" was vitally important in Kirk's mind—a sort of giant machine that made the air go, the lights shine, the ship itself move. But as with the implications of Spock's Vulcanness, the clusters of tiny facts surrounding the concept of Central Computer were difficult for him to interpret. He knew enough about the "computer" to use it to implement his plan for the ship, his plan that would save the world, that would keep the Hungries from tempting his people into destroying the beauty and wholeness of Rhea in which they lived, but there were other things which he simply had not had the time nor energy to pick apart.

"Good. See what you can get for me on a low-wave proton accelerator. If we know that it is manifesting itself near Central Computer, we can start our hunt for it there."

"Very good, Captain."

Spock inclined his head again, a gesture of respect. With the closing of the door, Yarblis heard the slightly uneven tread of his boots retreat down the hall; heard the boots pause, as a man might pause when caught by some thought, then start again and fade.

He had done something wrong.

Yarblis knew it, standing still in front of the door. His heart—the alien heart—beat fast with the rush of alien enzymes into his blood. He had avoided them whenever he could—the man Spock, the woman Helen, the physician McCoy—the others whom Kirk's mind identified as those who were most familiar with his mannerisms, though since these people lacked anything resembling a Consciousness Web, Yarblis could not imagine how they could truly know one another at all. He had hoped to be able to avoid them, or at least put them off, until they returned to his own world and he accomplished the plan that would put his people beyond the temptation of dealing with the Hungries forever.

O Rhea, Mother Spirit of streams and grass, he whispered to himself, *let me only last that long . . .*

Yet whatever he had said in this conversation, or in the one before, in the cold and sterile rooms that passed among the Hungries for a Healing Place, he had made some kind of mistake, and the man Spock was more suspicious than ever.

He would have to act fast.

The crew of the *Enterprise* felt little surprise when word came down that their course had been reversed and that the starship was en route back to Elcidar Beta III. In a number of quarters there was even a certain amount of relief that the ship remained on Standing Yellow Alert: confirmed reports of an intruder, precautions to be taken. Those who worked Central Computer late at night—Giacomo, Miller, McDonough—had for several nights already been doubling up on their shifts, those off duty, or friends in other departments, like Gilden and Brunowski, unobtrusively keeping those on duty company. A few questioned the fact that scans of the ship still revealed no evidence of an intruder's physical presence, but most had been in space long enough to realize the extreme narrowness of human experience. There were only a few who continued to claim that the intruder was, in fact, a ghost.

In other quarters, however, uneasiness remained.

"You can't deny there's something weird about the whole business, Spock," McCoy grumbled, perching on a lab stool and watching while Spock made adjustments on what appeared to be—and was in fact housed in the gutted casing of—a small laser cannon, hooked up to a modified nuclear accelerator and a proton converter. "If it's an alien—if it's something we picked up on the planet—what the hell is its aim? I still find cups and feinbergers moved around in the labs, and if there's any free liquids there, they get tipped over, but what's the point of that? And what the hell is that thing supposed to do, anyway?"

"This, Doctor," Spock replied, looking around the

workbench behind him—they were in the small ion-study lab on Deck 2—"is a low-level proton wave-induction generator."

"Oh," McCoy said. "Silly me; should have seen it in a minute." He crossed his knees and watched with a certain amount of interest as Spock turned around in what, had he been human, would have been irritation, and started a concerted hunt through the tools on the bench. "Lose something?"

"There was," Spock said, "a pin welder on this bench 2.7 minutes ago exactly—I put it there just before you came in." He straightened up, dark brows forming an even sharper vee than usual above the high bridge of his nose beneath the protective goggles he'd pushed up onto his forehead. "This is the fourth tool which has inexplicably vanished in the last eighteen hours. Yesterday a sonic wrench, a crystal-optic transmitter, and twenty-four centimeters of selenite wire all disappeared from this bench where I clearly remembered laying them down."

McCoy groaned. "Don't tell me it's starting here!"

Spock eyebrowed for amplification.

"Nurse Chapel tells me things have been disappearing out of the labs, and turning up in the damnedest places, like that note pad of mine that showed up in the decontamination room where nobody'd been for days . . ."

"Or a tube of methoamyline disappearing from the xenoecology stores and turning up in the ventilation ducts of Dr. Gordon's quarters?"

McCoy looked uncomfortable. "Well, there is that."

"How is she, Doctor?"

"Still pretty groggy. She says she has no idea how the gas cylinder got there, but she'd been asleep for a couple of hours when it was set off. The gas is odorless. It's only chance she woke up, only chance Uhura was awake when she signaled her room. Since there's no one else in sickbay at the moment, Chris and Lieutenant Uhura take turns staying with her. Considering she's our only source of information about Midgwis now, I think it's a safe assumption that our intruder's going to try again."

"I agree," Spock said, picking up a spot welder and squinting as he delicately collimated the beam down to approximate the vanished tool he actually needed. "Yet there is in fact very little evidence connecting the intruder—or the various poltergeist effects that have been reported on the ship—with the attempted murder of Dr. Gordon."

"Oh, come on, Spock," McCoy said. "You're not still claiming there's a Klingon spy on board, are you?"

"I would not be so rash as to theorize ahead of my data," Spock replied austerely. "But apports—objects appearing and disappearing—are fairly commonly reported in cases of poltergeist phenomena, and there has yet to be a reported case of a poltergeist wiping fingerprints from such an object." He pulled the goggles down over his eyes and bent over the induction generator; there was a sharp hissing as he pin-welded the delicate wires into place.

"It is for that reason," he said a few minutes later, straightening up again from his work, "that I wished to attempt contact of some kind with the intruder. At the least, we might gain some information about what it is and perhaps increase our knowledge of the fauna of Midgwis—if Midgwis is where it came on board, as seems to be the case. Certainly it seems to possess as high or higher levels of intelligence as the Midgwins themselves, and its skills at concealment would go far in explaining why it has not been mentioned in Dr. Shorak's reports. At best, we might gain a witness as to the real perpetrator of the attempt, provided, as I say, that the intruder and the perpetrator are not one and the same."

"And if they *are* one and the same," McCoy replied,

"you lay yourself open for God knows what. Some kind of alien possession, if Jim's right."

"If," Spock agreed carefully, "as you say, the captain is right."

There was a long and rather uncomfortable silence.

"Have you talked to him?"

Spock pushed his goggles up again, frowning a little, as if trying to fit together pieces of some complex puzzle which would not fit. "I have attempted to," he replied after a moment's consideration. "And indeed, it is difficult to find fault with his reasoning. The records of contact with alien species bear ample witness to the existence of life-forms with whom even the most careful attempts at contact prove quite rapidly fatal, not only to the single individual attempting contact, but to everyone in the contact party. And beyond this certainty—which could only be an exaggerated caution—he seems to be perfectly in possession of his senses."

"I dragged him in for a physical today, dammit," McCoy muttered, picking up a stylus from the bench and turning it restlessly in his hands. "His weight's down about five pounds, but other than that he's fine—physically. And if he didn't say two words to me . . . Well, he *is* dealing with an intruder, and one that can't be detected. And it *did* come damn close to killing the woman he loves. It's enough to make any man a little irrational."

"For which reason," Spock replied dryly, "I have always been profoundly grateful that I am a Vulcan." He returned to contemplate the awkward tangle of spare parts and wire on the bench before him.

"And this'll kill it?"

"Theoretically." Spock checked a connection, plugged in a gauge, and consulted the ruby numbers that blinked to life in the dark of the tiny screen. "It is difficult to tell in advance, as the life-form—if it is a life-form—is completely unknown to our records and does not register on scans. In theory, if the intruder is an independent neural-electronic infrastructure, the proton-induction field should disrupt its pattern long enough to neutralize it permanently."

He turned back to his workbench and moved his hand as if to lay it on something he knew precisely the location of, then paused, irritated, and began to hunt again. McCoy hopped down from his stool and walked around the induction generator, hands behind his back so Spock couldn't accuse him of poking things—he'd visited Spock while Spock was working before—examining it with interest. "So what was that *katra* thing Jim asked you about?"

Spock's back was to him, and he saw the shoulders stiffen. The Science officer's voice was arctic. "A theoretical concept in Vulcan metaphysics the captain and I had once discussed."

The intonation was as definite as the banging shut of a door, but McCoy persisted anyway. "He talked about it as if it were a type of life-form analogous to the thing we're dealing with."

"The analogy was in error." Spock removed his goggles, hung them neatly on the appropriate hook and donned a magnification headset, a pair of needle-fine manipulators in his right hand. "Now if you will excuse me, Doctor, the captain is very anxious that the generator be finished and tested this evening. Three more need to be produced tomorrow, so that the entire ship can be swept in sections, and I do need quiet to work."

"Well, excuse me," McCoy muttered, and took his leave. Spock was poking around in the innards of the induction generator before McCoy was out the door.

Back in sickbay, McCoy glanced through the door of the intensive care ward where Helen lay, dozing fitfully under the faint lights of the diagnostic bed. Beside her Uhura sat, the computer reader angled around toward her, and the muted amber lights of something on the screen turning her broad cheekbones to faintly gilded bronze. She looked tired. She'd had a full shift on the bridge already, McCoy knew, though he also knew the Communications officer did not grudge the time spent watching at the bedside of her friend. It was one of the worst and most annoying things of a Standing Intruder Alert, this doubling-up of watches. He couldn't ever recall one that had gone on this long.

On the other hand, he thought wryly, passing along the corridor to his office, he couldn't ever recall dealing with an alien who was nothing more than a pattern of neural impulses, if that. No wonder the researchers on Midgwis had never reported such a thing.

Or had they? Curious, he tapped a key to activate the reader on his desk, and after a moment's thought to remember some of the codes, punched into the reference computer. Would Input have gotten around to indexing Shorak's reports yet? Probably—they were usually pretty fast about things like that.

Letters swam onto the screen, amber in darkness.

SECURITY CODE REQUIRED FOR ACCESS.

Damn, he thought, cutting out; *Spock must have put a bee in Jim's bonnet about the Klingon conspiracy theory after all*. He debated buzzing Jim and asking about the access code, but glanced at the chronometer and decided against it. If Jim wasn't asleep now he ought to be.

He frowned, reflecting on that. Jim looked terrible. Was it the pressure of knowing the intruder was on his ship, somewhere, waiting to kill again? Or was it whatever the hell was going on between him and Helen? It sure as hell wasn't like Jim to take on that way over an affair that had turned sour, but then, Jim was generally careful to keep his affairs too casual to turn sour in that fashion . . . And in any case he, Leonard McCoy, Boy Divorcé, had no business setting himself up as a consultant to other people's love lives when he'd made such hash of his own.

Having him in for a physical had gotten him exactly nowhere. There was nothing wrong with him, except the lines of strain in his face, and that haunted look in his eyes. He'd tried keeping his friend off the bridge during emergencies before, when he was severely wounded; it hadn't worked. When he'd tried to talk to him he'd been met with monosyllables: *I can't talk about it now, Bones. Ask me about it later.*

"Maybe when we get back to that godforsaken planet," he muttered to himself, keying open his security safe and taking out a small, unbreakable container of bourbon to pour himself a glass, "we'll get this straightened out."

But the memory of Midgwis troubled him. The touch of the old patriarch's mind on his came back to him, like the balm of warmed oil on a half-healed wound—the sense of the burden of loneliness lifted. He remembered the molten amber moonlight, the smells of dust and whispering grasses—the sense of all things being at rest, being as they should be, without hurry and without stress, from the beginning of time. Remembered, too, the reflection of the firelight in Thetas's dark eyes, and the little Argellian's soft voice in the dancing shadows as he spoke of the strange beauties of the Midgwins' simple life, their elaborate structure of legends and faith, their spiritual philosophies and intricate, nonvisual arts, the deep calm of their civilization that came from the sense of lying utterly in the hands of Fate.

A structure fragile as glass, Thetas had said, which even change for the good might shatter irreparably.

He knew that none of the three researchers had mentioned any kind of Midgwin belief in spirits or invisible beings—which didn't mean there wasn't any, of course. It might be something the Midgwins hadn't mentioned to the researchers, or that the researchers wouldn't have thought to mention to the landing party if they considered them simply creatures of the imagination. Beings which moved and manipulated artifacts

would have damn little scope in Midgwin society, which
hadn't been able to come up with any greater claim than
a few sticks and a wreath of flowers to the instrumentality necessary to class them as officially a sentient civilization.

And yet, according to what Helen had told him in the
last few weeks about how cultural researchers operated,
it was not something they would disregard.

He got to his feet and walked back down the short,
brightly lighted stretch of corridor to the doorway of the
ICU. "Lieutenant Uhura?"

She looked up swiftly. Absorbed in her reading she
might be—novel, romance, fashion magazine, whatever
it was, piped up from the deep reserves of the library
computer's endless files—but she still knew herself to be
on guard. "Yes, Doctor?" She reached out to touch the
hand of the woman who lay in the bed, then to straighten
aside the dark cloud of hair that lay on the flat pillow.
"She's resting easier."

"Good." He came into the shadowy room. The air was
stuffy—because of the alert, the ventilators were double-
shielded. "Do you know if Dr. Gordon had any separate
set of notes about Midgwis? A separate wafer of her
researches, for instance? All the planet reports in the
main computer are under seal, and I'm not going to wake
Jim up to get them . . ."

"He sure looks like he needs the sleep," she commented. "Yes, Helen had a wafer. It'll be by the reader on
her desk in her room. It's got an orange label. It's all the
early reports on Midgwis—it's pretty complete. She was
looking for some kind of reference too, you know, about
a creature that was invisible, untouchable."

"She find anything?"

Uhura shook her head. "I don't know. But I don't
think she'd mind if you went into her room and got it."

But when McCoy went down to the visiting officers'
quarters—still feeling a little silly about going to all this

trouble for something he could probably get Jim to give him the access code to tomorrow, always provided he could track Jim down—there was no wafer with an orange label next to the reader. There was no such wafer anywhere in the room—in fact, there were no wafers of any kind in the room at all.

Restless, Helen moved in her sleep. Uhura looked up quickly and pushed aside the reader on its movable arm. The novel she was reading, about love amid the fall of ancient civilizations, was only to occupy her time—anything (*except a ghost story,* she thought wryly) would have done. She glanced in surprise at the chronometer in the upper corner of the diagnostic screen. Nearly midnight. Chris should be coming on duty here soon, and she could go to bed . . . not that it would be much of an improvement on sitting next to Helen. Because of the alert, even the officers, who had private staterooms, had doubled up quarters, standard procedure in the rare cases of an alien loose. She was sharing with Chris, and with Organa from Security, a woman with whom they both got along well. But one could have only so much of the cozy atmosphere of a slumber party. Here, at least, it was quiet. And, she admitted to herself, a little uneasily, remembering the strange feeling she'd had in the corridor, here things were very well-monitored indeed.

She bent over the bed, feeling Helen's face. Neither fevered nor cold, though her friend was turning a little in her sleep, muttering restlessly. She took the big, square hand in hers and said softly, "Helen, I'm here. It's Uhura . . . I'm here," not loud enough to wake, but enough, she hoped, to reassure.

Helen opened her eyes and stared at her in the dim glow of the diagnostic lights. Her voice, eroded by the harshness of the gas she'd inhaled, was almost unrecognizable as she whispered, "It isn't him!" Her eyes were blank, still dreaming—possibly even still asleep. She closed them again and a great sob tore her; the powerful fingers closed around Uhura's with a desperate grip. "It isn't him!" she sobbed again, and broke into a storm of weeping, turning her face away when Uhura tried to comfort her.

From weeping, she slid back into sleep.

Chapter Eleven

AFTER DR. MCCOY LEFT, Mr. Spock sat for some time at his workbench, magnification headset pushed up on his forehead, staring at the induction generator without really seeing it. His first flash of annoyance at McCoy he had repressed with reflex swiftness, and reproached himself now at the childishness of feeling it at all. What he felt about Kirk, he knew to be equally childish, and only to be expected, as his father would certainly have told him—and he could hear the Vulcan ambassador's deep voice and judicious phrasing in his mind—if one spoke to humans regarding Vulcan things.

In speaking to the captain at all regarding matters of his Vulcan heritage, he had behaved like a sentimental fool.

That katra *stuff* . . .

So that was all Kirk had gotten out of that conversation, one evening months ago in the deserted rec room when they'd finished a second game of chess and the captain had asked him about meditation, about the Vulcan philosophy. After several hours' more discussion about life, and why humans strive, they had reached—with the tentativeness of friends who are not quite sure

135

whether they wish to abandon the safety of super-ficialities—the concept of the soul.

It had been that hour of the night when the last of the off-watch crew members had trailed away to bed, when the lights had dimmed down to a few pools of brightness around the piano, the chessboard, the bank of food slots on the wall. A little to Spock's surprise, since the captain generally presented a facade of action and boldness, Kirk had spoken of his own soul, his own doubts. Spock had reciprocated with what he had himself been taught, and what he in fact believed . . .

It had been a side of the captain that he had rarely seen, and one which he had believed to be genuine. The anomaly was disquieting, but based upon matters notoriously open to misperception.

He went back to work.

The silence around him seemed suddenly profound. Straightening up, he looked about the ion lab, trying to analyze the source of his deep sense of unease. A lab, like any of the other small ones in the Science section, the bright lumenpanels prosaically illuminating neatly arranged tools on the workbench, the coils of wires and superconductor, the gauges on their shelf and, on the other side of the room, the brushed-steel cyclors and the gleaming computer terminal. Some imbalance of his circadian rhythms, he thought. It was only 2300 hours but it felt later, felt like the deeps of night . . . He had a flash of irrational dread that if he opened the door through which McCoy had passed, he would find only darkness there. And the room certainly felt cold.

The dread he felt, the sense of the uncanny, was certainly as irrational as his earlier annoyance had been. He reached for the spot welder he had collimated to replace the vanished pin welder—the tool he had placed on the bench behind him literally 8.3 minutes ago during his conversation with Dr. McCoy—and found it, too, gone.

"Curious," he said quietly. Getting to his feet, he made a slow circuit of the lab, checking—as they had all fallen into the habit of repeatedly checking—the ventilators behind their emergency baffles, the small, round electrical hatches, the corners that seemed somehow to contain strange feelings of congealed uneasiness. He found nothing. "Most curious."

He returned to work in a thoughtful frame of mind.

Dammit, Spock! Kirk screamed at him, voiceless, helpless, from the corner of the room where he stood; and he *was* standing, he told himself—feet on the floor, elbow a few centimeters from the wall—he *did* have the shadow of a corporeal body still . . . *Don't bend that fine Vulcan mind of yours to finding a reasonable explanation! You're the only one who might be able to hear me—who might be able to save me, to save Helen! He's going to try to kill her again* . . . And his own time, he knew, in this strange, bodiless state, was growing short.

But the sleek, dark head, bent over the innards of the induction generator cum proton cannon, did not lift again. And somewhere Kirk sensed the nearness of that other captain, that terrible alter ego who had done this to him . . . who was seeking to kill the woman he loved and use the ship that was his very life now for purposes unknown . . .

Somewhere that other self was walking, prowling the half-lit corridors on whatever errands had taken it nightly here and there about the ship, from the upper decks of the Science section down to the very bottommost of the cargo holds. Knowing he could not face him, he faded into the wall and fled down, following the computer lines toward the deserted lower reaches of the Engineering hull, where, if relatively unnoticed by any save Brunowski and Miller in the pursuit of their mysterious projects, at least for the time being he could be safe.

* * *

"Two generators," Mr. Spock said, "should adequately establish a disruption field on one deck of the ship, allowing for both the curvature of the primary hull and the length of the Engineering hull. According to what little research has been done in the field, my estimate is that ten minutes should be sufficient time to disperse an electrostatic life-form, though I have no data on the possibility of such a life-form reassembling itself. Perhaps you have an opinion on the subject?" And he regarded the captain, left eyebrow slightly raised, curious as to what his reply would be.

Kirk passed a hand over the lower portion of his face, a nervous gesture he had picked up in the last twenty-four hours or so, as if to vent some of the feverish restlessness which seemed, these days, to be consuming him. "Ten minutes . . ." he said softly, and for an illogical moment Spock had the impression that he was trying to call to mind precisely how long ten minutes actually was.

"It can—it might be able to—re-form itself . . ." The blinking amber lights of the Yellow Alert, still flickering on and off above the door of the small ion-study lab, increased the illusion of a strange animal heat in his eyes, as well as the way he held himself, with his head drawn down a little to his shoulders, as if for protection. "The *nialigs* of Rigel Five could re-form . . . Twenty minutes, the reports said." Then, with a visible effort, he drew a deep breath and made his shoulders relax. "What . . . what is your opinion, Mr. Spock?"

"I think that thirty minutes would be a guarantee of safety," he replied, a little surprised that the captain would have dug out that obscure report from the library section of the computer and consulted it, even as he himself had.

"Thirty, then," the captain said, with a sharp little nod that made him look again like himself. "We can't take chances, Mr. Spock. You were able to assemble two proton generators, then?"

"I was able, by cannibalizing the spare ion-frequency accelerators, to assemble three," Spock replied, worriedly observing how Kirk's hand stretched out to caress the gray housing of the laser cannon in which one of the generators had been constructed, and which now rested on the lab table before him. The other two generators stood near the door, clothed in the round, brushed-steel casings of the accelerators from which they had been constructed, barnacled with sprawling incrustations of the equipment welded to them to complete the transformation, the fruit of a long night's labors which had left the ion lab—and the physics workshops next door—strewn with gutted transformers and opened modulator housings like clamshells around a village midden. Even after he had completed work on them at close to 0400 hours, Spock had neither left the lab nor gone to sleep, half fearing they would play the same vanishing tricks as his tools had in the earlier part of the evening, or suffer the same inexplicable malfunctions that recording machines seemed to in the presence of the intruder's halo of poltergeist effect. When he had reported to the bridge at 0800 hours, he had left a security officer on guard over them—the woman was still waiting discreetly outside the door.

"Three?" Kirk's eyebrows pulled together slightly, questioning—then he nodded, though Spock had the momentary impression his agreement was pro forma, not because he understood the strategy. "Of course . . ."

He is tired indeed, Spock thought, his own eyes narrowing as he considered the strained harshness of the captain's face. "Had sufficient parts been available, or had Inorganic Fabrication had time to create them, I should, in fact, have built four," he said. "Naturally, we will need to stairstep our way down from deck to deck, disassembling the units on one deck while the deck below is being swept. Sufficient parts not being available, I was able to assemble two slave-relayed signal modulators which should extend the field to cover an entire deck and thus do the work of an independent generator, but it has left the physics laboratory completely depleted . . ."

"It doesn't matter," Kirk whispered in that low, tense voice. He did not even walk over to the two modulators that Spock had indicated—lumpy, bizarre bastardizations of assorted pieces of research equipment wired to the faceted shallow screens of pickup dishes. "The sweep has to be made soon, Spock. Soon—before we reach . . . Midgwis." He had been about to call the planet something else, Spock thought.

"Captain," Spock said hesitantly, "I am still of the opinion that some attempt should be made to communicate with the intruder . . ."

"No!" Kirk swung fiercely around on him. With an effort, he got a grip on himself again, straightened up, and said more temperately, "You don't . . . We don't know what we're dealing with, Spock. I can't take any chances."

Again, the sureness in his voice troubled Spock, the impression that his captain did, indeed, know only too well what they were dealing with. Had he seen something, Spock wondered, in the half-hour or so that McCoy had mentioned Kirk had spent walking alone with Dr. Gordon along the periphery of the thorn jungle that concealed and protected the Bindigo Warren? Seen, or sensed, or heard something that told him now what it was that had attempted to murder the only other witness to . . . whatever it had been?

But in that case, why keep its nature a secret? If it were a hitherto unknown form of life, to destroy it without even an attempt at observation would be monstrous, given the nature of their mission.

"Would it not be possible to use the generators to fence the intruder into a small area of the bottommost cargo hold until we reach Midgwis?" Spock asked reasonably.

"That way, advice could be obtained, either from the researchers on the planet or from the patriarch Arxoras."

"No!" Kirk insisted again. "It's—it's too dangerous." He passed his hand over his mouth again, fingers pulling twitchily at his lips as he thought. "Given time, it might be able to slip past the fields somehow, and we can't risk that."

"Perhaps," Spock said. "On the other hand, the intruder itself might be a creature known—and indeed revered—by the Midgwins, and there might be repercussions of some kind if we—"

Kirk laughed harshly, an abrupt bark abruptly cut off, then shook his head. "No," he said simply. "No, Mr. Spock. In fact, we have no way of knowing that Arxoras and the other *memmietieffs* aren't behind this. They could have been deluded into thinking . . . into thinking that the Federation means harm to the world . . . to Midgwis . . ." He shook his head again, the gesture of a tethered animal trying in vain to drive clouds of canker flies from its ears. The pain line between his brows stood out very clearly. "No. We are dealing with an Intruder Alert, Mr. Spock, and an alien which has proven itself capable of murder. For the safety of the ship we must do it this way, and must do it soon. How soon can the sweep begin?"

"The generators can be charged to full power by 1800 hours." Spock nodded toward the thick stringers of cable leading from the wall to the two chunky, brushed-steel globes, the savage triangular shape of the laser cannon. "Once charged, they will be able to operate on ship's power, though Mr. Scott is charging backup emergency batteries." Slowly, as he spoke, he began to collect the tools from the edge of the bench where they had ranged —the tools that had appeared and disappeared in so disturbing a fashion last night, always just after his back was turned . . .

Another manifestation of the poltergeist effect? But would a creature intelligent enough to know that the construction of the generators must be slowed down—intelligent enough to identify the sole member of the crew who might have information concerning it and attempt to dispose of her—have contented itself with merely stealing tools? For most of the night, in disregard of one of the standard Alert rules, Spock had been working alone . . . and the creature had allegedly attempted to kill once already.

He went on slowly, "Allowing ten minutes for setup and breakdown time, on either side of a thirty-minute run, I have estimated that the sweep should be accomplished in 15.666—"

"All right," Kirk said abruptly. "Set up your teams—have them in the main briefing room at 1800 hours." And turning sharply, he took his leave.

Thoughtfully, Spock summoned in the security officer to keep watch over the equipment once again, and descended to his quarters to complete his notes for the briefing and the assembly of the sweep teams. Allowing for the exigencies of sweeping the dorsal decks separately from the lower decks of the primary hull, for setup and takedown time—two more modulators, he realized, would have to be assembled in order to keep a continuous sweep going on Deck 7—the deck level at which the primary hull connected with the dorsal—the sweep, which would undoubtedly not begin until 1900 hours or later, would last through the night and well into the following morning. That meant a relief shift was needed, of two teams, perhaps three when they reached Deck 7 . . .

He paused in his note making and sat for a moment, his note pad on the small surface of the desk before him as he turned his stylus over in his fingers. The bright lights of his work cubicle gleamed off the faces of the three terminals on the immaculate desktop before him.

Beyond the little doorway his sleeping cubicle was dim, warmly red-lit in imitation of the world in which he had grown to manhood; the room was comfortably warm, and quiet, with a privacy which even in Standing Intruder Alert conditions he treasured above his own safety.

And in fact there had never been an occasion of the poltergeist—or intruder—manifesting itself in the primary hull during the first watch. Whatever it was, it was a creature of nighttime, a creature of darkness when no one was around. Like the *eschak*. Like McCoy's plantation-haunting ghosts.

He frowned, knowing that he should be contacting Mr. Scott and Mr. DeSalle to line up his sweep teams, which he wished to be comprised of Engineering and Security personnel—Scott in charge of one, Miller in charge of another. His mind roved over his own subordinates and protégés in Science for other possibilities . . .

But his eyes returned to the computer terminal.

After a moment he unshipped the keyboard from its recess and opened a screen. Clearing himself through entry and security programs in a second or two, he keyed through to the mainframe itself, using the keys rather than voice commands for greater speed and precision, as most of the Science personnel did.

Spock's interest in, and familiarity with, the *Enterprise* computer was as much with how it worked as with what it contained. He had found that by skipping the transliteration into standard English—and in fact skipping the voice programs altogether—he could access information far more quickly. Some of the Loglan didn't even translate. Sheerly out of curiosity, he punched through into the reference exec programs for a runout on all articles requested of the reference section in the past five days since they had left orbit around Midgwis. From there he narrowed to all articles requested from terminal PTQ-7767—the terminal in the captain's quarters.

The captain had summoned up and read all articles

referring to the possibilities of electron-state life-forms and how to combat them—including the obscure report on the Rigel V *nialigs*—within twenty-four hours of returning from the surface of Midgwis. A brief consultation with the captain's log—which was double security sealed, but Spock had long ago learned to make short work of any form of security seals—served to inform him that it had been nearly thirty-six hours before the first reports of the poltergeist effect had been turned in.

Rumor may have been going around before that time, of course. Spock was always startled by the speed with which information was disseminated in the rec room. But the overheard conversations of Reilly and Chekov caused him to doubt whether it would have been taken seriously at that point. And in that initial twenty-four-hour period, the captain had placed all reports regarding Midgwis under seal.

"'Curiouser and curiouser,'" Spock quoted from a piece of literature that nobody in the crew had any idea that he'd ever read, let alone liked. He keyed back through to the captain's log, winkled his way past the access codes, and studied the entries since the departure from Midgwis.

They told him nothing except that there was something that the captain was not writing about. Their terseness was very unlike his concise but thorough style.

He keyed out. Then, though he knew he was due back on the bridge, he turned his steps toward sickbay.

"Nothing." Helen's voice sounded a little better, though it would be weeks before the internal scar tissue disappeared—her entire respiratory system, Spock knew from McCoy, was similarly damaged. She still looked haggard, weak, and depleted, her body not responding well to either regenerative enzymes nor to the sonic rest treatments that usually accelerated natural healing. Spock wondered obliquely how a case like this one might respond to the Midgwin Consciousness Web McCoy had spoken about, then discarded the thought. According to Shorak's reports, the Consciousness Web itself was largely illusory and its effects in all probability psychosomatic. Even Vulcan holistic techniques did not excise disruptive organisms—merely tapped into the deep strengths of the patient's own immune systems and the regenerative properties of the mortal flesh. And it could well be, he thought, looking down at the woman's drawn face and bruise-circled eyes, that her lack of response to any kind of treatment did indeed stem from some private inner grief or confusion.

She cleared her throat a little, and as she concentrated on thinking back, on re-creating the events on the planet's surface, some of the pain lessened in her face. "Thetas and the captain were never alone together that I know about. Dr. McCoy talked to Thetas for some time by the campfire, but the captain and I were . . . walking. Seeing some of the planet."

A faint flush stained her cheekbones in the cool dimness of the convalescent ward, a reflex that Spock, standing with folded hands at the foot of her bed, knew to be connected in the human species with embarrassment. A little puzzled, he said, "If, as I assume, you were at that time attempting to make the decision whether to remain on the planet or to enter Starfleet and join the *Enterprise* as a permanent crew member, such an investigation would have been only logical, as would the desire to discuss the matter privately with the ship's captain." From the tail of his eye he saw Nurse Chapel, who had moved a portable work station into a corner of the room so that there would never be a time when Helen would be completely alone, pause in her analysis of experimental results. She half averted her face and brought up one hand to cover whatever expression tugged at her mouth, she and Helen carefully avoiding one another's glance. A little stiffly, Spock went on, "And during this time, neither you nor the captain saw any . . . untoward manifestations of a life-form that might have been similar to the one with which we are presumably dealing now?"

Helen pulled straight the sudden quirk at the corner of her mouth—a quirk that had abruptly lightened the weariness and strain on her face—and said, "No. But it was fairly dark, and the thing we're dealing with seems to be invisible, or at least very good at hiding."

"Indeed," Spock averred. He thought for a moment more, while Chapel made another data entry, fingers flicking over the small keyboard with barely a whisper of sound. At Helen's bedside a small earphone hung over the little reader screen—the convalescent ward was, like the individual crew quarters, equipped with plug-in ports for both readers and audiotapes, and the *Enterprise*'s library was fairly well stocked with both.

"And you're certain that at no time did the captain have any sort of private conference with Dr. Thetas, or with any of the other researchers?"

Helen shook her head. "No. Shorak introduced us to Arxoras, who . . . I suppose you could say he thought-scanned us. Not read our minds, really, but I had the impression he could have. More like taking a sample, testing the water . . ." Her dark, straight brows pulled down into a frown. "The other one, the Ghost Walker—Yarblis Geshkerroth—did that to him too. That was when he said that I should think about learning the same kind of mind-shielding techniques Shorak and L'jian use . . ."

"The Ghost Walker?"

"Dr. McCoy mentioned him." Nurse Chapel looked up from the tiny screen, crossed her booted ankles over a rung of her chair. "He's the leader of the conservative party in that warren, a complete isolationist. I think he'd been hurt by Klingon scouts, and wasn't making any distinctions between them and us."

146

"Indeed," Spock said thoughtfully.

"But we were all there," Helen went on, "and Jim didn't—didn't seem the worse for it . . ."

"No," murmured Chapel. "But . . . Mr. Spock, I don't know nearly as much as I should about telepathic technique, but is it possible the captain could have seen into this Ghost Walker's mind at the time of the contact, whether the Ghost Walker wanted him to or not? Could have read malice there . . . maybe even a plan?"

"In my experience," Spock said slowly, "something as linear as a plan is not something that transmits in chance telepathic contact, particularly between beings of such widely incompatible cultures and thought processes. But an isolated image or series of images can be picked up by a sensitive or skilled receptor from someone not skilled in masking his or her own mind."

"Not a description that fits the Ghost Walker," Helen whispered, sinking back against the pillow and frowning up at the tall Vulcan. "One of the great savants of their planet, they called him; one of the mightiest. And besides . . ." She hesitated, then stopped herself and shook her head.

"What is it?" Chapel asked.

She managed a weak grin. "Just being catty. Never mind." She thought about it for a moment, then shrugged and said, "Well . . . whatever else can be said about him, I certainly wouldn't accuse Jim Kirk of being psychically sensitive or skilled."

"No," Spock agreed. "But I have found him to be extraordinarily gifted in the interpretation of subliminal clues." He frowned again, folding his arms, wondering why the captain would have lied to him. To back up a deduction based upon unprovable hypotheses? Or to cement with fear an order that he was not certain would be obeyed?

Spock glanced at the chronometer visible on the wall

beyond Nurse Chapel's shoulder. It was 1340. The sweep-team roster needed to be compiled and its members contacted; a strategy meeting with DeSalle of Security was necessary to organize logistics, and he still needed to put together those two additional modulators . . . not to mention getting some rest himself, for he knew already he would be awake through the night again, coordinating the mechanics of the sweep and—the thought crossed his mind like a stirring of wind—keeping an eye on Captain Kirk.

He frowned, not sure why he had phrased it that way to himself and not comfortable with his own distrust. And yet . . .

He shook his head, dismissing the other possible course of action that had been slowly forming itself in his mind. He said, "Thank you, Dr. Gordon, for your help. Nurse Chapel, I will be transmitting a memo concerning the precautions to be taken to shield any scientific experiments in progress from possible effects of the sweep . . ."

"I've talked to Dr. McCoy about the possibility," she said, and added, with a rueful smile, "not that any serious experimentation has been going on with that—that *thing*—disrupting the labs."

"Indeed," Spock agreed quietly. "However, extra shielding may be necessary in view of the fact that, since the only communication between primary hull and the Engineering hull and dorsal decks is through Deck Seven, the proton-acceleration field will be in place on this deck while all decks of the primary hull below it are being swept—a matter of some two to three hours."

Chapel winced as she thought of what McCoy's reaction to that would be, then she nodded and said, "I'll tell him to take that into account."

"Thank you," Spock said formally. "The sweep on this deck will most likely commence at 2300 hours—my memo, once I have consulted with Security Chief

DeSalle, will give a more accurate indication of the precise time."

And turning, he started for the door. But before he had gotten close enough for it to open, he stopped and turned back. "Nurse Chapel . . . as the labs here have been one of the centers of the manifestations, there may be a recurrence of them as the sweep approaches. I realize you will be off duty at that hour, but . . ."

"I'll stay if you think it would help," she said quietly.

"I do," Spock replied, a little stiffly, for he knew of Chapel's affection for him and knew that under the circumstances, asking her for a favor of any kind was unfair.

"I'll get in touch with you if anything happens," she promised, herself withdrawing a little, growing more businesslike as she tried to answer his own formality. But her long hands, plucking nervously at the sides of the small keyboard on its stand before her, gave her away.

"Thank you," Spock said, and then, in a lower voice, added, "I appreciate it. Moreover, as the sweep drives whatever this creature is down through this deck to the ones below, I believe that it would not be a good idea to leave Dr. Gordon alone."

At 1800 hours the rostered crew members assembled in the main briefing room on Deck 4, thirty-six, all told, from the various watches. Fourteen were such members of Science and Engineering as Spock deemed able to deal with the proton-acceleration generators on both a theoretical and mechanical level—not always compatible, he reflected, considering the case of Lieutenant Maynooth, the head of the ion-study lab and one of the most brilliant ab-atomic particle physicists he had ever had the pleasure to work with, who could not be trusted to survive an encounter with a common stapler. The other twenty-two were selected members of Security, and the briefing included, as well as Mr. Scott and Captain Kirk,

Security Chief DeSalle, a big-framed, craggy-faced man who remained leaning quietly against the wall in the back of the room, saying very little but watching everything. Above the door the amber lights of the Alert still blinked, a constant, silent reminder that somewhere on the vessel an alien was hiding—invisible, silent, and potentially lethal.

Spock explained briefly the setup and takedown procedures of the three generators and four signal modulators, then outlined the leapfrogging strategy of the sweep, a pattern complicated by the necessity of keeping Deck 7 under a constant sweep while the decks of the primary hull beneath it were swept, then backtracking and sweeping the dorsal decks before moving on to the Engineering hull.

"What if it retreats upward from Engineering through one of the Jeffries Tubes to the engine nacelles?" asked Lieutenant Bistie, a middle-aged Navajo who was head of the Special Studies lab. "I mean, it can hang tight in the tube until the coast is clear, and then come down again."

"Insufflation tests with a number-seven neutral powder have indicated that the standing wave set up by the generators not only extends through walls, but is in some degree influenced by resonation patterns of the walls themselves," replied Spock, to whom Mr. DeSalle had already mentioned this rather daunting possibility earlier in the day. "We believe that a resonance column will be established for a considerable distance up the nacelle pylons, well into the region of the proton-disruption field of the engines themselves."

"But how do we know the disruption field of the engines will affect it?" inquired Organa, DeSalle's diminutive lieutenant.

Spock folded his hands on the top of the generator's polished steel dome which sat on the table before him.

"We have no way of knowing that the proton-acceleration fields of the generators will affect it," he replied. "This equipment is, you must realize, largely experimental, though it is based upon all information available regarding electrostasis life-forms."

"Well," Miller said hesitantly, "we know it can kill recording devices, and cause malfunctions in molecule-remix units . . ."

"Molecule-remix units?" Spock raised an eyebrow. "No report has been filed concerning—"

"Er, maybe that was just rumor," said Miller hastily. "But what if it can short out a phaser the same way?"

"May I remind you, Ensign," Captain Kirk snapped from the head of the briefing table, "that the induction mechanism of a phaser works on an entirely different principle from that of a recording device?"

Spock paused for a moment, his eyes going worriedly to the captain. Then he continued, "Indeed, we have little evidence so far as to what our quarry's capabilities may be, or as to what its reaction will be to being cornered. I can only recommend that all internal communications of the ship remain open, and that all life-support, engineering, and central computer functions remain double-manned until the sweep is completed. This may be particularly important the farther down the ship we go, as the intruder is—if my calculations are correct—driven into a smaller and smaller area."

"Captain," said Dr. McCoy, who stood, arms folded, in the doorway of the briefing room next to Mr. DeSalle. "Just out of curiosity . . . how are we going to know if we've gotten rid of the thing? It doesn't show up on any scans now. It isn't merely invisible, it's apparently literally incorporeal—we have virtually no proof that it exists at all. So how will we know when it ceases to exist?"

The captain turned to look at him, and Spock saw how yellow his eyes gleamed. "The proof that it exists," he said slowly, "is that it has tried to kill—and will try to kill again." His hands tightened, twisting at the metal stylus grasped between them so that the pale rod flexed and gave. "I'll know, Doctor. Believe me, I'll know."

Chapter Twelve

SPOCK, DON'T DO THIS TO ME! Even in the bowels of the Engineering hull James Kirk felt the sweep start, a nerve-jarring vibration in the molecules of air and metal that made up the bones of his body now, and knew that it would be his death. *God damn you, Spock!*

He wanted to rage, wanted to scream, as he had wanted to scream at him all through last night, while he'd patiently, fumblingly, moved and hidden every tool and piece of equipment he could manage to lift. He was close, he sensed, to dissolution already, his consciousness straining under the sheer weight of hours stacked onto hours, of consciously re-creating the parameters of the body he remembered: hands, feet, ears, toenails, the hair on his head . . . the sheer grinding eternity of keeping his mind alive. Now he felt in his shadow bones the chill shudder of the standing wave as the generators kicked in on the bridge and that first deck of the Science labs immediately below it, and knew there was no escape.

He had early found he could pass through walls only by his consciousness of their composition and of precisely what lay upon their other side—he could, he supposed, have passed through the outer skin of the ship itself. But beyond that skin lay the disorienting blackness of space, and that would destroy him as surely as the polarizing disorientation of the standing wave would.

Can't you see what's happening? he shrieked soundlessly, hopelessly, toward the groups of men—his own men, his own crew, his own friends—who would be milling around on the bridge and the Science deck below. *Haven't you caught on yet?*

And Laundryman Brunowski, checking the remix settings of one of the particle shakers that refabricated clean new uniforms out of the recycled molecules of the old ones, swung around sharply at the sudden drop in temperature and shivered, hearing, from among the vast banks of recyclers in the giant food-fab chamber beyond, the pounding begin, desperate, furious, and helpless.

Kirk fled upward, through the faint, shining pain of the superconductor cables and the wires within the walls, to sickbay on Deck 7. Being that close to the decks where the field had been set up terrified him—even with four decks between, he could sense it, like a piercing scream that shatters concentration and thought.

Frenzied, he called out to Helen, lying in her fitful sleep. *Helen, please . . . Helen, listen to me, can't you hear?* She heard him, saw him in her dreams, but he felt her mind flinch away in repugnance and terror as his face loomed mistily into her consciousness, felt her shoving him from her thoughts.

No, he felt the slurred and sleepy whisper of her dreams. *Not him. Not him . . .* And he felt, too, all the bitter and soul-deep hurt of that monstrous betrayal, and with it, her dark fear of madness, the horror she felt at the thought of the horror she tried not to know was true. Somewhere close by him Kirk heard the pounding start, not in one place now but in half a dozen, angry and uncontrollable; heard, too, something go crashing to the floor in a nearby office and knew that what psychokinetic powers he possessed were slipping from his conscious command.

Nurse Chapel started up from her chair in terror, staring wildly around the room as she flattened back against the wall. She would listen—he knew she would listen—but he knew of no way to break the silence between them, no way to bridge the gap between the material and the nonmaterial, between thought and operationality.

And he felt him coming. That eerie alter ego, that thing that had taken his body, felt him walking the decks down below the shrieking hypersonic whistle of the induction field. *He* had no fear. *He* need not dread the shattering vibration of the invisible air. The Midgwin patriarch had a house for his spirit, a system of nerves and cells in which to settle the electrical impulses of his being, a structure around which to twine the incorporeal vines of his personality—a material body to act as armature to the transient glitter of his soul.

And he was hunting him, tracking him, listening for the hammering of his despair, feeling for the telltale cold, the raging dread and terror . . . driving him into a corner until he could destroy him, as a shadow is destroyed when the lights switch on.

Despairing, Kirk fled.

Arms folded, Spock observed critically as Miller, Organa, and Fphargn carried the disassembled components of the proton generator to the far end of the physics lab, located the power source nearest the symmetry line of the ship, and began to set up. Miller worked quickly and neatly, his blocky, good-natured face set in lines of concentration, double-checking every connector, reading every gauge while the two security officers stood at either side, watching and listening in the silence of the enormous, dome-ceilinged room.

Spock cast a cursory glance around—all long-term experiments had been shielded, but he privately suspected that half of them would be severely disrupted by the presence of the proton-induction wave, and in any case all results would probably be called into question. He had spoken to the heads of all the labs in the Science section, and while no one had questioned the necessity of the sweep, he had seen a lot of gritted teeth.

What made it worse was that he did not agree with the sweep in the first place.

But it was one thing to question the actions of a commander whose obsession was putting the safety of ship, crew, and civilians in danger—as he had in the incident of the vampire creature of the Tycho System—and quite another to argue for the continued existence of a demonstrably deadly, unknown intruder. It was his instinct against the captain's, nothing more, and his instinct had been proven wrong before.

And yet . . .

He frowned, remembering unhealthy glitter in the captain's eyes, remembering a hundred indications of severe mental strain, of an almost unbearable secret. The captain, he knew, had gone on ahead of the sweep, prowling the decks below, looking for . . . what?

Again, Spock did not know.

But Midgwis had been its starting point. Of that he was now certain.

"Setup complete, Mr. Spock," Miller reported, and Spock, checking the assembly, nodded. The switches were thrown.

Spock's hyperacute hearing picked up the faint, whining hum, but the others seemed to notice nothing. Checking his chronometer and noting disapprovingly that they were already 2.3 minutes behind schedule, Spock crossed the enormous lab to the door, stepping out into the corridors that led around the turbolift banks to the small lounge in the center of the deck. Pausing in the corridor, he removed from the satchel that hung at his side a bulb insufflator—a slender nozzle attached to a round metal ampoule of number 7 grade neutral test powder. Holding the insufflator out before him, he tapped the button on its side to release a small, measured puff of powder into the air.

As it had in his laboratory tests, the powder—which would hang visibly in uncirculating air for thirty minutes or more—separated into unsteady bands, marking the frequency levels of the wave. Spock nodded to himself, and as the incorporeal bands broke, wavered, and began their slow drift toward the vents, proceeded into the lounge, where, just beyond the emergency gangway up to the smaller deck above, Mr. Scott and his team had assembled the other generator in front of the doors of the photon torpedo banks.

That assembly also looked in order. "Any significant problems, Mr. Scott?" he inquired, and the chief engineer flashed him a grin.

"Simple as one, two, three."

Spock nodded. "Indeed it is, provided one is not counting in binary. There are matters to which I must attend for the next hour or two. I shall leave you in charge until I return."

He returned, out of habit, to the ion-study lab where he had been working last night, which he knew would be vacant still; from the lab next door, though it was well after the end of the main watch, he could hear Lieutenant Bergdahl's voice: "Well, of course the experiments will all have to be done again, Ensign Adams. No data can be trusted after this kind of disruption . . ."

"I'd have thought that the solid-state crystallography wouldn't be affected by that kind of wave action." A woman's voice, abashed.

"Well, naturally it probably is not, but I want no chances taken." A heavy sigh. *"Why* they have to disrupt things in this fashion—"

"It tried to kill someone," Adams pointed out patiently.

"She was probably just careless—and do *not* put that beaker on that counter. How many times do I need to tell you that no organic experiments are to be brought anywhere in the vicinity of inorganic experiments?"

Spock sighed, remembering how whenever he entered Bergdahl's laboratory, the man unobtrusively followed him around, wiping whatever he'd laid his hand upon, even though sterile conditions were seldom required of geological procedures. He wondered how a reasonably young human male—Bergdahl was no older than Captain Kirk, and of the same sturdy, fair-haired stock—could so absolutely resemble the fussy, two-century-old Vulcan house steward whose constant, martyred criticism had made his own childhood a burden.

He flicked on the terminal, which, being one of the lab terminals, was capable of far greater access than, for instance, a library terminal or a simple reader. Since the information he wished to consult was classified, the distinction was a mere bagatelle, but a lab keyboard would be capable of greater exactness, and exactness was as necessary in breaking security codes as it was in programming a decent cup of coffee.

For a long moment he sat there, debating the ethics of the situation. It was a different matter from reading the Captain's Log, a document to which, as first officer, he himself would have access should circumstances place him temporarily in command. This was the captain's private realm, and Spock's own deep sense of privacy felt violated at the thought of entering it.

But matters had gone too far; his uneasiness over the captain's behavior was passing over into alarm. After a pause for thought, Spock neatly rerouted the information system around its guards, convinced the central security program that he had given it a password of whose identity he possessed no clue, reprogrammed a voice-code identifier, and finally keyed through into Captain Kirk's private, personal log.

There had been no entry made since Stardate 5947.3, the day of the expedition to Midgwis.

Unlike the official Captain's Log, Kirk did not make entries to his personal log every day. Such entries as there were concerned matters beyond the purlieus of official Starfleet notice, but of possible importance to the captain of a ship: repeated complaints about certain commodities in the galley selections; the disappearance of chemical samples from the Botany lab; the fifth request-for-transfer in eighteen months by someone working under Lieutenant Bergdahl; a quarrel that had broken out in the rec room between Ensign Phillips from Inorganic Fabrication and Yeoman Mendez from the galley, which had apparently been settled amicably but which, considering the volatile personalities involved, might flare up later. Kirk, Spock was interested to note, kept a far closer ear to rec-room gossip than he let on, which surprised Spock a little.

In several places the captain spoke of Helen Gordon:

In fairness I cannot ask her to consider staying onboard the *Enterprise*. She has her own career to forward, her own advancement to consider. And though long ago I consciously ruled out the possibility of such involvement, I keep coming back to the feeling that there is something important here that I would be a fool to let go of . . .

And, in another place:

When I was twenty, I was happy. With Ruth I had a sense of peace, a sense of belonging, that I have not known since. I have known many other things in the intervening years, happiness among them, but never that quiet joy, that rest, that sureness. When I left the Academy, she told me she would wait for me . . . maybe in my heart, even then, I knew that she wouldn't, not past a certain point. But I've always wondered what would have happened, had I gone back.

Past Kirk's mellow tenor in the earphone, Spock's quick hearing picked up Bergdahl's thin, complaining voice in the Geo lab next door: ". . . ion-study lab, which he is certainly entitled to do. I'm sure he realized just how important Dr. Maynooth's experiments are, and would be very careful not to disrupt them any further . . . Ensign Adams, you really must fully index those notes! I'm sure that with as little as you do around here, you can certainly find time to input them properly so that they can be retrieved at a moment's notice . . . Certainly, sir. If you care to wait for him I'm sure he'll be out soon, he's been in there for twenty minutes already . . ."

Spock flipped to another entry, returned his concentration to Kirk's voice, listening to the even, relaxed tone of the voice itself:

I have a sense of working one of Lieutenant Uhura's jigsaw puzzles, trying piece after piece, scenario after scenario, in my mind, knowing that somewhere, somehow, there has to be one that fits . . .

And after the visit to Midgwis, nothing.

He removed the receptor from his ear and sat for a time, looking into the depthless darkness beyond the neat amber letters of the screen.

The personal log revealed a good deal more about the captain than he had thought to find, and it articulated, in a curious fashion, the qualities that Spock knew made the captain an excellent leader, qualities he himself did not possess, and in some cases did not completely understand. Humans were, of course, irrational, the captain as bad as the rest—Spock was aware that in the earlier part of the mission his own logical reactions had made him less than popular with the crew. But in taking account of gossip that a Vulcan would have automatically considered none of his business and beneath his dignity, the captain was clearly able to tap this irrationality to his own advantage, to understand that strange, nebulous quality called "morale" or, simply, "feel" . . . something it would never have occurred to Spock to do. And part of that, Spock guessed, had to do with the relaxed quality of his voice, the easiness and openness with which he could pick up the slightest changes of circumstance.

That quality of voice, he realized, had been entirely missing from the later official log entries he had heard.

That easiness of voice was characteristic even of those entries in which he questioned his own goals and feelings, as if they too were matters to be looked at, if not with proper Vulcan dispassion, at least without either frenzy or rigidness.

Spock found it very curious that the captain would not have voiced his suspicions of the intruder—suspicions that were clearly driving him to the brink of physical breakdown—at any point in his personal log. Or had he feared that the intruder would break into it, and find them there?

A possibility, thought Spock, as he carefully worked his way back out of the program, remaking the security links around the captain's personal files and reassuring the computer that it must not, in fact, ever let anyone through without the proper code words . . . and that in fact it had not done so now.

Yet it argued for an intruder far more sophisticated than the precomputerized, preindustrial, preagricultural Midgwins, as well as for Kirk's inexplicable awareness that the intruder was, in fact, so sophisticated.

And it did not explain why the captain had not felt

called upon to comment in any fashion upon Dr. Gordon's decision to remain with the *Enterprise,* nor upon their subsequent quarrel, if quarrel there had been. Nor, for that matter, upon her near death at the intruder's . . . *hands?* The phrase snagged his consciousness. *Hands, fingers . . . fingerprints.*

There were matters here that did not compute.

Bergdahl was fussily checking a series of gauges set up along the back of a workbench in the Geo lab when Spock passed its door, while a thin, tiny woman with black Oriental eyes stood, a little awkwardly, to one side. "I don't care what they say, any kind of a field being generated automatically nullifies all experimental results. A duplicate set of all experiments will have to be set up . . ."

"Do we take down the tests in progress, then?" She had the air of one who has long ago learned to double-check everything out of sheer self-defense. Spock remembered that she had put in for a transfer to Input not long ago, at a half-step reduction in rank.

"Certainly not! One can learn from everything, including possible variations of results . . . or their absence. Please compile a list of all materials to be duplicated once we reach Starbase Nine—if we ever *do* reach Starbase Nine, with all this turning around and turning back . . . Oh, Mr. Spock!" He came hurrying out of the lab to catch up with Spock in the corridor. "Captain Kirk was here looking for you. He did not say where he was going, but said it was of no importance, and that he would find you later."

Natural enough, Spock supposed, crossing thoughtfully to the turbolift and checking the chronometer on the wall beside it. The captain would be checking the decks below for any sign of the intruder's continued presence . . . whatever those signs might be. He would not be difficult to locate. On the other hand, if the matter were of any importance at all, Kirk would have located him by comm link. And Mr. Spock did not particularly wish to encounter the captain just now.

The sweep team that had been stationed between the two emergency gangways had already descended through to the junior officers' quarters on Deck 4. If his estimate of time was correct, they would have the modulators in place and the generator going by this time. After a moment's further thought, Spock turned back to the ion-study lab, opened a locker there and took out a fresh bulb of number 7 neutral powder, and several plates for wave-activated and electric-field spectrography. These he snapped into a shielded case, tucked it into his satchel with the insufflator, and, emerging once more from the lab, took the turbolift down to Deck 8.

It was now close to 2130 hours, a time when the recreation areas of Deck 8 were normally at their heaviest use. Now the vast rec room's tables and couches were deserted, the room motionless save for the random, soothing swirls of various pieces of mobile art; the curved cavern of the gymnasium echoed emptily, bereft of its usual basketball game. In what was officially termed the "Entertainment Center" and unofficially known as "Central Park"—though the thirty-five-meter curve of grass and ground cover was, in fact, not central to Deck 8 or anything else—the fountain splashed dimly in the silence. Spock guessed that the converted cargo hold on Deck 7 that served as a cinema was vacant as well, a symptom of the uneasiness that pervaded the ship, the atmosphere of waiting to see how the intruder would react.

Carrying his satchel, Spock walked quietly past the shut doors of the main computer chamber. The enormous room, with its banks of information and terminals, would be not only manned, but heavily guarded, and judging by the slender information he possessed on the habits of the intruder, it was unlikely that it would manifest itself in the presence of so many onlookers.

According to some of the information on paranormal manifestations it might not even be possible for it to do so.

But most of the manifestations reported had been in or near the computer chamber, and there was a sixty-eight percent probability that the intruder was near that vicinity, at least for the next thirty minutes or so.

Keying his way through a minimum-security door, Spock entered the shadowy vastness of the automated food-prep facility, where bank after bank of molecular reconverters, like dim, square sarcophagi in some unimaginable necropolis, served the main banks of food slots in the lounge above.

All was quiet here, the murmuring hum of the raw-organics conveyor which, like a long, banded metal serpent overhead, fed the reconverters, sounding loud in the hush. Through the far wall Spock's sensitive hearing could pick up the modulated rattle of the laundry next door, where a long row of particle shakers formulated new uniforms to the indent specs punched in by those who'd turned in their dirty ones, and where three more conventional cleaning units meticulously extracted unwanted molecules of dirt and foodstuffs from the items of personal attire that crew members did not wish to have recycled, for reasons of sentiment which Spock presumed would be comprehensible to the captain.

He made his way over to a corner of the room, where the control terminal's green and amber lights gleamed like stars in the dimness next to a long worktable littered with hardcopy and velfoam plates. Spock settled himself in one of the chairs before it, uneasily aware that his actions were in direct violation of the captain's orders and, as such, qualified as mutiny. And it occurred to him that in his present, apparently irrational state, the captain might very well have him charged with it, if he found him here.

Spock's whole soul might revolt at the thought of

destroying an unknown alien life-form that had not yet been proven hostile—the attempt on Dr. Gordon's life being, for a number of reasons, suspect. But he had done such things under orders before.

But something about the whole situation bothered him, as even so prolonged and bizarre an intruder alert did not. It was clear to him that the captain was somehow linked with the intruder, if intruder it was. And at the risk of his career in the fleet—and quite possibly the risk of his own life—Spock had to find out what the nature of that link was.

He cleared a place for himself, frowning with distaste over the sloppiness of the chief cook and his assistants as he set aside half-empty cups of stone-cold coffee and data wafers whose covers—if they were in covers—were daubed with greasy fingerprints. It was already sufficiently dim in the room to comply with conditions of both the reported *Enterprise* manifestations and with similar phenomena mentioned in the records. He unshipped the protective case from his satchel, removed a photographic plate and set it on the table before him. Placing his hands outspread on either side, he shut his eyes, shielded his mind with every mental discipline he could muster, and waited, listening, his senses extended to catch the slightest shift of atmosphere in the room.

In the silence, he could hear quite clearly the deep heartbeat of the engines, the thrumming of the food conveyor that led down to the main recycling plants in the Engineering hull, the faint tap of two pairs of booted feet passing through the corridor . . .

". . . perfect time to take it to the storage compartment! The entire deck is deserted . . ."

"Yeah, but if we meet any of those sweep teams, how're we going to explain full-size sets from the Murlgau passion play?"

"We're not gonna meet a sweep team, and besides, I've

got a miniaturized remote motion sensor hooked up at the lift."

"A motion sensor?"

"Miller made some up for me. For God's sake, if you work for Birddog you've got to have *some* way of knowing when he's coming so you can look busy enough for him . . ."

The voices died away into the silent distances of the corridor.

Minutes passed.

Then somewhere quite close he heard a dim, hesitant tapping, as if someone were knocking faintly on one of the thick squares of the reconverters with a hard piece of metal, a ring or a coin or an old-fashioned metal key.

The room seemed cold to him, colder than usual, though not the bitter, malevolent chill of before. Attenuated, he thought, as if the center of the chill were some distance away. Eyes still closed, he sat listening, not daring to speak, trying to analyze why he felt that the room was occupied by someone other than himself, though he had heard no footfall, no pressurized door hiss, no breath. Keeping the inner fortress walls of his mind still guarded, he opened out the channels of telepathic communication that the Vulcan mental techniques so stringently taught. He tried to transmit openness, willingness, and hoped obliquely that the intruder —if the intruder was in fact near—was not one of those beings capable of coming through such guarded channels into the mind of the listener after all.

But there was nothing, only that vague sense that he was not alone.

Then the chirp of the comm link broke into his thoughts, and, immediately after, Captain Kirk's voice. "Mr. Spock . . ."

Spock opened his eyes. The room before him was empty. The photographic plate on the table before him was blank.

He flipped open his communicator. "Yes, Captain?"

Kirk's voice was harsh but low, tense, breathless. "It's here, Spock. The hangar. It's trying to communicate . . . get here, fast."

"I'm on my way, Captain." He slipped the plate back into the case as he strode from the room, directly across the corridor into the turbolift. "Hangar deck."

The doors of the hangar deck slipped soundlessly open before him, revealing a huge expanse of empty darkness. Only the dimmest of emergency lights glowed high overhead; under the overhanging shadow of the observation gallery, all was pitch-black. The *Copernicus* was a solid rectangle of darkness directly before the vast clamshell doors which were all that separated the *Enterprise's* fragile atmosphere from the black vacuum of space.

Spock took a few steps into the room, listening, wondering if the captain had deliberately reduced the light levels in anticipation of his own encounter with the intruder. It was logical, if in fact he was as familiar with its nature as he appeared in fact to be . . .

Then from the shadows of the shuttlecraft he thought he heard Jim Kirk's voice call out "Spock!" in a tone of unmistakable fear.

He slipped free of the satchel over his shoulder and crossed the huge expanse of floor at a run.

"Captain . . ."

There was no one near the shuttlecraft, which was docked and dogged firmly down, its doors sealed shut. Spock slipped a handlight from his belt and flashed it around him, but there was no sign of Kirk—no sign of anyone. He called out again, "Captain!" and heard the flat slap of echoes ring back at him. Overhead, the bare rafters made a harsh latticework of shadows, and his light gleamed back off the tough plex windows of the dark gallery, the round glint of the vent shields below them.

A noise in the blackness under the gallery made him

turn—for a moment he saw a dark shape outlined against the whiteness of the corridor lights as the door opened, then shut again.

It did not open again when Spock approached. Swiftly he pulled aside the cover panel for the manual release, and discovered that the handle had been removed.

As he started toward one of the other doors—though he knew within a few percentage points of certainty that it had been likewise sabotaged—the soft whooshing of the vents began, a trickle of sound that quickly swelled to a whispering, deadly gale.

Someone outside had hit the controls to cycle air out of the hangar, preparatory to opening the clamshell doors and letting whatever was inside be pulled out into the freezing black eternity of space.

Chapter Thirteen

"FURNITURE STARTED FLYING around the room yet?"

Christine Chapel looked up, startled, from the last of her data corrections to see Lieutenant Uhura leaning in the doorway of the convalescent ward. She laughed ruefully and pushed the small roller table aside. "Believe me, I've been listening for it."

Uhura nodded back down the corridor toward the door of the O.R. and the various labs. "Everything seems intact so far. They're just setting up on the deck above this one—I think everyone's a little nervous." She still wore her duty uniform—she must have put in a considerable amount of extra duty, Christine reflected, trying in every way she could think of to raise the silenced transmitter on Midgwis.

"Not nearly as nervous as some of the lab chiefs. Emiko Adams told me Bergdahl's putting in for duplicate *equipment . . .*"

"Oh, plague, plague!" Uhura widened her great brown eyes in mock horror and made ritual signs of aversion. She noticed that Nurse Chapel, with her odd, old-fashioned formality, was the only member of the junior crew to refer to the unpopular Anthro/Geo chief by his right name when not on duty.

From her bed Helen asked, "Do you think it will work?" Her coloring was a little better, but her voice still sounded like it had been gone over with scour solution.

"Mr. Spock seemed pretty sure of it when I talked to him last night." Uhura shrugged. "But you can't really know, can you? You just take aim and hope."

"Besides," Chapel pointed out, rising from her chair to help Helen sit up and pull a garnet-red robe over the blue and black medical smock, "you're the expert on the life-forms of Midgwis."

Helen chuckled wryly. "So expert they try to gas me in my room. Which is ironic, because there's no mention of any intelligent creatures on Midgwis that can do the things this one does. Or at least," she added, thanking Chapel with a haggard grin, "maybe there is and it just hasn't had things like labs full of beakers, or walls to pound on, or cylinders of toxic gas to demonstrate its capabilities on before this." The dark level of her brow twitched down. "Which is one of the weirdest things about the whole business . . ."

Down the hall, in one of the labs, the sudden crash of equipment falling made all three women swing around with a gasp. Helen, pallid already, went white—Chapel thought she was going to faint, and sprang back to her side, while somewhere close by the lunatic, frenzied crashing continued, as if a maniac were tearing McCoy's personal lab to pieces. After a frozen instant Uhura plunged for the door; Christine gasped "No!" and the Communications officer snapped back, "Stay with Helen!" The room had gone deathly cold.

"Come on!" Helen rolled over and scrambled out of bed, staggering and nearly falling, so that Chapel had to catch her. The red flash of Uhura's uniform had already vanished around the lab door. "Dammit," Helen gasped, holding herself upright against Chapel's strong shoulder, *"don't* let her go alone!"

Chapel gripped the other woman tight around the waist; the two of them nearly ran into Uhura in the corridor.

"Come in here," the Communications officer said softly. She looked shaken as she led the way back to the Medical officer's private lab, and for a moment Chapel's mind groped in panic for the experiments she and McCoy had taken such care to seal and batten and shield.

"Look at this," Uhura said.

In the doorway of the small lab they stopped. Helen, holding unsteadily onto Chapel's shoulder, asked in her raw voice, "Where did the water come from?"

"It blew out a vent filter." Uhura nodded upward to the vent, long since locked and fitted with baffles and guards. All its complicated covering had been ripped away, and the accumulated water vapor that always collected under the dehumidifier screens was spattered over the surrounding walls. The vent cover itself, filmed with a delicate mist of infinitely fine water droplets, lay flung in a corner against the legs of the lab table. Helen took a second look at the half-meter square of reinforced duraplast and whispered, "What the Sam Hill . . . ?"

Written in the vapor film, huge and ragged, as if scrawled by a demented child, were the letters, SPOK— HNGR DEK—HURRY—DEAD.

The three women were in the streaking turbolift before Chapel said, "We—we should tell the captain."

"No!" Helen's voice was a harsh gasp.

"It—it might be a trap . . ." Chapel's face was as white as Helen's had been earlier. "Or it might have wanted to lure us away and leave Helen alone . . ." She had been first one out of sickbay, literally dragging the others down the corridor in her fright.

Floors flashed past them, blurred bars of greenish-white in the dark of the lift shaft. Uhura, her hand on the control, frowned, struggling within herself with some thought. Then she said, "I don't know. The thing is . . . the night Helen was poisoned I . . . I was wakened by something falling, something making a noise—if I hadn't wakened, I wouldn't have seen her comm light, and nobody would have gotten to her in time. Chris, what woke me up was that bronze *calot* of mine falling on the floor from the middle of my dresser. The things around it weren't tipped over or brushed aside or anything; it was like the thing had been picked up and dropped."

Slowly, fumblingly, knowing what she was getting at but unable to fit it with known facts, Chapel said, "But it . . . it tried to kill Helen . . ."

"*Something* tried to kill Helen," Uhura pointed out. "Something, as Mr. Spock pointed out, that wiped its fingerprints—or wiped something—off that cylinder."

"Then there might be—be two intruders?" Chapel turned her head, hearing the thin sound that came from Helen's throat; saw her friend pale again, her face twisted with inner pain. "Are you all right?" And Helen nodded, her black hair hanging down to hide her face.

The red warning lights of the opening cycle were flashing above the door of the hangar deck, visible as the three women burst from the lift doors. "Go!" Helen gasped, balking and struggling out of their grip; they left her slumped against the wall and ran for the doorway as the lights went solid red.

Chapel whispered, "Dear God . . ." and heard Uhura say something considerably less refined as she slammed over the Abort toggle; for a horrified instant she stared up at the bar of warning lights, her mind blanking on how long the cycle lasted, on whether the lights going from flashing to red meant that the outer clamshell doors had already opened or were going to open in . . . how many seconds? "God, God . . ." She seemed to be hypnotized by a single, small yellow light blinking in the panel next to the door. Blinking amber meant a malfunction somewhere . . .

Uhura was already hitting Re-Ox buttons, then calling up the malfunction cues to the gauge screen.

Pressure evacuation malfunction—the bay had never completely lost pressure. The oxygen-drain mechanisms had jammed.

And a slight mechanical glitch had prevented the outer doors from cycling open.

In addition to which, Chapel read over Uhura's shoulder on the amber screen of the gauge readout, the internal comm link, abort panel, and manual override systems operative from within the hangar had all been tampered with.

They had to use the manual release in the corridor wall to get the bay open.

Mr. Spock was lying across the threshold as the doors slid open. With the reoxygenation of the hangar deck, he was already starting to come to. Chapel dropped to her knees beside him, feeling for pulse and cursing herself for not bringing a tricorder. His skin felt cooler to the touch than she had ever known it, almost human-cool . . .

"It knew English," Helen said softly.

Chapel looked up. Helen, holding herself upright against the corridor wall, had staggered after them to the open doorway of the shuttlecraft hangar. She stood leaning there in her crimson robe and blue pajamas, her black hair hanging down in an unruly cloud over her shoulders, her eyebrows standing out like a scar above her deep-sunk, tired eyes.

"The intruder," she explained, slipping down to sit beside Uhura's booted feet. "It knew English. It wrote, 'Spock, Hangar deck, Hurry . . . Dead.' Meaning, I suppose, if we didn't get here, he would be dead . . ."

The three women looked at one another, Uhura hunkering down beside the other two. "We have to tell the captain," she said. "Call off the sweep. Whatever is going on around here, it isn't the intruder that's been attempting the killings."

"I doubt that he would comply."

They all looked down. Mr. Spock rolled up onto one elbow, wiped away the drying trickle of green blood from his nose, and felt at his head—Chapel knew he must have had a terrific headache, if nothing worse. The pressure drop had bruised the capillaries around his eyes, smudging them with dark green shadow as if he'd been struck. She tried to help him sit up, but he politely but firmly drew away and sat himself up, his back propped against the doorjamb of the bay, the bay itself a chasm of shadow behind him.

"The captain is obsessed," the Vulcan went on clinically. "Though personally I am still inclined toward the theory of a Klingon-paid conspirator among the crew, the captain insists upon blaming—and destroying—the intruder, and is behaving with a degree of irrationality most uncharacteristic. In fact I would almost say . . ."

He paused. His dark brows slanted more sharply down over the high bridge of his nose, and from the sunken and discolored sockets, his troubled, coffee-colored gaze met Helen's and held it.

Softly, almost inaudibly, Helen said, "It's because it's not really Jim . . . isn't it?"

There was silence. Chapel looked, confused, from Spock's face to Uhura's to Helen's, and saw that it was an idea new to none of them—something toyed with, discarded for the best of rational reasons, yet never entirely dismissable from the dark at the back of the mind. Far above them, though it was impossible that she should either hear it or feel it, Chapel was aware, as if by emanations through the walls, of the steady downward working of the proton-induction sweep, the shattering wave that was designed to destroy whatever it was that had apparently saved Helen's life by waking Uhura, and which had certainly risked itself to save Spock's.

The sweep had been only a deck or two above them when the warning in the lab had taken place—who knew how far through the floor the disruption radiated?

At length Mr. Spock said, "It is a difficult contention to prove."

Helen shook her head. "I knew it," she said softly. "I knew it the first night after we left Midgwis. It wasn't him."

Uhura swore, softly, horror and compassion in her eyes.

"It would certainly explain his turning the ship around, and returning to Midgwis," Spock went on, getting slowly to his feet. Chapel rose also, and went to pick up the equipment that lay on the floor just within the doors of the bay, a carrier satchel stuffed with an insufflator and a protective case of the sort that electrospectrographic plates were carried in. "Though it leaves unanswered the question of why a substitution—if substitution it is—was made in the first place. Thank you, Nurse Chapel."

He slung the case straps over one shoulder, and offered his arm to help Helen to her feet. Though Chapel knew that Spock preferred not to be touched, he put an arm around Helen's waist and a shoulder under hers. Leading the way across the hall, his strength made no more of her solid weight than it would have of a child's.

Chapel, hurrying to keep up, asked, "Then the intruder . . . the ghost . . . the poltergeist . . ."

Spock's voice was matter-of-fact. "Is in all probability Captain Kirk."

They opened a channel into the main computer from a reader port in the tractor-beam machinery room on Deck 23, a deck otherwise given over to the dim-lit silence of cargo holds. The terminal had probably never been used for anything except replays of fastball games and the perusal of sports magazines in the ship's extensive library, but Spock deftly disencoded all security and access-limitation programs in it, and proceeded— with startling skill, considering an extremely limited keyboard—to open routes straight to the mainframe, while Uhura dug in the wall locker for a small kit of tools.

"What's that for?" asked Chapel, who had posted herself unobtrusively in the doorway, watching the empty hall. No one came here except, now and then, a duty officer in charge of repairing the tractor beam, and occasional maintenance personnel. With the lights turned up full power, the gray-walled room with its bulbous wave generators looked sterile and sordid; greasy napkins lay dispiritedly in one corner, with several blue-gray velfoam cups whose rims had been methodically picked to pieces by someone's nervous fingernails. The place had a smell of staleness and disuse. All around this deck the unpressurized hull sections contained raw materials for recycling, either organic or inorganic, and the smells of them were a faint, unpleasant backtaste in the air. Dark and silent, the cargo holds kept their prosaic secrets: boxes of soil samples, examples of alien machinery to be taken back for analysis at Federation starbases and universities and institutes, alien flora and fauna cryofrozen wholesale. The deck below contained nothing but cargo holds and storage. This was the last corner of the ship where a terminal of any kind could be plugged in virtually secure against intrusion, at least until such time as the sweep was almost at its end.

"We'll need an outpost guard," Uhura said, removing the cover of her personal communicator and, after a moment's thought, reaching into its infinitesimal guts with a needle-fine magnetic switcher. "I'm cutting out the ship's pickup channels—I'll do the same for yours and Mr. Spock's. That way nobody will be able to hear us."

"I suggest, Nurse Chapel, that you return to sickbay and bring Dr. McCoy here." Spock, laboriously coaxing the limited-capacity screen to cut in a second screenful of notes to remind him of half a dozen artificial-intelligence programs not committed to his memory, spoke without looking up. "We will need as much help as we can get in keeping track not only of the sweep, but also of the captain's movements. And I would be very much surprised if the good doctor does not have suspicions of his own."

He cut in a chronometer reading and tightened his lips—the well-bred Vulcan equivalent of sizzling oaths and hurling the keyboard against the wall—when the overtaxed screen cleared itself of everything save a small, blinking 110.

"He's known something was going on," Chapel said slowly, keeping her voice soft—with the door held open to facilitate reconnaissance, voices would carry in these echoing halls.

"By this time the sweep should be finishing the primary hull and beginning to clear the dorsal sections," Spock went on, touching his way neatly through the computer language that was so much swifter than the voice activation most people used, and far more precise. Uhura, her lips taut, had gone back to her tinkering with the communicators.

"It will take me approximately thirty-two minutes to access and disconnect the slave relays that control the electronic shielding of the central computer; nearly three hours to tailor and implement an artificial-intelligence program theoretically capable of sustaining an entire pattern of human thought. During that time it is imperative that we be neither disturbed nor suspected. And," he added, half turning to look up at the three women behind him, "we will need to find the captain, wherever his—his consciousness, his awareness, the electron shadow of his entity, is centering itself. Find him, and bring him back here—if it is, in fact, the captain, and not an intruder after all."

Chapel shivered as the full import of the dangerous game they played came to her. *Was* it the captain who had tried to kill Spock—to kill Helen? Or was it an alien who had so obsessed him that he had turned himself into a stranger? She had known Jim Kirk for years—he'd gotten her transferred to the *Enterprise* when she'd decided to enter the space service to look for her fiancé, Roger. She trusted him implicitly . . . Only, which of them was really Kirk?

Uneasily, she asked, "How . . . What happened to you?"

"The captain told me that he had cornered the intruder in the shuttle bay," Spock replied, as calmly as if he had not come within a few microns of switch-gap of being dragged out into the freezing vacuum of space. "I thought that I heard him call out to me from the back of the bay; when I entered, the door slammed behind me. Door controls and communication had been cut— manually, the wires disconnected and the cover plate replaced . . ."

"But the outer doors didn't open." Uhura glanced up from her work, the sweat of concentration shining on her face in the bleak glare of the lumenpanel overhead. Though the Communications officer was theoretically able to break down and repair any piece of comm equipment in stock, few of them were actually called upon to do so once they'd passed their entry tests. "I didn't check on why . . ."

"Another one of those inexplicable malfunctions that seem to be part of the poltergeist effect," Spock replied evenly, turning back to his screen. "Certainly at odds with the decidedly manual efforts of the would-be assassin."

"What was the equipment for?" Helen asked, nodding toward the insufflator and the case, which lay on the floor at her side.

"I had gone down to the computer decks to attempt contact with the intruder," Spock said, "having for reasons of my own come to the conclusion that the captain had been behaving in a fashion aberrant enough to warrant investigation."

"Did you make contact?"

He did not reply for a moment, only continued to check programs, moving files and directories to other sections of the computer and occasionally tapping in instructions of his own. At length he said, "I don't know. I brought the electrospectroplates along in the hopes that the intruder—who had seemed all along to be attempting to write something in the spilled liquids in the sickbay labs—would be able to write on the plate . . ."

"He did write," Uhura said, looking up again. "He wrote in the water vapor of the vent filter. That's how we found you. And, as Helen pointed out, he wrote in English."

"Fascinating," Spock murmured. "Unfortunately, the plate was blank when I—" He broke off, looking around at the abrupt clatter as Helen dropped the case on the floor.

"I knew it," she whispered, and turned her face away, tears forcing themselves through the thick black fringes of her shut eyelashes. "I knew it, I knew it . . ."

Uhura, looking down over her shoulder, gasped.

While Spock had been speaking, Helen had opened the case and taken out the single used plate. In the center of it, shadowy black on the gray, was the ghostly image of a man's face.

The face was Captain Kirk's.

Chapter Fourteen

THEY HAD SWEPT THE DORSAL—running one generator per deck, it had not taken long—and the long, narrow hold full of air-circulation machinery, visicoms, and pumps that ran along the top of the Engineering hull. They were assembling the generators on Deck 16 for the final phases of the sweep.

In the darkness, Jim Kirk felt the thin shivering vibration that shredded at his nerves and consciousness, and knew he should move again, move downward . . . Downward to where? He could no longer remember, nor recall where he was—a dark place full of machines, he thought, that shivered with the throbbing of the engines; but that told him little. He was lost, and even if he moved on, it would only be to wait for death.

He was tired, very tired. The screaming haze of the proton-acceleration field extending through the ceiling of Deck 7—extending down from the generators on Deck 5—had battered him, disoriented him; he had fled straight down the nearest emergency gangway to avoid it, only to realize that below Deck 7 there was no connection between the primary hull and the dorsal that led down to the deeper safety of the Engineering hull. He had been trapped.

For a moment fear had seized him as he'd realized there was little he could do except descend, driven by the sweep, down through the recreation decks, the fabrication rooms and cargo holds, until they cornered him in the auxiliary fire-control room of the phaser banks, down on Deck 11 . . .

Cornered him. Scotty, and DeSalle, and the others he'd worked with, been friends with . . . Using the machines Spock had made for them . . . Spock, whom, at this point, he didn't even know whether he'd been able to save.

But even as he thought it, he remembered the cautiously prowling specters of Ensigns Gilden and Adams, lugging the first of what he had later seen was many loads of supernumerary original hardcopy to his secret cargo rooms in the outer skin of the ship . . . remembered Gilden saying, "And furthermore, I think it's ridiculous that there's no corridor, or lift, or anything between Deck Eight and the dorsal . . . What do they think we're going to do, raid the food remixers?" And Adams replying, "There's the food conveyor . . ."

And through the food conveyor he had gone, desperately holding the shadow shape of his body around him, desperately remembering to create, in his mind, the contact of his knees with the ridgy rubberized floor of the repair duct that ran along the top of the conveyor, the way his arms would brush the metal sides.

He was safe, he thought now.

But in the darkness he knew he had only purchased a handful of minutes for himself, and what did it matter?

He wondered if the women had been in time to save Spock, if the malfunction he had caused in the bay-door mechanism had held once he'd fled upward to the perilous brightness of sickbay, where he knew at least

Chapel and Helen had to be. Wondered if the malfunctions on the oxygen and pressure systems had been sufficient to keep his friend from perishing of hypoxia and cellular collapse.

He thought he had had some notion of returning to the hangar deck to see. But all his thought, all his perceptions, were darkening, collapsing in on themselves with exhaustion after that final, desperate effort of concentration required to blow the vent covers in the lab, the excruciating exertion of forming letters in the water-vapor mist. He had no idea of where he was now, this place full of whispering machinery, nor of how he'd gotten here.

He was only smoke and memory, and soon that, too, would be gone.

"Jim?"

The voice was soft, somewhere outside the place where he was. He recognized it from somewhere in his past . . . It was so difficult to remember who he himself was now, so difficult to recollect, to re-form, the parameters of his body, the dim clamor of memories that made up his life. But he recognized that it was someone he knew.

"Jim, I know you're here. Jim, come with me, follow me. Spock's worked out a way to save you."

Spock must have survived. Good.

And he sank a little more in on himself, like the settling debris of a dying star after all its light and heat are gone.

"Jim, follow me. We're down on Deck Twenty, behind the shuttlecraft maintenance shop . . ."

Shuttlecraft maintenance shop? Recollection stirred, putting itself cloudily back together—the shape of that giant chamber under the hangar itself, the storage rooms behind it, the cargo holds behind that . . .

"We know what happened to you. We can help you . . ." The voice was farther away. He heard the hissing of a door. Kirk stirred, trying to summon back the memory of his legs, his arms, trying to collect a way to walk after that speaker. He could have drifted, he thought, passing like a cloud . . . only once he forgot what it had been like to walk, he knew he would never remember again. And he hadn't the energy to do both.

Footsteps, walking away. The voice whispered again, much farther off . . . stealthy, surreptitious, like the voices of Gilden and Adams in the dark of the Deck 7 main corridor; like the voices of Brunowski and Miller as they tinkered with their vast bank of computer controls, trying to get the recycler machine to form individual coffee beans instead of the "slab coffee" usually produced; like the voices of the lovers who occasionally walked, in order not to meet whoever it was they did not want to meet, in the dark bottom corridors of the ship.

Of course, he thought. If the intruder, the Ghost Walker, the creature who had raped him of body and mind, were to learn of what they knew, it would certainly find a way to kill them, as it had tried to kill Spock and Helen. At the very least, as captain, it could have them jailed until it was too late . . .

And it was very nearly too late now. He felt the hurt in him grow sharper as the sweep moved down a deck, as the reassembled induction generators powered up again, as the standing wave came closer. And in any case, where could he go? It was only a matter of time . . .

Time until what? They had turned back toward Midgwis. Planetfall would be in three days.

The Ghost Walker—the thief who had stolen his body, who had taken his ship and his command, who had raped the woman he loved and tried to murder his friend—had something in mind.

The thought stirred anger in him, anger and the old stubbornness, the old pride. *I am James Tiberius Kirk,* he thought. *I am captain of the* Enterprise. *You may have taken my ship, you may have turned my crew against me and have them hunting me like dogs, but by God, I'll destroy you if I can.*

That had been McCoy calling him.

Bones.

Now he remembered.

He looked around him, turning the shadow shape of his head. He saw he was in the machine room that operated the clamshell doors of the hangar deck. He must have come one deck farther down than he'd intended, stumbling blindly, trying to see if Spock had survived.

Slowly, atom by atom—had his body and flesh still been composed of atoms, and not the electronic shadows of memory—he drew himself together, clothing himself again with the memories of his flesh, the memories of his ship. The blinding scream of the proton field on the decks above made it difficult to concentrate, but he pulled to mind the access doors connecting this room with the cargo holds beyond and the deck hatches leading up into the hangar deck above . . .

He had hands again, he had feet. He dragged them back into existence by an act of will. Slowly, blind and hurting with fatigue, clinging to the bones of his ship as he would have leaned upon the arm of a lover, he began to make his way along the decks, following the voice of his friend.

It would end soon. It had to end.

Captain Kirk— *No!* he told himself, shaking his head blindly. *Yarblis—Yarblis Geshkerroth . . . I am Yarblis Geshkerroth the Ghost Walker . . .* stared with glazed, aching eyes at the red-shirted Hungries as they dismantled, for the twentieth time, the unwieldy proton cannon, preparatory to carrying it down the turbolift, down two more levels. At first he had been revolted at the mere concept of creating a machine that would mimic the vibrations of the mind. Now he was fascinated. There was something delicate, something hellishly precise, about that kind of understanding of the way the universe worked; about coming at it from the outside rather than from the inside.

He turned his eyes away, knowing that the Hungries became uncomfortable if one stared too long.

Around him his crew—*Kirk's crew! Hungries! Opaque and greedy and dull*—moved, male and female, their voices hushed as they had been hushed since the sweep began. That, too, he had only realized belatedly, had made them nervous. They were not entirely comfortable themselves with the world they had created, the capabilities of the things they used. At the sight of one of the security officers, a dark-haired female leaning on the wall, speaking to one of the males, the human body which he had taken for his own whispered a greedy wish. Shocked, Yarblis thrust the thought aside. Yet it returned, with the intrusive memory of the woman Helen.

He shook his head and moved away, sickened beyond reason both at the thing he had done and the way he had enjoyed that dark violence. He had little experience with controlling such wishes, little knowledge of what he should and should not do. The memories of such matters were clouded, jumbled, distasteful to him, for they were memories of the body and not the mind.

"Captain . . ." It was Mr. Scott, the engineer—Scott/ Scotty of Kirk's memories, who looked at him with deep concern in his coffee-black eyes—hoisting a piece of the generator by a strap onto his arm. "I never asked—did you manage to locate Mr. Spock?"

Kirk—*Yarblis! I am Yarblis . . . Who was Yarblis?*— nodded. "He said he was going to check a report of manifestation down on the shuttle deck, but that was nearly two hours ago." *How perilously easy it was becoming, to speak in hours and minutes . . . how simple to think in them, when there was no sun, no moon, no wind to mark the turning of the day!* He frowned, as Kirk did, and after a moment said, "And that in itself bothers me." When they found the bay doors open, he thought, when they reached the shuttle deck, only a few decks beneath them now, the sweep would be simpler. They would ask no more questions, have no more doubts. They would be avenging one of their own.

Kirk, the real Kirk, had saved Helen. Since he had slipped out of the shuttle bay—and causing Spock to think he had called him from the shadows of the tiny ship had been a simple illusion, of the type he had used to lure many of the dark Klingon Hungries to their deaths—he had been worried that, somehow, what was left of Kirk had been able to save Spock as well. But there had been no outcry, no summons for the bone setter McCoy, so he did not think Spock had survived.

Instinctively, he knew that Spock had been a danger to him.

Like all the Hungries, he thought as he walked down the corridor to the lift, Spock worked from the outside rather than from the inside. But he was aware now, as he had not been aware when he had first conceived the idea of taking over Kirk's body, of using the ship of the Hungries itself to implement the terrible plan by which he would save the world from the pernicious effects of their influence, that his masquerade was not as thorough, as complete, as he had thought it would be. Though they had no Consciousness Web—something he still found hard to picture, with the pain of separation from the web an agony he lived with, as he would have lived with a gut wound—they nevertheless knew one another better than he had thought they could. He knew he had made mistakes. And Spock, the Counter of Everything, had counted those as well.

He paused, looking around him at the sterile white

walls, the flat floors, flat ceilings . . . hating, with all the passion of his soul, this flat place that stank everywhere of the Hungries. They made their world into this, he thought. And they would lure his people into making the true world, the real world, the beautiful Rhea, the Mother Spirit place, into this as well, this hateful place where everything was divided into Mine and Not-Mine, into Me-Don't-Touch and Others-Not-Me . . . lure them with promises of how easy life would be, how good.

Life was not supposed to be easy or good. It was supposed to be beautiful, and beauty lay in peril, in cold, in hunger as well as in rest and comfort. It was something they clearly did not understand.

And in a generation, or two, there would be many in the world who did not understand either. And in time they would all become Hungry too.

And beauty would begin to disappear.

But he would keep that from happening.

He looked around, even reached out his hand—*Weak little hand with tiny fingers!*—to touch the flat, cold wall that had never been organic, never been made *from* anything, and smiled a taut, exhausted smile.

This place, this ship, was his now. If only he weren't so tired, if only his bones did not hurt with bitter, consuming loneliness, he would have laughed his triumph. For when he was done, there would be no question, then or ever again, of the Hungries being able to violate the world and offer their dream of satiation in trade for his people's souls.

"The sweep's down to Deck Nineteen," Lieutenant Uhura reported, from the doorway of the half-deserted rec room, thumbing open a channel on her communicator and hoping to hell she'd disconnected the right switch and the conversation wasn't being picked up on the bridge. "Any word?"

Helen's voice, gritty with the aftereffects of the gas even if there hadn't been a world of static and the buzz of a loose connection, replied, "Nothing yet. He's just sitting in the machine room in the dark, waiting. It's so cold down on this deck, it's hard to tell if . . . if anything's happening." She still couldn't bring herself, Uhura observed compassionately, to mention the captain's name.

"Keep me posted," she said, her voice soft, and keyed out. At 0735 in the morning—and Uhura groaned when she thought about having to be on the bridge after a night like the one she'd just been through—though the rec rooms of both primary and Engineering hulls were usually vacant, the gyms and exercise rooms invariably were in use by those who either enjoyed getting their blood well and truly circulating first thing in the morning, or by those who wanted to "get it over with" before starting their day. At this hour the pool deck—in whose doorway Uhura was now standing—was generally stirring with men and women, its ceiling echoing with the voices bounced back off the water. The sharp slap of feet and steady beat of music would be drifting in from the gym, where the martial arts enthusiasts would be striding through their before-breakfast katas, and the dance room where Organa would be drilling her students in pliés and stretches.

But the uneasiness Uhura had noticed last night on the crew deck—and in the rec rooms—was still in force. A lone swimmer stroked his way steadily through the pale aquamarine glimmer of the pool; gym and dance room were swathed in hush like a sheet-draped empty house. The crew members who used the Engineering hull facilities might, Uhura supposed, have gone up to the primary hull this morning . . . she didn't know. Tension cannot be sustained over long periods of time—a good deal of the air of nervous waiting had abated from sheer exhaustion—but she deduced that the crew in general were taking no chances until the intruder was pronounced good and dead.

She sighed. It was as late as she could let it get. She rubbed her face wearily and headed for the nearest lift, her boot heels echoing in the empty spaces of the rec room, in quest of a quick cup of the strongest coffee she could get, a shower in her room, and the hopes—probably vain—that it would be a quiet day on the bridge.

"Nothing." Bones McCoy spoke barely above a whisper, looking down at the woman who sat on the floor just within the machine room door. "I've been through every back corner and service hallway of the ship—places I didn't even know *existed*—and I haven't felt a thing. Not that I'd really know it if I felt it . . ." He hesitated, thinking about that. Then, slowly, he added, "But I think I would."

Helen nodded. "I think we'd all know, now."

Oddly enough, McCoy saw that she looked far better than she had even that afternoon. Still exhausted, stretched to the limit of her physical endurance, yes . . . but that dead look, that hopeless weariness, that glint of haunted fear in her hazel eyes, was gone. She still had the look of a woman who had been badly hurt, emotionally even more than physically; but life was back in her face, life that had been gone, buried under hopeless confusion and the fear that she was insane, since they'd beamed up from Midgwis that last time.

The communicator chirped softly. Helen flipped it open.

"Sweep's down to Deck Twenty," said Uhura's voice softly. It was past 0800 hours, and McCoy guessed she was monitoring audio pickup from the comm links. "Anything yet?"

"Not a thing."

McCoy sniffed, and looked away. "I always knew there was something about that damned transporter I didn't like," he grumbled. "Scrambling a man's atoms like a bushel of rice . . . it must be how the Ghost Walker killed the Klingon scouts, back on the planet."

Helen nodded. "All he'd have to do was wait till they transported down and take one over on arrival, then wait his chance."

"But on the other hand," McCoy went on, "I suspect that it was only because of the kyrillian stabilization effect of the transporter beams that Jim was able to survive at all."

Helen's mouth quirked. "Which leads to some pretty unpleasant speculations about why Yarblis Geshkerroth decided to take over the position as captain of a starship."

Then, from in the dark machine room behind them, they heard Spock's voice whisper, "Captain?"

Helen and McCoy looked back. The little room was nearly dark, illuminated by the faint amber glow of the reader screen and the dim light of a burning candle—begged from Gunner's Assistant Barrows, who had a stock of them, though whether for religious or erotic purposes, Helen didn't know—which picked out the angles of Spock's aquiline face and left the hollows of his eyes in darkness. Spock had read, conscientiously, the literature involving the manifestations of nonphysical beings, and one thing mentioned repeatedly was the necessity for low lighting—possibly to give greater scope to charlatans, he had remarked, though it was equally possible that light waves themselves had the effect of confusing and lessening the powers of a creature that existed as no more than a collection of electrostatic impulses itself.

The Vulcan sat like a strange, impassive idol in the

candlelight now, his bony hands outspread, palms upward, on the grubby drekplast of the tabletop, his eyes shut. The room was chill—Helen could not tell, as she had said to Uhura, from what cause.

Softly, the Vulcan spoke again. "Captain, are you here?"

And from somewhere, dimly, there came a knock, like the dropping of some hard object onto a concrete floor.

"Come closer to me," said Spock softly. "The *katra* . . . the essence of the soul. The inner being. It can be transmitted from body to body; it can be held in the mind of another for a time, as Sargon's *katra*, his personality, was held within yours. My mind is open to you, Captain . . . Jim. Come closer to me—enter the part of my mind that is open and ready. I have removed the electronic guards around the central computer . . . I have programmed a bank of artificial-intelligence programs to store your self, your knowledge, your being . . . until we can restore you to what you are. Do you understand?"

But there was no reply.

"We can save you," said Spock, his voice barely above a whisper. "Programmed into the computer, you can exist indefinitely . . ."

The silence in the room continued, but Helen could feel an emptiness, as if something that had hovered there was beginning to depart. The sweep, she remembered, was only a few decks above them now; Jim would have existed without his body for over a week. It might very well be that he had not the strength to return, or had forgotten how.

Quietly, she reached up and took McCoy's hand. It was something else she had read, in the literature of séances; something Spock had mentioned, but had not understood. Now, suddenly, it made sense to her. With McCoy's help, she rose to her feet and drew the doctor farther into the darkened room. Without a sound they took seats on the other chairs near the table. Helen's hand closed gently around the Vulcan's strong, slender fingers—startlingly warm with the higher temperature of his blood—and after a moment McCoy took Spock's other hand in his. As he did so, completing the circle, Helen felt immediately that Kirk was somewhere near.

Closing her eyes in the dark, she could feel him as a living presence. *Standing close to Spock,* she thought . . . *standing just behind his shoulder.* She didn't try to form any thoughts, any images, in her mind; just sat in the hard-backed plastic chair and relaxed, letting her mind open, her thoughts reach out, to give him one more thing to touch, one more thing that was familiar to him . . . one more thing to orient himself, to draw himself back. In the deepening silence they sat, a ring of energy, of friendship, of offered strength.

Then she heard Spock's breath catch and felt the tightening of his fingers on hers. Gently he disengaged his hand, and, as she opened her eyes, he turned away to the reader once more, spreading his palms over the housing he had opened above its tangle of cable and superconductor, his eyes still closed in meditation.

Across the table she met McCoy's eyes, but he said nothing. She eyebrowed a question to him, and he nodded.

At the reader's simple keyboard, Spock began to type. For a long time there was no sound but the deep, throbbing hum of the engines, a bone-shivering tapestry of half-subconscious noise down here, and like a dry counterpoint, the quick tapping of Loglan keying through. In the gold candlelight Spock's face had a blank look, though his eyes were open now; he worked without hesitation, sure and calm and detached, and behind him his shadow wavered hugely on the blank, grease-stained wall.

Quietly, McCoy and Helen rose from their places and stood behind him, looking down over his shoulders at the screen.

Beneath long columns of Loglan he had typed a question in English: ARE YOU THERE?

And after a long time, words formed themselves below.

YES. THANK YOU. THANK YOU ALL. CAN SLEEP NOW.

And the screen went dark.

Chapter Fifteen

"BY THE WAY, SPOCK . . ." McCoy's deep, slightly drawling voice broke the long silence of the candlelit machine room. "Do you remember you're dead?"

"Indeed, Doctor." Spock brought one hand up and gingerly rubbed the back of his neck. Now that he was no longer locked in the concentration necessary to write and set up an artificial-intelligence program—not to mention compacting every other program in the computer to make space for something that extensive, and programming the computer to lie about how much space was in use—and no longer immersed in the deep meditation needed to accomplish the state of shared *katra*, no matter how briefly, he realized his head still ached from the pressure drain in the shuttle bay. Reaction, long delayed, was setting in, reaction to those endless minutes of near-panic as he'd tried to operate first the manual overrides to get himself out of the bay, then the alarms to summon help before the pressurization cycle was complete and the outer bay doors opened. He had blacked out, he recalled, in the midst of it. Even at the time, he remembered thinking, with a final flash of logic, that this was probably preferable to being conscious when the blinking red lights went solid and the slow, freezing drag of space's utter vacuum began to pull him toward the opening doors.

He shook the thoughts away, and the cold seed of remembered fear they brought with them, as irrelevant. McCoy's communicator chirped; at a button's touch Chapel's voice said, "Sweep down to Deck Twenty-one—have you had any word? Anything at all?"

"We're safe," McCoy replied shortly. "Rendezvous in sickbay . . ."

The reader beeped softly. Though equipped, like most readers, with a limited sound-effects capability, there was no voder-vocoder attached to this, primarily an entertainment and schematics terminal. Turning, Spock saw written on the screen:

HE'LL LOOK THERE FOR YOU AS SOON AS THE SWEEP IS DONE. A HULL SECTION HAS BEEN PRESSURIZED 30 METERS DOWN THE STARBOARD CORRIDOR ON THIS DECK—YOU CAN RECOGNIZE THE BULKHEAD THAT CONCEALS IT BY THE SCRATCHES ON THE BOLTS. THE COMPUTER TERMINAL THERE IS LAB-QUALITY. SPOCK CAN HIDE OUT THERE. THE REST OF YOU RENDEZVOUS THERE AT 1800.

They all stared blankly at the screen; then McCoy blew out his breath in a sigh. "Well, if I didn't believe it before," he said wryly, "I do now. Nurse Chapel . . ." He spoke into the communicator. "I'll be up to sickbay in a few minutes with Helen . . ."

Helen's communicator beeped also; they heard Uhura say, "He's in the lift with the first of the generators, on his way down to you . . ."

"We're clearing out," Helen responded swiftly. "Jim's safe."

"He was murdered." James Kirk—*Had he another name?* he wondered, with clouded and aching mind . . . Surely he had . . . Gesh . . . Gesh . . . Yarblis Geshkerroth . . . He shook his head, turned slowly to scan the faces of his senior officers, grouped in the small briefing room, trying to read them and failing. "This . . . this creature, this intruder, that we destroyed with the machinery Spock made, even as we were hunting it, destroyed him." He rubbed his hand across his face, the alien flesh aching. Yes, he thought, he was Geshkerroth, Yarblis Geshkerroth the Ghost Walker. He had slain Hungries, defending his people, defending the world, defending Rhea. He remembered that now. As he was defending her again.

His body hurt with a dull, continuous pain, and words were increasingly hard to find, but none of the men and women gathered seemed to find that strange. Scotty's dark brows were drawn together, forming a small upright line between them, his black eyes following Kirk's every movement. On the other side of the table, Bones McCoy and Lieutenant Uhura were alike wrapped in silence, though he saw a glance flicker between them—communicating . . . but how could they truly communicate without the Consciousness Web? Mr. DeSalle, next to Scott, clenched his fist convulsively and hissed beneath his breath.

"What—what happened, sir?" That was Sulu, the navigator, the muscles of his face pulling a little, as the faces of the Hungries had when he had turned on them, slain them, in the forest.

Memory of that grounded him a little more into himself, and he was able to steady his voice and fish forth Kirk's patterns of speech. "As far as I can tell, Spock was lured into the shuttlecraft hangar—we'll probably never know how. The lock was depressurized, the doors were opened."

"But that's not possible!" protested Scott. "Not while traveling at warp speed—every alarm in the ship would have gone off!"

"All alarm systems connected with the bay were disarmed," Uhura said, folding slender hands the color of thorn tree stems. "It didn't register anywhere, except as a note in the systems computer."

"Dear God . . ." Scott whispered, appalled.

"He would have been unconscious," McCoy said to him quietly, "by the time the doors opened . . . There are worse ways to die than anoxia."

"But the important thing is," Kirk—Yarblis—continued, pacing restlessly across the front of the room, "that the sweep was successful. The intruder—the murderer—was destroyed, there is no sign of it anywhere now on this vessel."

"There was no sign of it before," Sulu muttered, sotto voce, to Uhura. But his black eyes slid sidelong to his captain, the look of pain and shock replaced by another which Yarblis could not read.

Yarblis passed a hand across his face again, as if touching the flesh, the skin, would make it hurt less. "I'll make . . . the announcement . . . to the crew . . . Mr. Sulu, we're to make all speed back to the world . . . back to the planet Midgwis. We're clearly dealing with creatures who would stop at nothing, and I fear what the silence of the research party may mean. Gentlemen, dismissed."

They rose, casting quick, furtive looks at him as they filed from the room. He waited while they did, then stepped across to touch McCoy's sleeve. He had debated, seeking in the captain's memories for what the man would do in the circumstances of his first officer's murder. The reaction was different from those of the other Hungries, the dark Klingon Hungries he had taken over, and he was not certain whether this was an individual difference or one common to their family. It was harder for him to think now, harder for him to remember, to sort through those murky areas of emotion and instinct. The strange urges and fevers of this human body were pulling stronger and stronger on his mind, the alien food he ate clouding his awareness, the killing need for sleep that he barely dared take . . . and above all, the overwhelming, hurting loneliness, the isolation from the web. He had not spoken to another true soul, had not shared his self with any other, in day after endless day.

Only a little longer, he promised himself quietly. *Only a little longer, and I will be back in the world again . . . the world that will be safe, and true, and whole.*

"Bones . . ."

McCoy halted, his head tilted slightly. Yarblis was aware of the Speaker with Everyone, the lady Uhura, pausing just outside the door as if to listen.

"How's Helen?" he asked, catching Kirk's softer inflections just so.

McCoy's thin mouth tightened. "I meant to tell you when this was over, Jim," he said quietly. "She's not well—she's taken a turn for the worse."

He made his brows pull down and his breath catch a little. "Can I see her?"

The doctor shook his head. "I'm afraid I've had to put her back in ICU for continuous monitoring. I don't think there's anything to worry about, but . . . she was badly hurt, Jim. She's just not able to get over it."

"I see." He did his best to sound worried, as indeed he was. She might yet die without further help from him, but it was clear that under continuous monitoring, it would be very difficult to make sure that she did, in fact, die. He shook his head again. In two days they would return to the world. After that, whether the woman lived or died would not matter. All that mattered was that she was not able to be up and around, that she was not able to speak to the others . . . and that the others not believe her.

"Jim, I'm . . . I'm sorry about Spock."

Still not entirely clear as to what the man Kirk would have responded, Yarblis spoke from what he recalled of the other Hungries, and only said, "He was revenged. Let us hope we will not need to avenge those back on the . . . the planet."

And turning, he passed Uhura in the doorway and walked away to Kirk's quarters. Perhaps, now that he could discern no trace of his ghostly alter ego anywhere upon the ship—now that Kirk's lingering self had been at last dispersed—he would be able to sleep.

"Surely there's something we can do!" Christine Chapel looked anxiously from Spock's face, austere in the dim glow from the computer screen and the yellowish glare of a low-powered lumenpanel—the only lighting wired into the dark cave of the hull section—to McCoy's, then back to Helen herself, who sat in one of the hard flexiplast chairs at her side. The doctor was slouched in the other chair, as befitted his rank as a senior officer; his blue eyes looked hard but very tired. Helen felt in complete sympathy with him—she herself was exhausted almost beyond thought, hurting for sleep in spite of the stimulants she'd bullied McCoy into giving her to attend this conference. She could see Chris glancing worriedly down at her from time to time, clearly of the opinion that she should be in bed, a judgment call with which Helen one hundred percent concurred . . . Except that nothing would induce her to return to sickbay, even to the Special Observation Ward, without one of the others as a guard.

Politely, Spock inquired, "Such as? Possession is at best a tricky legal concept, and nearly impossible to prove . . ."

"And considering how long it took to remove it from standard jurisprudence," Kirk added, "I would almost rather . . . remain as I am . . . than have it be returned." The voice that issued from the voder-vocoder was almost like his own had been, with only the tinny flattening and expressionlessness to betray its artificial nature. Uhura had smuggled the voder down from Communications stores immediately after Yarblis/Kirk's post-sweep briefing, and Spock had put in twenty minutes or so, in the midst of his endless tinkering, in lowering its pitch from the standard female register to a close approximation of Kirk's steel-flexible tenor.

The remark itself, Helen thought, was so absolutely typical of Jim that, like McCoy, she thought, *If I didn't believe it before, I believe it now.*

He's there. He's in the computer, alive . . .

She didn't know why the knowledge brought a hot lump of tears to her throat and a burning to the scorched-out membranes of her eyes. She turned her face away, so that the others would not observe . . . and wondered how much Kirk could see.

"Except that there's no question of you remaining as you are." As always when he was tired, McCoy's southern drawl had deepened. "He didn't steal your body and your ship for a joyride. We're heading back to Midgwis full-bore. He's got to be doing it for a reason."

"I know," Kirk said. "Believe me, there were times when I think it was only that thought that kept me hanging on."

There was a moment's silence, save for the rattling hum of the jury-rigged air circulator which kept the aromatic smells of coffee and chocolate, with which the room was replete, from drifting into the corridor outside. Then McCoy chuckled softly and said, "Give it up, Jim. You're not going to convince anybody who knows you it wasn't sheer stubbornness."

There was a faint noise, a sort of brittle crackling, from the voder. Spock frowned sharply and turned from the schematics he was calling up on the screen of the portable terminal—which Chapel had brought down from sickbay to hook into Miller's existing tangle of components—to examine the circuitry.

"Are you there, Captain?" he asked. "Are you all right?"

"Fine, Mr. Spock. What's the problem?"

"A fault in the voder, I believe . . ."

But Helen, smiling a little wearily to herself, realized that the sound had been the closest approximation the voder could summon up to Jim's laughter.

"According to the computer's internal log," Spock continued after a moment, "Yarblis has been spending five to six hours a day studying every operation of the ship, with special attention, it appears, to the computer itself. Computer schematics and manuals are among those programs which he has caused to be printed out in his cabin . . ."

"No wonder he looks like he hasn't slept in a week," McCoy muttered.

"That," Kirk said, "and the fact that he's been prowling the corridors, either looking for something, or re-familiarizing himself with the layout of the ship."

"That means potentially he could figure out that the captain's hiding out there," Uhura pointed out from her post by the door. At either end of the dark corridor the miniature sensors borrowed from Emiko Adams kept unseen watch. In the hull section itself the food remixer that filled two thirds of the space—and where Brunowski had acquired it was a mystery, as no such equipment was listed as missing from Stores—had fallen silent after its last self-clean cycle had spun through, the ends of its cable leads looped neatly out of the way.

"Potentially," Spock agreed, returning his attention to the portable terminal and keying in a long sequence of commands. "However, I took the precaution, when I allotted space for the artificial-intelligence program that currently serves the captain as a pseudobody, of compacting all nonessential programs and library reserves in the computer, so that the additional usage would not be noticed, and of programming the computer itself to report no change in its spatial allotment."

"I always thought you'd make an efficient criminal, Mr. Spock," said Kirk's voice from the voder.

Spock stiffened. "Considering the trouble I have gone to to save your life, Captain, there is no need to insult me."

"Insult?" McCoy grinned. "That's a high compliment."

"To a human, I have no doubt," Spock replied blightingly. "Nevertheless, crime is the refuge of the unresourceful; a retreat from perfect logic."

The grin in Kirk's voice was almost palpable. "I beg your pardon, Mr. Spock—I only meant that you would exercise your customary efficiency in whatever field of endeavor you undertook."

"Thank you, Captain." Spock bridled a little, like a dandy who possesses fifteen mirrors and claims to be above looking into any of them—if he'd been a cat, reflected Helen, he'd have washed his whiskers. "That is a compliment indeed."

"But Bones is right," Kirk said quietly. "I can't stay as I am. And certainly none of us can afford to let him remain as *he* is. Bones—Spock—Helen—is there any way, anything you can think of . . ."

"Short of murdering him," McCoy said, "no. And I wouldn't even advise that, since I have no idea how this mind swap works . . ."

Spock looked up again from his primary keyboard, which, as Kirk had promised, was of the highest lab quality or better, thanks to Miller's adept tinkering. "I estimate that if Yarblis Geshkerroth can be induced to abandon the captain's body and mind, we will have fifteen or twenty minutes' leeway to return the captain's consciousness to it without physical deterioration of the brain tissue."

"You could stretch that out further with the stasis chamber," McCoy added. "But how're you going to induce him to leave? Serve him eviction papers?"

"He may leave on his own," Chapel said, shifting her shoulders uneasily against the wall. "By the way he looks, I wouldn't be surprised if Yarblis is having his own problems maintaining his hold on your body."

"We must hope that he does, at least for the time being," Spock responded. "For should Yarblis abandon the captain's body at this point, and the captain return to it, Yarblis will have no choice but to take the captain's place in the computer—something he could easily do, now that I have removed the electromagnetic safeguards."

"That's all we'd need," Uhura muttered. "He sure wouldn't have any problem protecting his planet from us *then.*"

"An unwarranted assumption, Lieutenant, if you believe that from his position in the computer Yarblis might destroy the ship. There are extensive backup systems within the computer itself to prevent a failure of that kind. Even with the amount the Ghost Walker has learned about the makeup of the ship, he would not be able to turn the computer against us. On the whole, Captain, at the moment I consider yours to be the superior position."

"Unless there's a power cut," Helen pointed out quietly.

Spock shook his head. "Power failure to the computer itself is virtually impossible. The backup batteries—"

"I didn't say 'failure,'" she replied, her eyes somber in the grimy shadows. "I said 'cut,' as in, 'cut with a sharp instrument through an access hatch.'"

She looked inquiringly up at Uhura, who nodded. "A few minutes of complete down-power at most will crash the nonessential systems," said the Communications officer. "You don't 'hold' even the essential ones in a crash—they're automatically replaced from a hard-wired digital backup two nanoseconds later, and nobody knows the difference."

"And that's fine," Helen said, "for a system. But can you do that with a . . . a living entity?"

There was a long and intensely uncomfortable silence, which Spock eventually broke. "The power core of the computer is extremely well-protected . . ."

"But the lines leading into it from the converters aren't," Uhura said. "The wiring conduits run straight up the back of the dorsal infrastructure. You can get to any of them through those doors beside the food slots in the observation lounges—or, on Deck Eleven, through Gilden's office. It would be fairly easy to know exactly what to look for if you consulted the engineering files, which you say is exactly what the Ghost Walker has been doing."

Helen looked from Spock's troubled face to the silent stack of components on the table, as if that, too, had a face . . . though it was a face her mind shied from remembering. "Couldn't he have turned back—couldn't he have made the attempt on my life an excuse to turn back—because he wants to be in orbit around his home planet again when he destroys this vessel in order to keep his world safe from Federation interference once and for all?"

Chapter Sixteen

"BUT THAT WOULDN'T WORK," Chapel protested faintly. "Destroying a ship would never keep the whole Federation away. If anything, it would bring them down on Midgwis full-force."

"Does he know that?"

"If he knows what the captain knew, he does," Uhura pointed out.

"Maybe," Helen said, sinking back into her chair. "If he's rational, and not a fanatic. But the Federation's only detailed reports about Midgwis at the moment are in the *Enterprise*'s logs. They wouldn't become common knowledge until they were transshipped from Starbase Nine. And if destroying the *Enterprise* wouldn't buy complete noninterference in his planet's affairs, at least it would buy him time."

"Time for what?" Uhura demanded. "Isn't it obvious to him that unless they accept at least some of the techniques the Federation is holding out to them, they're going to starve? Or risk becoming subject to Klingon protectorate?"

"And in fact there are a number of Midgwins who are coming to just that conclusion . . ."

"They've dealt with the Klingons before . . ."

"Helen's right." It was Jim's voice, quietly, from the computer. The anthropologist shivered, hearing his voice in the dim-lit room, more than ever like a haunting . . . She found herself looking around, expecting to see the traditional pale ghost-shape of him, floating in a corner. And dreading it. Dreading the memories—good and bad—the sight of his face might bring. But there was only the angular collection of spare scanner drives and data cubes, cable and screens, that Ensign Miller had borrowed from Stores, for whatever Brunowski's secret purposes were, green and amber lights on the remixer glinting like spectral eyes.

"The population of the Midgwins is split," Kirk went on . . . Helen could almost see the gesture of his hands. "Geshkerroth's party—the out-and-out isolationists—are in a minority now, or were in a minority when we left, but we have no idea what's been happening on the planet in the past week, nor why communication was severed with the research party."

"My guess is that Geshkerroth's accomplices in the warren trashed the transmitters as soon as we left orbit," Helen said.

"Did he have them?" Uhura asked.

"According to Thetas, there are about a dozen shades of opinion over what should be done with the Federation's offers of assistance," added McCoy, folding his arms and leaning his flat, bony shoulders against the wall at his back. "Most of them have to do with acceptance on some kind of terms, but at heart none of them are really willing to give up the old way of life."

"Nor should they have to," Kirk said. *It must be driving him crazy not to be able to pace,* Helen thought, amused in spite of weariness and strain. Or perhaps the kinetic portion of his brain *was* pacing. "Nor will the Federation require them to, if that's their choice. Unfortunately," he continued, "their old way of life is in danger whichever way they slice it, now that the Klingons have put in for rights of protectorate over the planet. My impression is that very few of them realize that, or want to realize it, but the Klingons may very well make a case for the fact that having no agricultural development, they should not be considered a 'culture.' Given time, the Ghost Walker might amass considerable support for complete isolation. In any case it doesn't matter whether he actually could or not, but only that at the moment he thinks he can. And time may be what he's playing for."

"Most illogical," Spock said disapprovingly.

Abruptly, the red light on Uhura's small hand-held scanning panel blinked on with a soft chirp. "Someone coming," Uhura reported. "They're past the sensor out in Corridor Six . . ."

Spock cut to visual monitoring on the portable screen. In the off-duty quarter-power lighting of the corridor they could discern a short, burly figure wearing the red coverall of L&R, striding along with, incongruously, a dancer's lightness.

Uhura identified him. "It's Yeoman Brunowski."

Spock switched off the screen, and Uhura flicked the makeshift toggle controlling the lumenpanel wired overhead, leaving the room in the darkness in which they had originally found it.

"Stay where you are, everyone," came the Vulcan's deep, slightly grainy tones out of the blackness, and Helen heard the faint swish of his clothing as he crossed the room to the hinged bulkhead that had at one time—before Brunowski had talked his friend into tinkering with it—formed a part of the internal pressure skin of the ship.

The dim lights of the corridor seemed very bright as the door swished open, outlining the blocky silhouette. Like the jointed limb of a spider, Spock's arm intruded into that rectangle of light, resting lightly on Brunowski's shoulder. The hapless laundryman's knees buckled and he collapsed without a sound.

"I suggest he be given an injection of trichemizone and be kept under sedation for forty-eight hours, Doctor," Spock said as he reached up to turn on the lumenpanel again and pulled the bulkhead shut. "No one must know of our headquarters here . . ."

"You'd better get Miller too, then," Kirk put in. "I see him rostered as off duty tonight, since he was up all night running the sweep, but I can hear his voice through the voder circuits, down in Central Computer having a cup of coffee with Ensign Giacomo."

"You don't think they've told her about this place . . . ?" worried Chapel.

"Now, wait a minute," McCoy protested, his grizzled brows descending sharply. "Maybe this isn't the time to balk about ethics, but I *did* take an oath once upon a time not to use medicine as a means of imprisoning the innocent."

"Perhaps," Spock agreed quietly, kneeling once more at Brunowski's side. "But logically, this man is scarcely to be described as 'innocent.' Moreover, should he be imprisoned in any other fashion, he and his accomplice would both be in the severest danger from an alien who has already attempted two assassinations in order to preserve his secrets, to say nothing of the danger thereby resulting for all of us."

McCoy's mouth quirked dryly. "I should have known you'd come up with a logical reason." He fished a hypo from the case at his belt and fitted an ampoule to the gun.

Spock regarded him in some puzzlement. "If that is the case, Doctor, then why—"

The hypo hissed venomously; Brunowski sighed and seemed to settle like a beached whale. "We'd better get him out of here," McCoy said, and between them, he and Chapel hauled their patient to his feet. "I don't like it, but—"

"Take Service Lift Three," Kirk advised. "It's never in use this time of night." And, as they were manhandling Brunowski's not insignificant bulk out the door, he added quietly, "Helen?"

She paused, half turning back. In those few minutes of complete darkness she had felt the eeriest sensation, the impression that Jim was in the room with them, was standing close beside her . . . though her common sense told her that Jim was, in point of fact, really up in the Central Computer room on Deck 8, only listening to them, speaking to them, through the threads of the computer's superconductive nerve endings which ran down the dorsal wiring pipe to the redundant computer chamber on Deck 19, and thence, through finer nerve endings into which Miller had shamelessly tapped, to this darkened hold.

But still, she felt that he was there.

His voice continued to issue, eerily, from the tiny black box plugged into the terminal's side. "Thank you," he said. "For helping me . . . for saving me . . . for believing. And for choosing to be here on the ship, for choosing to stay, for giving up what you did. I'm sorry beyond words that it's cost you what it has . . ."

She shook her head quickly. "Jim, I . . ." How did you touch a computer? How did you put into words what couldn't be said? She felt tears burn at her again, and realized she was trembling with sheer exhaustion, the efforts of the past twelve hours falling on her in a single slamming tsunami of fatigue. She wanted, more than anything else, to lean on his shoulder, to feel his arms around her, to feel the protection, the warmth, of his caring, the way it had once been.

But it was something she had put away from her, in those hellish days of knowing that Jim was not Jim, and though she reached for it now, it still wasn't there. Only an eerie proxy, a disembodied voice—Eric in that ancient story singing to his beloved Christine from behind a wall . . .

But there was an analogy in that she didn't want to pursue. She sighed, bracing herself against disappointment and weariness, pushed back her black hair from her face and straightened her back.

"I can't talk," she said simply. "I'm tired . . . But I'm glad, I'm so glad." And turning, she stumbled after Chapel and McCoy and their unconscious burden. Uhura was waiting outside the nearly shut bulkhead, to put her arm around her waist and take her weight on her shoulder, helping her back down the corridor toward the service lift that would carry them all to sickbay's problematical refuge.

Spock rested his elbows on the table's edge and folded his hands before his chin. "Most interesting."

"Dammit, Spock . . ." The voder was not capable of registering the complete vocal inflections of irritation and fatigue, but it came close.

"I refer to Dr. Gordon's capacity for faith in an apparently illogical conclusion, based upon subliminal cues. It is very similar to your own."

Kirk's voice was weary. "If you knew what I had to go through, trying to get your damned attention, Spock . . . trying to get you to listen in spite of your logic . . ."

"My apologies, Captain." The Science officer inclined his sleek head. Then, after a long moment, "And my . . . gratitude. Both for your efforts in saving my life in the shuttle bay . . . and for the fact that you are still with us at all."

"Oh, go to sleep," said Kirk. "We all need it. We'll figure out what Yarblis is up to in the morning."

Spock remained hidden in the hull section until the *Enterprise* was in orbit around Elcidar Beta III— Midgwis—once again. Deck 23 was a portion of the ship unfrequented by anyone even during the main shift, only a deck above the dark cargo holds of the hull bottom. They were undisturbed.

Much to Mr. Scott's distress, Ensign Miller fell victim to the same mysterious virus that had incapacitated his disreputable friend Yeoman Brunowski. Dr. McCoy tested a dozen other crew members for signs of the virus and published a list of twenty or so symptoms. Lieutenant Bergdahl promptly appeared, claiming fourteen of them, plus several which had not been listed, but was released after examination, to the considerable disappointment of his staff. Aside from the fact that more uniforms had to be returned as improperly fitting due to the usual slight intolerances of the molecular remixer programming, and a tendency of starch-based substances in the food slots to be flaccid and rubbery, not a great deal was affected, but among the junior members of the crew there was whisper that a jinx had been put on the ship.

Whether the captain knew of this or not was unapparent. On the bridge he was silent and withdrawn, but in that he was no different from the rest of the bridge crew. Unemotional and precise, the Vulcan had never been universally popular with the crew, but among those who had worked with him for three years, his absence—his murder—was deeply felt. There was a fanatic glare in the captain's fatigue-shadowed hazel eyes as he stared at the fore viewscreen, or endlessly studied ship reports and voyage logs on their proximity to Midgwis. "And no surprise," said Mr. Sulu quietly, over an after-dinner cup of coffee with Chekov in the main rec room. "First Spock, and now Helen. Chris Chapel says she's doing worse . . ."

Chekov cursed in Russian. "I saw him this way when he went after that thing that destroyed half the *Farragut*'s crew. If that's what the Midgwins can do, no wonder he's worried about that research party."

The object of these concerns himself passed his time, in partnership with Jim Kirk, in communion with the *Enterprise*'s computer. Since the adjoining bulkhead section contained the raw carbon-hydrogen-oxygen-nitrogen from which all food on the *Enterprise* was formulated, it took only a determined study of the remixer tech manuals in the ship's library computer for Mr. Spock to manufacture his own food, and with a little experimentation, he discovered that the breadboarded dials permitted a far finer adjustment of flavorings than the digitalized program settings in the rec room, with the result that, for the first time in three years, he was able to get really edible Vulcan *m'lu*. Lieutenant Uhura and Nurse Chapel smuggled him blankets, upon which he slept in a corner of the room, when he slept at all. Mostly he and Kirk scanned through the files of the computer itself, investigating anything that might assist them in second-guessing Yarblis's intentions when they reached their destination.

With a little coaching from Spock, Kirk was able to enter even the most highly classified of files, to circumvent voice-code locks and retina scans and display anything for perusal on Miller's terminal screen. But nowhere did they find any program, any file, any comment regarding the intentions of the Ghost Walker, the pseudo-Kirk who controlled the ship.

"And I doubt we will," Kirk commented, while Spock tinkered with a third work terminal which Uhura had smuggled down to him from Stores. "He can use the computer, and understands how it works, but he doesn't think in terms of it. It doesn't come as second nature to him, to keep a log, or make files of information, as it does to you and me."

"No," the Vulcan observed, tapping his way neatly through the more stringent of the computerized safeguards set on the inner core of the ship's utility programs. He was currently engaged in finding and removing his own specific sensory parameters from the computer's memory so that another life scan of the ship would not register his presence, even as a scan of the computer's directories would not register Kirk's. "It was, in fact, one of the things that served to confirm my impression that you were—in the old Earth parlance— not yourself."

"Confirm," Kirk repeated thoughtfully. "I'm curious, Spock. Did you suspect before that time?"

Spock was silent, surveying the two screens full of figures and directory paths glowing before him. The room's original screen—the terminal connected to the voder—was, as usual, dark, save for a blinking cursor light and a few cryptic symbols concerning the misleading directory paths behind which the A.I. program hid.

"I knew that all was not well," he said slowly. "Though I hesitated to ascribe such a comprehensive dislocation of your customary reactions to so illogical a cause as your involvement with Dr. Gordon, I was also aware that I was dealing with a matter which in my observation always causes extreme irrationality in members of your species. But I believe that my first definite suspicions came from playing chess with your alter ego. In spite of knowing everything about the game which you knew, he did not have your . . . adeptness."

Spock frowned, leaning forward a little on his elbows, his hands framing the glowing screen before him as he cast his mind back. "He was . . . more ruthless than you. And less careful to conserve his pieces. His attack was more reckless, his guard weaker. And he had no interest in the strategy of the game, beyond winning it."

"I know," Kirk said softly. "And that's what worries me about the fact that the ship is still under his command."

Kirk was also, again with coaching from Spock, able to cut himself into all the intership monitoring and communications devices, permitting him to observe what was going on in nearly any part of the ship he chose, though only able to do so in one location at a time, as he had been able to hear the voices of the staff in the Central Computer room. On the whole, this required such effort on his part that they still relied on Emiko Adams's miniature sensors for their first line of defense.

"He still walks the ship at night," Lieutenant Uhura said, perching on a corner of the crowded computer bench, long legs crossed gracefully while McCoy unwrapped the assortment of small tools from the clean uniform shirt he'd brought for Spock. "But whether he's prowling, looking for something, the way he did before the sweep convinced him you were no longer a threat to him, or whether he's doing something—cutting wires, planting charges, whatever, as Helen suggested—there's no way of telling."

"Can you pick him up on a monitor?" McCoy suggested, as Spock examined the shirt—slightly too short, like so much of what was coming out of L&R these days. "Run a sensor sweep and find him?"

"I'm afraid not, Bones." Even in twenty-four hours Kirk had acquired more control over the nuances of the voder—Uhura would have sworn the captain was in the room with them. If she closed her eyes, she could almost see him, sitting on the other end of the table, just behind Spock's shoulder, where the Vulcan sat in his hard duraplast chair. "For one thing, something that large would show up on the computer's internal log. For another, Spock could be picked out on a scan because of the specific differences in a Vulcan/human physiology, the same way an alien intruder could be—because they're unique. Physically, I'm standard-issue."

"And the damn thing is," Kirk went on after a moment, "nobody thought to put video pickups on the inside of walls or hatch covers the way they did at all the intersections of the halls and in most rooms." Spock, when he had gone to reroute the visual pickups that covered the starboard corridor of Deck 23 to simply repeat the image of the portside corridor, had discovered that Miller had already taken this precaution. ("We ought to put that boy in Security," Kirk had remarked, to which Spock had replied austerely, "We ought to put that boy, as you call him, in the brig.") "If anything *has* been planted, we'll have to look for it."

"Considering that there are 1,576 access hatches and service ports on board the *Enterprise*," Spock said, "of which, at my best calculation, 342 could be deemed of critical importance for the safety of the vessel, this could be an extensive task."

"Can't we do this the easy way?" Uhura asked, with a gesture of one slender hand. "Can't Dr. McCoy here declare him unfit to continue his duties, and put him away like we've done to poor Danny and John? He's certainly given us enough evidence of irrationality, you know."

"For one thing, sickbay is *not* an auxiliary brig!" McCoy retorted—he still felt vaguely uneasy about the Hippocratic oath. "For another, since there is nothing physically wrong with him, and since he's not in any way endangering the ship or the crew, it would take a couple of days of hearings, and we're now less than twenty-four hours from planetfall on Midgwis."

"Not to mention the fact that Yarblis appears to be in sufficient command of himself to talk his way out of such charges," Spock added. "Moreover, such action would not put us any closer to reversing the exchange of personalities between him and the captain."

"That doesn't matter, if the ship and its personnel can be kept out of danger . . ."

"Permit me to disagree, Captain. No proof exists that such an exchange took place. He could, with very good reason, claim that you are nothing but a highly sophisticated artificial-intelligence program invented by me,

216

with the aim of usurping his authority. Such an action would only result in tipping our hand. We would very likely find ourselves in the brig for mutiny, he would still remain captain of the *Enterprise,* and he would assuredly attempt his scheme again. No." Spock shook his head. "Our sole logical recourse is to wait, and to thwart whatever scheme he has as best we can."

I will destroy them, he thought, his boot heels clicking on the hard slick surface of the starship's deck, the cold white lighting that, on these levels, never changed nor failed, glaring hurtfully in his tired eyes. *I will destroy . . .*

Long ago, he remembered being taught by Arxoras that to destroy life, any life, was bad. And something inside him hurt, for he had loved Arxoras then, loved his old teacher deeply. And he loved him still, for all that he had given, for the wisdom he had shown him, and the never-failing luminous serenity of his spirit. Looking back on those days, the hurt returned, but like a wound which, after a time, scars over—a profound loneliness that had replaced his longing for the old comfort of the Consciousness Web.

The hurt changes, he thought to himself, remembering the hideous burns the weapons of the Hungries had left upon him, the twisted faces of his comrades when he had found their shredded bodies in the woodland glens. *But it never ceases to hurt.* Sometimes even now, in this new, sleek, alien body, it seemed that the scars left on his old body, his real body—asleep deep in its cave beneath the canyon rocks, and tended by Yngash and Ka'th Ka'who, his accomplices and nest siblings—still ached.

As he entered the Healing Place, a glass observation window caught his reflection, clumsily elongated and huge in his dull and ugly wrappings of yellow and black, with its featureless little bulb of a head, its pathetic rag of hair, its tiny and feeble hands. Yet at the same time he saw, beyond the window, the woman Chapel, and beside her the bed where the woman Helen lay, and the alien flesh he inhabited warmed with the thought of them.

No! he thought, in sickened disgust. *To want such as they—smelly, vapid, lifeless . . .* But he did want them, with a hunger that was not unlike a pallid echo of his own desperation to join with the minds of his friends, with the minds of his people, the true submersion in the caring and concern of others.

Soon, he thought. *Rhea, Mother Spirit, soon . . .*

In the Special Observation Ward he saw the woman Helen reach up and clasp Chapel by the hands. They were speaking together, Chapel and this woman whom they had told him was so ill that she could not be left unattended; Helen gestured with her hands as she spoke, and shook back the dark torrent of her hair. They seemed almost like two people of his own warren, happy together in one another's company, and he hated them for that, hated them for having, somehow, what he was denied.

No, he corrected himself. *They do not have it—had never had it—do not even understand what it is, without the Consciousness Web.* Through the glass he heard their voices, faintly, though the hearing of the Hungries was so thick it had taken him days to get used to it.

". . . shuttlecraft down to the surface. You can wear one of my uniforms and get on early; we'll need someone down there who understands a little of what's going on. Do you feel up to it?"

"Pretty much." (They had told him, he thought, that Kirk's woman was too far gone to speak.) "Has any contact, anything at all, been established?"

Chapel shook her head. "Uhura's been trying since we came down out of warp speed. The planet's on the fore viewscreens now, we'll be making orbit in twelve hours. Not a sound. She thought she might have picked up traces of an ion trail from some other ship, but can't be sure . . ."

Helen's face tightened with pain. "Dammit . . . Nomias was a pain in the neck sometimes, but the thought that even *he* might have met with some harm . . . And Chu was like a mother to me."

"We'll be taking two security guards . . . Dr. McCoy thinks it's best," she added as Helen made a quick gesture—like a denial, Yarblis thought. "Whatever's going on down there, we don't want to take chances . . ."

Take them or not, he thought, *it will do you no good.*

Quietly, he slipped away. So they suspected, he thought. They—or Chapel on her own, though most likely the physician was in it too—were lying to him to keep him away from Helen, and would lie tomorrow, to get her down to the surface of the world and supposedly out of his reach.

Well, let them, he thought, ticking over in his mind all he had studied, all he had learned, about the ins and outs of this queer floating warren, this terrible thing like a giant flendag nest of metal, floating, as Arxoras had said, upon the waters of eternal night. *Twelve hours* . . . The part of him that was Kirk knew how long that was, and something in him flinched in agony. Every hour, every minute, was a trial of endurance to him now, a race against the pain of holding to this flesh until his goal was accomplished, until the world was finally made safe.

Whether or not the woman Helen went down to the world with McCoy, he thought, they would still be caught in the destruction he would cause; they would still die in the midst of the terrible thing he knew he had to do.

Chapter Seventeen

"WHERE ARE THEY?" Helen ducked under the lintel of the deserted hut. Ms. Oyama—one of the three security personnel who had, against Helen's better judgment, accompanied the shuttle party—followed close at her heels, phaser in hand. Latticed peach-colored daylight filtering through the round window showed them the two piles of flattened grasses that made up Thetas's bed and that of Shorak and his wife. A bag of plaited vines hung from one of the bent saplings that supported the low ceiling of mud-covered thatch and daub. When Helen had last seen it, it had contained the few research items the party had used—tricorders, the first aid and medicines—keeping them off the ground and safe from dust and the local dirt crawlers. It was empty now, as were the shelves that had held spare clothing, the mini-computer, and the repair kit. Like the Midgwins, Shorak and his party had dispensed with bowls, pots, or dishes, and had eaten the slender yield of the grasslands as Rhea chose to give it.

It still seemed to Helen a reasonable thing to do, if one were to live among these people as closely as possible, a necessary procedure for a contact team. She thought, *I'll have to ask Chu how it is, getting used to it,* and then her lips tightened hard at the thought of the austere little Chinese.

Dammit, please *don't tell me she's dead* . . .

She ducked again, to leave the hut.

"Nobody in there either," McCoy informed her, gesturing toward the squat shape of the newer hut that had been erected for Chu, Nomias, and, she knew, herself. The daubing of the roof thatch had not even been completed, and inside, the dust glittered in a hundred mottled slits of uneven light. "The beds look like they've been slept on, but there's no bedding—the whole place has been stripped."

"How could you tell?" Security Chief DeSalle muttered, looking around him at the stillness of the clearing. His red shirt, and those of Oyama and Gomez, made dark scarlet splashes against the purple-brown stems of the surrounding thorn trees, the pale rocks in the soft amber haze of the light. The savannah beyond them stretched away to shimmering distance, harsh and almost white with summer, marked here and there with the low spinneys of dark foliage, the lumpish red-barked barrel trees and the occasional insect hill. Seeing it for the first time in daylight, Helen realized how naked the landscape looked, like an overgrazed pasturage, every food-bearing stem picked clean. The air felt hot and close, weighted with a soft humming that at first she thought must be insects. Nothing moved except, far out over the veldt, the indistinct, loping shapes of a small herd of pfugux, with the attendant gray rustle of small predators—licats or sheefla in this country—gliding in their wake.

Then she remembered that Midgwis had no flying insects.

"Could the Midgwins have overpowered them?" Chapel asked, shading her eyes as she looked around at the sun-drenched stillness.

Security Officer Gomez raised one black brow. "Those little things?"

DeSalle shook his head. "If they did, they did it without shedding anybody's blood," he pointed out, squatting to study the ground around the burned-out firepit. "These ashes are four, five days old . . ."

"Over here," McCoy said, beckoning from the rear of the original hut.

There was a sort of alcove there, like a little shed built of thorn stems and roofed with mud-daubed grass. Helen remembered Thetas telling her that though it was no secret to the folk of the Bindigo Warren that the researchers had a transmitter, they generally kept it out of sight to lessen the sense of their alienness. What was heaped on a torn blanket on the floor of the shelter was clearly the remains of both the Institute's old subspace transmitter and the newer device Chu and her party had brought with them. Most of the parts were jumbled together in the center of the blanket, mixed with dirt and pebbles and twigs, but some had been neatly sorted into a pile on either side.

"Old transmitter and the new," DeSalle remarked, turning a flattened microchip over in his fingers. "They were trying to repair them."

"Here's where it was done, sir," Oyama called from a dozen feet away, among the boulders at the head of a nearby gully. "Scratched-up branches used to lever it to pieces, a couple of big rocks and a boulder they pounded it on . . ."

DeSalle went to check, leaving McCoy, Chapel, and Helen—their blue Med Section uniforms dyed a dull olive by the brazen light—under Gomez's watchful care at the shed. He came back with Oyama a few moments later, saying, "By the scratches on the boulder, it looks like it was done a week ago." He frowned, and pushed back his thick, brown hair from his forehead. In general he remained on board the *Enterprise*, Captain Kirk

222

preferring to head planetary details himself. But like most Security chiefs, he was meticulous and observant, and a childhood spent on various Class-3 colonies had given him considerable experience in rough country, as well as a rather empirical outlook on life.

Helen found herself wondering what the interloper, the pseudo-Kirk, had told him, to justify the departure from the norm. Technically, of course, any senior officer could head a landing party—some ships in the fleet routinely assigned the job to the Science officer (who might or might not be second-in-command). It was, in fact, largely a matter of temperament who headed landing parties, and among the senior officers of any starship, it was generally obvious who should be doing the job. Kirk was one of the few captains who made a habit of taking the position himself, because, as he'd told her once, he wanted to have firsthand knowledge of the situation if it turned ticklish. ("The hell you do." Helen had grinned up at him, lying against the hard muscles of his chest, and had reached up to tweak a lock of his hair. "You just can't stand to be left out of things." And he'd grinned back, and confessed, "Well . . . that too.")

She looked at DeSalle now, over the smashed remains of the transmitters, and his face was grim. "By the tracks, there were two or three of them . . ."

"You said Geshkerroth had accomplices in the warren," McCoy murmured to Helen, and she nodded.

"Looks like they did it as soon as the *Enterprise* was well away," DeSalle remarked, and cast another glance up the narrow path through the thorn trees to the towering rocks around the box canyon, his light eyes narrowed. "I think it's time we went up to this warren of theirs."

"No," Helen said quickly. She shuddered at the thought of what Shorak would say to the armed invasion of the warren whose trust he'd worked so desperately to win. "I'll go . . . alone. These people could barely be talked into having researchers here at all; they're very much of two minds about any kind of contact with the Federation . . ."

"Looks like they came to some kind of decision," McCoy remarked grimly.

Their eyes met, his wary, warning. Helen remembered Yarblis, and the fanatic, haggard gleam in the eyes of the man who had once been Jim Kirk as his face bent over hers. Remembered the shut door of the shuttle bay, the red bar of lights over it; remembered the blinding sense of total evil that had wakened her from her dreams. Remembered, too, that Yarblis had accomplices in the warren of whose capabilities—and intentions—she was ignorant. But she remembered also Shorak's reports, the painstaking patience required to establish contact with the Midgwins at all. It had been almost axiomatic in every class she'd taken how easily a careless word, an action wrongly performed, could give everyone in the community under study a contempt, or a fear, or a distrust of the researchers, which would take months or years to repair. Shorak had begged Kirk not to send security down on the *Enterprise*'s first reconnaissance of the planet. *We're having enough problems getting them to distinguish between you and the Klingons as it is,* he had said.

"No," she said, shaking her head so that her thick, dark braid slapped at her shoulders. "I'll be careful—I won't approach the place unless it looks safe. But I need to talk to Arxoras, and I'm not going to undo everything Shorak and his party worked for by walking into the warren with a bunch of armed guards."

"Let me follow you, then," DeSalle said reasonably. "I'll keep my distance in the bush, if it looks like I won't be needed. There may be a perfectly simple explanation for this. But until I know what it is, I don't want any of us going around alone."

* * *

"Spock!" The urgency in the captain's voice broke him sharply from his meditations—meditations he was certain he would need, as much as he would need the information on Midgwis that he had managed to dig out of the computer's backup memory. Rising from his kneeling position on his blankets, he crossed swiftly to the worktable, the screens of all three terminals dimly glowing in the low light.

"Yes, Captain?"

"Computer sensory cutoff on Deck Five. The whole area's blacked out of communication."

"Officers' quarters," Spock said automatically, cutting in the second screen. "Also all emergency battery rooms for the primary hull, upper phaser banks, and air-circulation systems for decks One through Seven . . ."

It was odd, thought Spock, to hear a computer swear.

"Where does the cut-through have to be, Spock? The auxiliary lines have to have been severed as well . . ."

"Once out of the dorsal column, access tubes Four and Seven," the Vulcan said after only a moment's hesitation —having logically deduced the danger areas for sabotage, he had taken the precaution of refreshing his own memory of the schematics of the ship. "Though with a cutoff from computer sensors, I doubt that Mr. Scott's repair crew can find the breaks before Yarblis makes his move."

"Particularly since we've taken the precaution of keeping his best assistant under sedation? You may be right . . . I've patched through. Mr. Scott?"

There was no hookup to hear the engineer's reply, but a moment later Kirk said, "We've got a report of computer blackout of Deck Five, main system and auxiliary as well . . ."

Spock, knowing the Scots engineer, could almost hear his shocked protests of there being no way it could happen short of—

"I thought that too. Get some personnel to find the cut,

but more important, get whoever you can to the air-circ pumps and the battery rooms to check for possible malfunctions there as well."

Aye, Captain, thought Spock, mentally providing the other half of the conversation, and nodded concise approval to himself for the captain's deft manipulation of the voder mechanisms, which permitted him to transmit his own voice over the comm link. He had learned quickly.

"With the personnel at Mr. Scott's disposal," he remarked, "the chances are at least twelve to one against finding any act of sabotage in so many areas before it happens—forty-three or more to one against if Yarblis attempts something outside the immediate area of the life-support system."

"Greater than that," Kirk said grimly. "What would you do if you were some Engineering ensign checking around an emergency battery and you met the captain of the vessel down there and he said, 'I've already checked this area, you go that way and check out the latrines.'"

Spock raised a brow. "I see, Captain, that I am not the only senior officer of this vessel who would make an efficient criminal. Since the order of probability is high that the threat will involve Life Support, if you will excuse me, I will take the precaution of securing an oxygen mask from the nearest emergency station." He paused by the corner of the worktable to check the small hand screen that was currently monitoring the sensors at either end of the corridor, then worked the lever to open the bulkhead and slip out. Moving with quick stealth, he slipped down the hallway to the emergency station at the foot of the gangway by the doors of the deserted cargo-transporter room.

Even in the middle of the main shift, no one was there—the room was seldom in use, and Kirk, from his position in the computer, would have picked up any communication requesting bulk shipment from the surface. Still, he listened carefully from the shadows before moving into the open. It would scarcely do, he thought, for reports of sightings of his own ghost to follow so hard upon those of the ship poltergeist.

The emergency station was recessed behind a panel in the bulkhead beside the turbolift doors. Spock glanced swiftly in one direction, then the other, listening especially for the sound of the turbolift descending. But all was still. With the small sonic extractor he'd brought with him, he unfastened the alarm panel that would have registered breakage of the safety seals on the station itself, then opened the panel and took a mask from the neat row within.

The oxygen bottle attached was empty. Frowning at the carelessness of the Security patrol responsible for checking such things—though it was easy enough to neglect, down at this untenanted level—he replaced it, drew out another . . .

And that bottle, too, was empty. All of the eight in the station bore the small red gauge light of critically low supply.

And all of them had been turned so that those lights would not show through the clear plex inspection port on the bulkhead.

He prowls the ship all night, Uhura had said.

His heart cold within him, Spock strode back to the concealed hull section. McCoy was on the planet. So were Chapel and Helen. Uhura would be on the bridge at this time, though it was a safe guess that Yarblis would not . . . not if he was working his way systematically from air-circulation pump to air-circulation pump, directing ingenuous ensigns to investigate latrines while he himself sabotaged the oxygen of the entire ship . . .

"Lieutenant Uhura?"

"What is it, sir?" Her voice was normal and absolutely

calm, though she had to be aware that he wouldn't contact her on the bridge, even using the doctored communicators, without urgent need.

"Is Yarblis on the bridge?"

"No, sir, he isn't."

"It appears likely that there is going to be an attempt on the ship's oxygen systems within the next fifteen minutes." That was the soonest, Spock estimated, allowing for the minutes occupied by his own check of the emergency station, that major damage to the air-circulation pumps could be done, even by someone who knew what he was doing, as Yarblis by this time undoubtedly did. "It also appears that some, if not all, of the oxygen masks in the emergency stations have been tampered with. Bring as many operative ones as you can locate down to Deck Twenty-three immediately."

"Yes, sir. Right away, sir. Should I contact Security, sir?"

"And tell them what, Lieutenant?" Spock inquired a touch acidly. "That someone who has been in clandestine hiding in an illegally pressurized hull section containing misappropriated Starfleet property alleges that the captain of the vessel is about to commit an act of sabotage? And in any case, we have no proof of what is about to occur."

"Very well, sir," Uhura replied in her most neutral tones. "I'll see to it at once."

"And let's hope," the Kirk voice remarked from the computer as Spock keyed off, "that she doesn't meet me in the turbolift on the way down."

The soft humming that filled the air grew stronger as Helen climbed the path from the Research Institute's little clearing among the thorn trees to the tall rocks surrounding the Bindigo Warren itself. She and DeSalle walked half bent over, keeping to such cover as they could; the Midgwins, of course, with their short stature and tough hides, found in the shoulder-high thorn forest more than adequate concealment from the airborne Hootings, the long-necked and thoroughly repulsive predators of this part of the world. The Flaygrubs, the major predators of the planet—for years regarded, along with the Bargumps, as its predominant life-form—were seldom to be found this far south in the relatively waterless savannahs; the only real dangers to the Midgwins in their clustering warrens of mud shelters were the licats, shaggy and long-bodied and hideously fast. Helen recalled in Shorak's preliminary report an account of an attack by a pack of them on the Bindigo Warren; how the Midgwins had crawled to safety in the tall rocks of the canyon and had huddled, jammed together in their thousands, for most of the day in thirst and hunger until the predators had gone away. He had noted that Arxoras and the other patriarchs had forbidden the researchers to defend the warren, and Shorak, as any researcher would have, had agreed, even at the risk of his own life.

Helen hoped no ill had now befallen them.

The hot gold sun beat upon her face, warming her; she had forgotten how much she missed the touch of air moving on her skin. Whatever was going on here, whatever peril had cleared the research camp, here on this planet she felt a curious sense of release. Here, at least, she would be in no danger of meeting that terrible pseudo-Kirk, the very sight of whom made her flesh crawl.

We have to find Arxoras, she thought, striding up the dusty path. *Patriarch and memmietieff, he will know what to do, how to return Jim to being who he was . . .*

The soft humming increased, a curious sweetness in the dusty air. To her nostrils came the musky pungency of the Midgwins themselves, and another sound, the dry, scaly rubbing of their hides that she associated with the whisper of the night wind in the long white grasses, the deep scents of evening on the veldt.

She realized then what the humming had to be.

The entire population of the warren, nearly ten thousand of the pear-shaped, wrinkled little Midgwins, were formed in the thick concentric rings of the Consciousness Web, skeletal hands entwined, round eyes closed, rocking gently from side to side and humming in the thrall of their dreams. The delicate folds of their faces, the wrinkles of the skin around the little beaks of their mouths, were utterly relaxed. Hot sun shone on the knobby little purple-brown shoulders beneath the long cloaks of spidery hair, and the golden air seemed to pulse with some alien peace, some deep union born of contentment and the acceptance of fate.

Helen signed to DeSalle to remain where he was, and stepped clear of the shelter of the thorn trees. None of the Midgwins opened its eyes, or seemed to hear, despite the fact that she knew that licats hunted during the day, and that the Midgwins generally posted guards to flash telepathic warning signals from the rocks above the camps. But she saw no such guards. No sound broke the amber brightness of the afternoon, save for the deep, purring hum of the web.

As quietly as she could, Helen walked toward the thick-braided lines of bodies and arms.

The patriarchs of the warren, she knew, started the web, sitting in its center, near the rocks that marked the village spring. She could get nowhere near that point, so close were the Midgwins packed around it, but she climbed up on one of the immense, bubble-shaped red boulders that littered the ground all around the warren, and from that vantage point scanned the purple-brown faces near the center for the telltale white muzzles of the patriarchs, and most particularly for Arxoras's milk-white hair.

But nowhere did she see him, or any other of the old ones of the group. And, if she remembered Shorak's reports correctly, it was most unusual for the warren to enter web in the daytime, when the danger of predation was greater and the sun shined so hotly down. Yet even the children of the warren were there, rocking and swaying in the lines beside their parents, infants rolled close in their fathers' pouches—not an unusual circumstance for a web, she thought, but the children, being without armor and unable to run, generally stayed in shelter during the day.

Her sense of foreboding increased. She dropped back off the rock and returned to where DeSalle waited in the shadows of a barrel tree a dozen yards beyond the warren's edge. "He isn't there," she said softly, wondering what the hell they were going to do now. Surely Yarblis couldn't have gotten rid of all the patriarchs . . .

DeSalle frowned, recognizing the anomaly even from the little he knew about Midgwin society.

"Is there any way we can wake one of them up and ask?"

Helen shook her head. "They're not really asleep . . . and I doubt that we could bring one of them out of it, or that doing so would be a good idea. Thetas told me they stay in the web for three or four hours at a time, sometimes longer . . . I don't know whether any of them ever tried to break into the trance. It would be horribly bad manners at the very least . . . I'm not even sure whether it might be dangerous."

DeSalle's mouth twitched. "Sounds counter-evolutionary to me," he commented, scanning the harsh thorn jungle around them as they turned back down the trail. "As far as I can tell, there are no guards posted, no lookouts . . ."

Helen shook her head. "I didn't see any, and Shorak said there usually are in the daytime. It's odd . . ." She looked back over her shoulder at the tight-crowded bodies, rocking gently like the lapping of a calm sea, her heart sinking within her. Her boots scuffed the thin dust of the trail, the scent of it mingling with the dry, strange smells of the thorn jungle, of the spring around which the warren was built. Curious, she thought, how the village itself didn't stink, the way so many tribal villages did— the Midgwins were fanatically clean. With that heavy a population, she thought, you'd have to be, if only to avoid disease and drawing predators to the spot . . .

"It's odd that they'd be holding web in the daytime," she said after a moment, her anthropological training puzzling over the problem even in the face of what might mean serious trouble—for Jim, for the ship, for them all. "And odder still that the patriarchs would be gone."

DeSalle was scanning the low thickets around them as they walked, his phaser held ready, his eyes narrowed against the hazy golden light. "One might have something to do with the other."

"Maybe," Helen agreed worriedly. "And both might have to do with—"

They stepped into the clearing in front of the Research Institute and stopped dead. Standing in front of Shorak's hut, wearing the mottled gray-and-bronze camouflage of a battlefield unit, were two Klingons.

Chapter Eighteen

"ATTENTION . . . INTRUDER ALERT! Repeat, intruder alert! Red Alert!" Pacing the narrow confines of the hull compartment, Spock looked up sharply at the sound of the captain's voice. "All Security personnel report for search of decks Fifteen, Sixteen, and Nineteen immediately! Repeat, all Security personnel report for search of—"

"Is that you, Captain?" He turned swiftly back to the computer. "What proof have you that—"

"It's not me," replied Kirk's voice from the voder. "It's the false me—or the real me, whichever way you want to look at it. The computer wouldn't have accepted a voder voice for an Alert command—that's one thing you can't tamper with either."

"Of course not . . ." Spock frowned. "Nor could it have been overridden. An attempt to throw Mr. Scott off the track, and to divert personnel from a search of Deck Five and the air-circulation equipment on Eight . . ."

The warning light Uhura had installed blinked suddenly on. Spock crossed to the locked bulkhead in a stride, listened, and recognized Lieutenant Uhura's characteristic swift step, but native caution made him wait until she herself opened the panel.

"These were all I could find on Deck Four." She held out three masks to him. "I couldn't wait to search further, but everything on the bridge level and the Science section has been emptied." Her dark eyes were wide and grave in the flashing red light of the hall outside. "I'm going back up—if there's going to be a pressure drop, some kind of alarm has to be sounded, and I don't care how much trouble we get into because of it."

"I agree," the Science officer said, taking the masks— triangular face shields of the immemorial pattern equipped with small bottles of highly reduced oxygen and a CO_2 filter system—and hooking their straps to the utility satchel he had had with him during the sweep. "And I believe that it is now incumbent upon me to come with you. There is little to be gained by my further concealment, since I believe that, logically, Yarblis has violated any further possibility of retaining the illusion of normalcy on this ship."

Uhura rolled her eyes. "Yes, I'd say that when the entire life-support system goes down, that *does* blow the illusion of normalcy . . ."

Spock paused in the act of gathering tools and slipping them into the satchel at his side. "Remember that even if there were a major rupture in the pressure skin of the ship, or a serious drop in pressure, the bulkhead seals would activate automatically to contain the danger areas. In the event of pump failure, sufficient oxygen would remain in the ship to permit evacuation to the planet long before the emergency masks would be needed. The fact that the masks were tampered with indicates—"

"Spock . . ." Kirk's voice from the voder cut into his. "We've got another blackout . . . on the Auxiliary Phaser deck, this time. All computer control to the main phaser banks has been cut."

Dimly, from the corridor, a warning siren hooted; Spock stepped to the bulkhead and put his ear to the thick wall, listening through it—Uhura shouldered him aside and opened the bulkhead a slit so that she too could hear. Through the crack the red flash of emergency lights spilled over their faces like intermittent lightning.

"Pressure drop alert," the computer's female voice intoned. "Pressure drop alert on decks Nine and Ten . . . Emergency situation on decks Seven and Eight. Immediate evacuation procedures on decks Seven and Eight . . ."

Uhura swore.

"Sickbay," Spock said. "Main transporter room, galley facilities, Security, all recreation areas—"

"Spock!" Kirk's voice called out of the computer. "Get to the bridge! Internal sensors are picking up coolant gas flooding those decks!"

"I shall contact you from there, Captain." Spock slung on the satchel and, with Uhura at his heels, strode out of the bulkhead room, locking its hidden panel behind them. As they hastened through the flaring splash of emergency lights toward the forward turbolift, Spock conducted a rapid mental inventory of his tools and the time it would take him to use them, to break through the sealed pressure doors, to repair whatever had been Yarblis's precise target. He wondered too, as he and Uhura rounded the corner, whether the temperature controls had been likewise sabotaged, and how long the hulls would retain heat.

He stopped before the doors of the turbolift.

Nothing happened.

The turbolifts were dead.

"We arrived not more than forty-eight hours after Dr. Chu's transport ship departed," Commander Khoaltar said, shaking his head politely as Dr. McCoy waved him toward a seat on one of the log seats around the Research

Institute's long-cold fire. "No, thank you . . . we have better means of displaying our civilization than by sitting in the mud with the . . . I suppose they must be called 'natives' now, instead of 'local fauna,' since the United Contact Council seems disposed to vote with the Pan-Sentients." He rubbed his slender hands—he was small, almost delicate looking, and his bronze-and-black field-combat uniform was foppishly neat. But there was something in the dark eyes that told a different story: McCoy reflected that he wouldn't have wanted to have to patch up what was left of anyone foolish enough to pick a fight with this man. Among the several combat badges on his sleeve was the small gold insignia of a high-ranking scholar.

"Oddly enough," the Klingon added, looking around him at the circle of *Enterprise* medical and security personnel, "I'm beginning to believe that such a designation might be correct."

"Now, whatever led you to that conclusion?" McCoy asked sarcastically.

"And what happened to Dr. Chu and the others?" Helen put in, sitting on the log at the doctor's side. She looked exhausted, even from the short walk up the trail. Though she could not have been left on the ship, McCoy thought, she should have remained on the shuttlecraft to rest. "Did you . . ." She hesitated.

". . . have anything to do with it?" Khoaltar raised one carefully trimmed brow. "In a manner of speaking, yes."

"We can surely find a more comfortable place to discuss this than here," his companion added, a taller and somewhat older man named Urak. He was more obviously a scholar, despite the mottled camouflage garb. Probably, thought McCoy, a civilian who'd been pushed through the same kind of remedial physical training he'd had to put up with when he'd joined the fleet. "Our own research station is just on the far side of the hill; though it's not completely set up yet, we can at least offer you chairs to sit in, and something civilized to drink."

DeSalle shook his head. "I think we'll stay here, thanks." Oyama and Gomez, unobtrusively stationed a short distance away in the brush, were visible from the camp but too far off to be caught in any single line of fire. Though DeSalle had appeared to accept completely the Klingons' assurances of peaceful intent, he wasn't a man to take chances.

"We'd need to in any case," Helen added quietly, "as we need to speak with the patriarchs of the warren as soon as they come out of their trance."

"Don't plan on it being soon," Khoaltar warned, folding up his slender form to sit on the logs at McCoy's side. "They've been in that trance, on and off, for over a week now, ever since news of the plague reached them."

McCoy and Chapel glanced at each other. "Plague?"

"In, I believe it is called, the Walpuk Warren," the Klingon said. "It lies downriver not far from here—I suspect they will be returning at any time now. We had been here, as I said, less than twenty-four hours when word first reached the patriarchs here of it. They must have meditated, trying to heal from a distance, as it is their belief that they can do . . ."

"I think it's more than a belief," Helen remarked softly.

"But less than a certainty," Khoaltar replied, "as even they were willing to admit after a day and a night. There is only so much one can do against the effects of prolonged starvation and undernourishment . . ."

McCoy's fist clenched sharply on his knee. "Dammit, I tried to tell Thetas that . . ."

"He did not disbelieve you, Doctor," the Klingon replied in his soft voice. The slim brown hand picked up a twig from the ground, scratched a random, shuffling pattern in the sulfur-colored dust. A crimson lizard skittered along the thorn stem behind him, regarding the strangers with a bobbing blossom of stalked, black, hysterical eyes. From the warren the soft hum of the web continued, gentle and buzzing in the heavy heat of the afternoon.

"And in time, even the Midgwins themselves apparently believed. Because their patriarchs went to Dr. Shorak asking for his assistance in the matter—medical assistance, and technical knowledge, for a matter which, for the first time, was beyond the limitations of whatever psychic powers these creatures may possess."

McCoy sighed bitterly. "I told him. I told him it was only a matter of time . . ."

Helen looked curiously across at the slender form in its mottled black and bronze, sitting, almost invisible, in the harsh patchwork of shadows at Dr. McCoy's side. "But Shorak didn't have anything in the way of medicines," she said. "Medical knowledge, yes; L'jian is a doctor. But not the medicines, the antibiotics necessary to stem that kind of an outbreak. It was their commitment to living truly among these people, to teaching them and working with them. Even L'jian couldn't have done more than advise."

"No," agreed Urak, from his standing position, gently stroking his short, soft black beard, behind his aristocratic colleague's shoulder. "He couldn't. However, *we* had no such commitment . . . and we did happen to have a certain amount of pan-biotic medicines, as well as concentrated nutrients to temporarily combat the starvation in that area of the planet that was one of the chief causes of the plague."

"And you *gave* it to them?" McCoy asked, deeply suspicious.

"We are not monsters, Doctor," Khoaltar replied with a haughty inclination of his head. "As well as researchers, we are in a way of being diplomats. And, since the United Council seems disposed to regard the Midgwins as sentient, and will very likely so vote, it behooves us to present our own case for the development of this planet in the best possible light. Very likely we will be censured by the Ministry of Expansion for wasteful expenditure, but in ten years, or twenty, it may be an investment that will pay well."

"Then it wasn't you who wrecked the transmitter?" Chapel asked doubtfully.

Khoaltar turned upon her a smile of surprising sweetness. "My dear lady," he said, "if a Klingon wishes to wreck a transmitter, believe me, he will go about it with more efficiency than a wooden lever and a rock. According to Dr. Thetas—who for the first day of our stay here was the only member of the Federation party who did not avoid us with hostile glares—both transmitters were found demolished the morning after you left the planet. I suspect that after a state of détente was reached, Dr. Shorak would have unbent sufficiently to request the use of our transmitter—he is shockingly prejudiced for a Vulcan."

"That may have something to do with his wife's sister having been taken prisoner at the battle of Plethak," DeSalle remarked, and Khoaltar made a deprecating gesture with the twig he still held in one graceful hand.

"As I myself was only five years old at the time of that battle, I would not know," he said. "Urak, perhaps you would care to go back to the encampment and bring us all something to drink? Mr. DeSalle, if you find this activity suspicious—as you very well may, this being a disputed world—you may wish to send one of your guards, either with him or behind him. But I assure you that if we were to destroy your party—and if we had destroyed Dr. Shorak's earlier—the consequences to us would be . . . unpleasant in the extreme."

"From the Federation? Or the Organians?" McCoy asked thoughtfully, as DeSalle nodded to Oyama to follow the Klingon at a careful distance, back through the hot, spiky fringes of the bush, toward the site of their alleged research camp. "Or from your own Emperor, for complicating an already complicated situation?"

Khoaltar was silent for a few moments, dark eyes returning to the patterns he sketched, with a calligrapher's light hand, in the dust. Then he said, "All three, certainly, but . . ." He glanced up, and there was worry in the onyx gaze. "But mostly from the Midgwins themselves."

"Damn you, man, what d'you mean, the programmin's been blanked?" Scotty shouted into the intercom on the emergency bridge, his accent, like McCoy's southern drawl, becoming far more marked under stress. "It's a bluidy utility program, man!" His blunt fingers stabbed another toggle as lights on the small unit on the arm of the chair in which he sat—the captain's chair, smaller than the one on the main bridge, but like it, equipped with full input from every intercom on the ship—flared on again.

Sulu's voice was clipped and terse with tension. "Mr. Scott? Any word from the captain? We've got everything below Deck Six evacuated—we're running an accountability check . . ."

"To hell with the accountability check, are you gettin' the air-circ feeds straightened out?"

"As well as we can, sir. But they were booby-trapped—as far as we can tell, they were set up to reroute the xyrene gas until the doors of the systems rooms were opened—then they blew. We've got Bray on repair of one of them, and he says the damage isn't too bad . . . Can you get up here?"

"And how am I to do that with the turbolifts shut down and Deck Seven swamped in gas? You know there isn't a—" He broke off and swung around as there was a stir in the crowd around the emergency doors into the bridge. The crowd of security personnel, originally sent to chase the putative intruder from decks 15, 16, and 19, had been gathered on the auxiliary bridge—which was far too small to hold that many people—ever since the start of the alert, unable to make their way back to the primary hull where the trouble now seemed to be. The harried engineer opened his mouth to demand who the hell that was, and left it open.

"Status report, Mr. Scott?"

It was the late Mr. Spock, looking very much his usual calm Vulcan self, with a flustered and rather rumpled Lieutenant Uhura in tow.

After one swift gulp of astonishment, Scotty vacated the command chair, in which Mr. Spock seated himself as if he had never been on the shuttlecraft deck in his life. "All turbolifts are out, sir," he reported, making a heroic recovery. "The engineer in Turbo Control reports the operations program that guides them has been taken out of the computer—not only the main computer, but the backups as well. We've had power blackouts all over the ship—all owin' to cuts in the communications lines . . . decks Seven and Eight are flooded with xyrene, and there doesn't seem to be a full oxygen mask on the ship . . ."

"Leaving the auxiliary phaser controls isolated at the bottom of the primary hull," Mr. Spock concluded. "Can the turbolifts be operated manually?"

Scott shook his head. "Not a chance, Mr. Spock. And the captain's gone missing . . ."

"Mr. Spock . . ." Kirk's voice cut in from the intercom on the arm of the chair, and even with the flattened quality of the speaker, Spock's sensitive hearing identified the limited range of a voder-manufactured artificial voice.

"Yes, Captain?"

"I've found it. Among the programs Yarblis copied for

his own reference onto wafer was the entire inventory of all the main phaser-bank programs. He can now upload them into a 590-capacity or higher portable computer— of which the ship has two, and three 670s, counting the one Miller borrowed to program Brunowski's remixer . . ."

"Captain," Mr. Scott broke in, "where are you? They've been lookin' high and low for ye . . ."

"I'm quite safe, Mr. Scott, but I'm trapped where I am on Deck Eight," he replied, quite truthfully. "You've done an excellent job of coping with this—thank you . . ."

"And who's this Yarblis fellow?"

"The intruder," Kirk said quietly. "The intruder who has been with us since Midgwis . . . an intruder who may very well be capable of mimicking my voice. He has, as I have said, every ability to take over the main phaser deck now. And by linking back the program into the phaser controls at their source, he can either use the phaser banks himself . . . or override the damper backups, and blow up the ship."

"Do you know, Doctor, what it was that disposed us to take seriously the claims that the Midgwins were sentient at all, and not the . . . subsentient primate species that everyone—including Federation researchers— originally thought they were?"

McCoy glanced back up the path in the direction of the towering rocks that marked the warren. The soft, humming coo of the Consciousness Web could still be heard, though it was growing softer now, sinking into a whisper. He remembered the preliminary reports which described it as herd behavior, possibly having something to do with mating or the protection of the old and the infants of the warrens, for those were the ones closest to the centers of the webs. Even after Dr. Shorak had discovered the largely telepathic nature of Midgwin communication, the Klingons had continued to claim that the Consciousness Web was more analogous to the swarming instincts of various forms of hymenoptera or espikotherae than to anything relating to sentient beings.

"Because they were able to kill your scouts?" He had begun to speak sarcastically, but didn't, for it suddenly occurred to him that such might very well have been the thing that had won the Klingons' respect.

"Not the fact in itself," Khoaltar said. "That definition would qualify Denebian slime devils for sentience—though I do not doubt that there are some bleeding hearts in the Pan-Sentient League who eventually will attempt to claim exactly that, and file suit against everyone who has mined the swamps of Deneb Cantios Four for violation of the Prime Directive. But the *way* in which that killing was done."

DeSalle, who had been leaning against the trunk of one of the stunted trees and unobtrusively watching the 360-range sensor in his palm, frowned. "I thought they were just reported as . . . killed."

The Klingon shook his head. "There is evidence that one or more Midgwins . . . in effect, took mental possession of the bodies of members of the scouting parties. This we have deduced from analysis of transmissions of the various parties' reports. It appears that at least some of the Midgwins could—possess—control—our men, knowing what they knew, understanding what they would have understood. And thus disguised, they bided their time, and waited for unguarded moments."

"Yes," McCoy said softly. "Yes . . . I know."

DeSalle looked startled—Khoaltar turned his head sharply, his dark eyes narrowing. "Do you?"

But McCoy made no further reply. After a moment Khoaltar continued, "But you see, to understand, and to use, the information they found within their victims' minds, they had to be . . . sentient, surely. And almost certainly intelligent. And to tell you the truth, Doctor . . . in spite of the fact that it is our mission to learn as much about them as possible, to establish communication and trade with them if we can, I am just as glad that they have kept their distance from us."

Chapter Nineteen

"YOU'RE SURE THIS IS how you want to do this, Mr. Spock?" Scotty's voice echoed strangely in the long, narrow hull of the machinery room which ran the length of the Engineering hull's uppermost level—Deck 15, whose dim shadows pulsed with the faint throb of the air-circulation machinery for all the decks below, and whose curving walls seemed to reverberate with the power of the twin engine nacelles on their pylons far above. "I mean, I could handle the repair of those air pumps mesel' and let you take a security guard with you instead of me bringin' along Bistie to make my job quicker."

Spock shook his head, and slipped the oxygen mask down over his eyes and nose, transforming his head, in the uncertain light, into a strange insectoid shape of straps and bulbs and monstrous, crystalline eyes. "Repair of the air-circulation system is of the first priority," he said, "followed, as quickly as possible, with the reprogramming of the turbolifts. From there help can be gotten to us."

"But if the captain's trapped on Deck Eight—that area

of the ship's flooded with gas." His dark eyes were filled with concern.

"The captain is quite safe where he is," Spock replied evenly, and turning from the still-baffled chief engineer and his assistant—one of the few who could repair one air system unaided while Scott worked on the other—he opened the repair hatch that let into the food conveyor which ran all the way up from the main recycling plant on Deck 21 up to Deck 8. He switched on the sharp white beam of his mask light, contemplated the narrow, pitch-dark, and rather slimy tube with its linked ladder of bucketlike carriers, and with stoic distaste climbed in.

In any environment but that of a starship, he thought, rapidly ascending the steep-slanted tunnel by means of the stilled conveyor chains, such a place would invariably have been the haunt of both vermin and molds of every description. Despite meticulous sealing and sterilization procedures, the place seemed to be faintly coated with a thin organic residue, the dark semiliquid of pure CHON that could be theoretically recombined to form anything from the most delicate of blancmanges to Romulan chili, though in practice the results were frequently less than inspired. Spock was well aware that the stuff was perfectly clean, and that neither rats, nor insects, nor Antraean garbage worms, nor molds of any kind, existed on the ship . . . nevertheless, the long, dripping passage stretching away into the darkness above him looked like the sort of place that might contain all of them. He was glad he was wearing his oxygen mask. Pure CHON might be absolutely clean and healthful, but its odor was scarcely aesthetic.

Moreover, there was no telling how far the coolant gas had leaked down the tube from Deck 8.

Xyrene gas was heavy and tended to flow downward; the first drifts and filaments of it were detectable in the glow of his mask light and the crisscrossed, swaying beams of Scott's and Bistie's, four or five meters below the place where the tunnel itself leveled out to pass above the remixer room in the primary hull. By the time they reached the level stretch, the concentration was high enough, according to the gauge of Spock's tricorder, to have caused unconsciousness and rapid death in anyone breathing it. The deck below them must be heavily flooded.

"There should be another repair hatch about five meters ahead," came Scott's voice in his earphone.

Spock moved his head; the beam of his mask light flashed across the access port, through whose unsealed edges the pink gas was leaking in a wavering veil. "I see it," he replied. "Mr. Scott, I believe matters would proceed most expeditiously if you and Ms. Bistie both proceeded up the gangways to Deck Five and effected repairs on the pumps controlling Deck Seven, rather than attempting to repair those on this level that control the decks below."

"I'm not sure I've got enough oxygen in this little bottle to do a major repair anyway," came Bistie's voice through Spock's earphone.

"Indeed. I shall proceed downward to the main phaser deck . . ." He opened the hatchway and put his head cautiously through. With the failure of the pumps, the lights had cut out too. Only the ghastly reddish glare of the emergency systems glowed, intermittently illuminating a hellish swamp of shifting pink mists drifting between the dark islands of the remixers below. Spock reached up to adjust the beam of his mask lamp to widest scan. It showed him no danger, and his sensitive hearing picked up no sound of footfall or breath. Sitting up cautiously in the narrow space, he dangled his legs through the aperture, let himself carefully down by his hands, and dropped.

"You be careful, Mr. Spock." Scotty dropped down

after him, his red uniform shirt, his trousers, his hands and face—where his face could be seen through the strapwork of the mask that covered it—all smeared with a brownish film of CHON in the bloody glare. "I don't want to be losin' you again before I hear how you got out of that hangar deck in the first place."

"It was elementary, my dear Mr. Scott . . ." They halted before the emergency gangways that ran up either side of the silent turbolift shaft—massive pressure doors had slipped from the walls to seal them off. "The pressure drop, of course," Scott muttered, unshipping the pin laser from the utility satchel he wore and going to one knee to begin cutting at the locks. "And good odds the one above this'll be the same . . ."

"As indeed it should," Spock replied austerely. "They are designed to prevent loss of atmosphere, or, conversely, the sort of contamination that would occur were the deck above us not already thoroughly flooded."

"But it means the deck below'll be sealed too. Shall I come down with you to cut that?"

There was a swift crackle of the intercom near the turbolift door—Kirk's voice came on, the voder voice, the computer voice, as far as Spock could tell. Of course, he thought. From the safety of the computer, the captain was perfectly capable of tracking them through the in-ship comm link. "It'll take too long," Kirk cut in crisply. "The hull storage compartment behind the forward emergency transporter room has been pressurized, and there's a trap down into a hull section below that—also pressurized—and one below that. They're a little cold, but they're livable. That'll put you on Deck Ten, below the level of the pressure drop . . ."

"Pressurized a hull section?" Scott demanded, shocked that anyone would take such liberties with his beloved ship. "Now who the divil . . . ?"

"Just don't trip over Mr. Gilden's collection of magazines—we owe him that at least."

"Very good, Captain." Spock switched off the comm link and turned to Scott. "Get Deck Seven cleared and bring Security through to the phaser deck as quickly as you can," he said, his deep voice quiet. "If you have any communication from the captain while you are repairing the pumps . . ." He hesitated, wondering what he would do if the pseudo-Kirk started giving orders again. Wondering what he would do if it was *not* the real Kirk, the computer Kirk, who had just guided him by that perilous route . . . it was very difficult to identify a voder voice as such on the tinny comm link. He knew too that Yarblis had been prowling the ship, seeking out its secret ways, for nights. If Yarblis had guessed that someone was using a voder to replicate Kirk's voice . . . "Ask him which side of the ship Yeoman Brunowski's chocolate factory is on, and upon what deck. He should tell you Deck Twenty-three, starboard. If he does not, distrust whatever he says."

And with that Spock turned and strode off down the circular corridor toward the emergency transporter room, his angular figure quickly swallowed up in darkness and bloody murk.

The time was at hand.

Yarblis Geshkerroth the Ghost Walker sat in the deepest chamber of the floating warren of the Hungries, staring into the screen of the Arkresh-670, the auxiliary portable into which he had downloaded all the killing-ray programming . . . the terms for these things, even, were beginning to cross and meld in his mind. The Hungries, who counted everything, measured everything, had made machines to ape the powers of the mind and the body, had more words than his own people did, and those words were easier to say with the mind than to use the longer, slower terms that forced the mind to consider what it was that was actually being done.

It would be so easy, it would be so pleasant, not to consider what it was that he was about to do.

Around him the red lights flared on and off, like the rising and dying of hideously shortened days, and with every glaring blink of red, there followed a swoop back into eternal night. Beyond the wired plex interior windows, the machinery of the phaser banks themselves was dyed a gory crimson, from which lines of scarlet eyes stared at him with the single-minded intensity of madness. There had been sirens hooting a warning like the mating cry of a Bargump, but he had, at least, found the tannoy speaker for that—his hand still bled a little from the rage-induced strength with which he'd ripped it out of the wall.

The silence was balm to his soul as he worked, programming in those things that he had written down, studied, memorized all these endless, hellish days and nights—plans assembled from all the schematics he could find in the computer, all the data and skill he could glean out of the memory of James T. Kirk.

Soon he would be free.

And Rhea would be safe.

Rhea.

He could see her in the forward viewscreen, as he had seen her yesterday from the bridge—as he had seen her for one blinding, heart-breaking moment that first day of his masquerade, as the *Enterprise* left orbit. He had barely been able to force himself to tear his eyes away from her—barely been able to act as he knew the captain would. And that, too, had angered him . . . that they had become casual about the soul-hurting beauty and wonder of seeing a world.

But she filled the viewscreen now, and he was free to look his fill. She was so dark, so golden, with her silken oceans and the soft chevelure of saffron clouds. The infinite beauty of her mottled colors, amber, smoke, the chocolate-brown of bare rock and the purpled hues of the

seas; snowfields like the bloom of frost upon a ripe and
delicate fruit. Had it been possible, he would have
broken out the windows of every observation port on the
ship, so that he could lean out and hear her sing.

He worked deftly, the small, soft little hands that it still
amazed him to see, adept on these keypads of letters,
forming concepts precise enough in their detail for these
hateful counting machines to comprehend. He had cut
through the leads from the main computer, the open
access port gaping like a wound in the wall behind him,
just beneath where the tannoy speaker dangled on its
faintly sparking wires. He had plugged in the secondary
computer and used his voice—the voice of the bright
warrior Kirk—to route his way through the guard on the
program. It would be, he estimated, a long while before
the evil air could be coaxed away from the decks that
separated him from the redshirt guards, as long perhaps
as it took to gather a double handful of edible seeds in a
dry summer. They would come as swiftly as they could,
knowing their computer had lost touch with the killing-
ray place, but the gangway doors were sealed, and it
would take them time to cut through.

More than enough time.

Then Rhea would be safe, and he could go home.

Home to the Consciousness Web. Home to those who
loved him, and whom he loved. For one instant at the
thought of it, though he clamped the disciplines of his
soul down upon it immediately after, something inside
him cried like a child.

Later, he thought, later there will be time for relief . . .

He had explored this vessel thoroughly enough that he
knew that, even when he abandoned this abominable
alien body—consumed now with fever and exhaustion
as it was—he could find his way to the transporter room
and operate its controls. It was harder to think than it
had been, harder to remember everything. Perhaps it
would be easier, better, when he was clear of this

poisoned, exhausted body, this sink of instincts and memories and lusts that were not his own.

Now he concentrated his mind on the task ahead, referring at times to the notes he had made and brought with him, programming in the proper commands, the proper numbers, the grid sequences having to do with things that as Kirk he understood but that as the Ghost Walker he did not . . . orbital shift and firing order, power levels and primary ignition. So intent was he on this that he did not hear the stealthy creak of boot leather in the corridor outside until it was almost upon him; it was in fact the faint, preliminary grind of the manual door control that made him swing around in his chair and duck behind the console even as the doors slammed open and the white beam of a phaser stabbed into the alternate glare and darkness of the room.

Furious and shocked as he was that any could have avoided his precautions—he had not fought the Hungries for years for nothing—his mind, the trained psychic skill of a *memmietieff,* slashed out in defense, slamming the doors like pinching jaws at the intruder's arm and body. As the intruder sprang and rolled free of them—into the room—in the bleeding glare of the lights he saw that, impossibly, it was the Vulcan Spock, the Counter of Everything, and at once many things became suddenly clear.

He had not died in the hangar deck, and the attempt had crystallized his suspicions of his captain. He knew what his captain had become—he had used his logic to discover the nature of the threat.

Rage exploded in Yarblis, rage fed by loneliness, by grief, by all that he had done—rage and fear that at this late moment his plan for the saving of Rhea would yet be crossed. This rage gave strength to the psychokinetic abilities latent in the brains of all these alien beings. As Spock flung himself along the wall to get a clear shot at him where he crouched behind the console, Yarblis reached out again with his mind and ripped the dangling tannoy speaker away from its wires, sent it hurtling through the half-dark air at the back of the Vulcan's head.

Spock tried too late to duck, the corner of the speaker gouging into his shoulder, tearing the blue shirt he wore and bringing blood green as keval sap welling from the flesh beneath. The room was almost bare, containing little beyond the phaser control console, the two chairs before it, and the small computer that Yarblis had used to bypass the ship's main controls; they could hide from one another on opposite sides of the console, but Spock was armed. Staggering with shock, the Vulcan rose to fire straight down across the console at him, but Yarblis reached out with his mind again, this time catching him in the same whirlwind of angry force that he had used to hurl the speaker, flinging him back against the far wall of the room with bone-cracking force. The phaser fell from his hand, clattering on the floor. Even so, Spock tried to get up again, groggily fighting unconsciousness, and Yarblis flung at him all the smashing impact of his mind.

Spock's body hit the wall with the hard crack of a skull striking metal. He slid to the floor.

Yarblis picked up the phaser, set it to kill, and walked around the console to where the Vulcan lay, beneath the vast viewscreen filled with Rhea's gold and damson face.

The grinding whir of the doors alerted him again. He swung around, leveling the weapon . . .

But there was no one framed in the hard, open rectangle of flashing crimson light. He took two steps toward it across the round chamber, moving cautiously, listening for the whisper of breath, the rustle of clothing . . .

And then he saw it. Stepping forth from the wall that held the open access port he'd used to cut into the computer leads, he saw him, as he'd seen him for those few hours in the moonlight down on the world . . . the ghost shape of James T. Kirk.

He saw the shape quite clearly, though he knew it was not his eyes that beheld the strange, elongated body, the tiny head with its fair hair, the hazel eyes and decisive chin which stared back at him unbelieving from the mirror every morning.

That Kirk's spirit, his mind, should have retained its cohesiveness after this long away from his body was impossible, unbelievable. A few days, a week perhaps . . . He had searched the ship, time and time again, after the sweep, searching for the whisper, the faintest clue, as to the presence he had felt in its shadows every day, every hour before. And he had felt nothing. Shock held him speechless.

"Don't do it, Yarblis," he heard Kirk's voice in his mind. "Destroying this ship will gain you nothing—nothing but the possibility of war between the Federation and the Klingons, because neither side is going to believe that the Midgwins were capable of blowing up a starship. And your people are going to be caught in the middle of any conflict."

He drew his head back into his shoulders, an instinctive gesture of defense, and hissed, "Destroy this ship? Do you think I am a fool? No, they would never believe . . . they think we are fools, and children, who need only to be guided into the right way, the way of Yours or Mine, the way of first seducing the Earth Spirit Mother and then raping her and making her their slave . . . Your way. The easy way of the Hungries, the way of the full belly and the empty soul. It is not this ship, this . . . this metal driftwood floating on a sea of nothing with its cargo of dirt crawlers, that I will destroy."

The very gesture of his head was the same, remembered, re-created, in the faintly glowing shape that the mind can be trained to retain when it leaves the body. "What then?"

"What do you think?" Yarblis demanded savagely, his very soul hurting as he pronounced the words. "The Bindigo Warren—the tumor where the poison is growing—the place where your seducers have started already on the souls of humankind. My people have begun to listen to what yours have to say. You have taken the soul of our greatest, of my friend, my father, my brother, Arxoras the Wise . . ." His voice broke with the hurt of it, with the grief at killing his friend, the greater grief of seeing what he would become. He shook his head violently, tears of that grief, that fury, filling his eyes.

"And when they see the warren destroyed by the bolts from out of the heavens, never will they trust you anymore. And that is as it should be, for you will turn our people into what you are."

And he saw Kirk's face first stunned, then slowly change with shock. "They're down there," he whispered.

"A mother can transmit disease unto her child with a kiss, golden captain," Yarblis said, his borrowed voice cracking under the strain. "It is better thus."

"And you would murder your friends . . ."

"My friends in the warren who are helping me with this, who concealed my body and cared for it . . . they would rather die in Rhea's defense than live to see what would become of her, when the beauty of living dies. And those others . . . If they knew what they would become in time, after your ways have taught them to say Mine and Yours, after your ways have killed the warmth of the web that binds us all each to each, they would thank me, and welcome the fire. If Arxoras could see what he will become, as I can see it—"

The red lights flashed, on and off, on and off. Kirk was silent with horror, and Yarblis remembered, dimly and belatedly, that the woman Helen had gone down to the planet, and also the healer McCoy, whom Kirk cared for . . . But that was impossible, he thought in the next second, impossible to truly care without the Consciousness Web . . .

"You don't know the future, Yarblis."

"I know what you are!" Yarblis screamed back at him, at that impossible, glowing shape in the scarlet-drenched darkness, at that alien mind that should have dissolved shrieking as the other Hungries had dissolved into the soft golden air of the only world worth having, the only world worth saving, the only world worth living in. "I know what you have done to yourselves, and what your people will do to mine! You will feed them the food that makes them Hungry inside, that makes them forget what Beauty is. You will deceive them into asking for that death! And I know that my people would rather die than become as you are!"

He felt Kirk's mind grope out, seizing at the broken piece of the tannoy speaker to fling at him, and with his own mind he hurled it aside. Then like a splintering crash of light, he threw his strength against the strength of Kirk's mind, tearing at it, like the scream of the induction field from the sweep, seeking to break it impulse from impulse, spark from spark. The power and rage of his mind were such that the wired plex of the internal windows bulged and shattered, fragments of it showering across the floor of the room and rattling like scarlet hail upon the machinery beyond. He felt Kirk cry out in pain and felt the wrenching twist of his despairing strength, flinging the debris of the speaker at him, trying to strike him with it, to break his concentration . . . to kill him perhaps. He struck the speaker aside again, and Kirk retreated before him into the hallway, trying to pull the doors shut, to protect himself . . .

The blast of Yarblis's mind wrenched the doors from their sockets, sending them clattering on the hard and flat and hateful floor, and over them he strode into the hall in pursuit.

He caught a glimpse of Kirk's glittering shape near the door of one of the storage holds which were the only other rooms on this level, fumbling with the limited strength of his mind to open the door, to get at the objects inside—alien weapons, stones for analysis by the Geo lab, boxes of samples of earth. Yarblis had seen the inventories, as he had seen the inventories of every storeroom on the ship. Though he had very little control over it, Kirk's electrostatic spirit shadow had the random strength of psychic energy—and obviously, thought Yarblis, he had more power than he had given him credit for. He must be destroyed, and destroyed quickly, before he found another way to thwart the plan.

The door gave suddenly, crashing open; Yarblis saw Kirk duck inside. He still followed the routes of human form and flesh, as if instinctively knowing they bound him together. Yarblis strode after him, slamming the doors back with his mind as Kirk tried to get them to remain shut against him. The white blaze of his mental energy he threw at that flickering ghost, shredding at it, weakening it, distracting it, and somewhere in the darkness of the hold he heard the violent, random knocking of that embattled soul's terror and rage. A heavy box of soil samples bounded down from a shelf, missing him by yards, rolled like a leaf across the floor of the hold.

He swung around again, sensing where Kirk had to be hiding among the banks of shelves, the stacks of boxes in the shadowy gloom. Outside, Yarblis could hear the dim throb of the warning sirens from elsewhere on the deck, reminding him that time was short—that he must accomplish his deed soon. He knew where Kirk was hiding, and his own fury and desperation swept the shelves between them aside as if they had been dry weed stems, sending them crashing down in a shower of rocks and dust and bursting crates. Kirk tried again to hurl a massive sample of some kind of ore, some rock that smelled of distant worlds and alien seas, at his head, but his strength was lessening, his control almost non-existent. It was not a matter of hiding, of dodging, as it had been with the Vulcan Spock and his phaser—it was a matter only of strength to strength, of will against will, and Yarblis knew his will was stronger.

He smashed at Kirk's will with his blind brute strength and felt him stagger, felt him founder and slip. His will he sent forth like the blasting roar of a battle cry, the battle cry of the will that had shattered the dark-skinned Klingon Hungries when they had materialized on his world in a shower of sparkling bodiless fire. He felt Kirk cry out in pain, and stones sprang from the shelves that remained, whirled in the air like blown leaves and then fell clattering on the floor. Before him he could only see the glowing form of Kirk, flung back against the wall as Spock had been flung, arms raised as if they could protect him . . .

Spock, he thought. Spock was in the room with the phaser. If he revived, he would come seeking him again, seeking to kill this body, and he could not stand against them both.

He flung one more blast of his mind against Kirk, and saw the pale glow of him flicker and fade. Turning, he fled from the storage hold back toward the phaser control chamber, remembering suddenly all the precepts of gunnery . . . Had Kirk been trying to delay him, deceive him, trick him into abandoning his post until the planet's orbit had taken the Bindigo Warren out of his range?

He would do it, he thought, to save the woman Helen, and his friend McCoy, down there in the warren—down where the fire would fall.

But it would not save the warren from destruction. He, Yarblis, would not allow this chance to be wasted, this last chance to cut the cancer from the body of Rhea, this last chance to awaken those he loved to the danger in which they stood.

Spock still lay unconscious where he had fallen, the broken crystal of the window glittering all around him, green blood leaking from the cut in his shoulder and the savage gash on the side of his head.

Gasping with his exertions, barely able to walk, Yarblis leaned his short human arms upon the console and looked down at the readings.

The Bindigo Warren was still within range.

He raised his head and looked up at the viewscreen, where Rhea still hung against the darkness, the face of beauty, of love, of song. For a moment the thought of the Consciousness Web overwhelmed him, and a despairing gladness that the Bindigo Warren was still in daylight—that they would not be in the web when they were destroyed. But the other warrens would know. And he would spread the word, would tell them what the Hungries' ship had done—he would force them to turn aside from that soft, sweet poison forever.

And he himself would have peace.

Behind him, dimly, Yarblis could hear the far-off knocking of a poltergeist, like the last helpless cries of the dying. His mind was James T. Kirk's, clear and concise and knowing what he did. He finished setting the coordinates to take in the Bindigo Warren and an area ten miles around it, flipped the primary ignition switches, waited while the lights behind the shattered spiderwebs of the internal windows blinked from red to green.

He would go home. Back to the Consciousness Web . . . back to the love, the strength, the sweetness of Rhea—Rhea as it should be, and now always would. He could see his hands—Kirk's hands—trembling, felt the sweat running down his face, and recognized that the last effort of will, of psychokinetic energy, had sapped the final strength from this borrowed body. *Good,* he thought, with a final burst of rage at the creature who had so nearly thwarted all his plans. *I have not only defeated you, I have hurt you . . .*

He was thinking of James T. Kirk as the last lights went from red to green and he hit the firing switch.

On the forward screen he saw the red beams lance out into darkness, and a moment later saw the pinprick of fire blaze forth on the planet's shadowy flank.

Then he sank his head down to the controls, and closing his eyes, gratefully embraced the dark.

Chapter Twenty

"FOR THE DEAR GOD'S SAKE, would you mind tellin' me what that was all about, Mr. Spock?"

Spock looked up from the diagnostic gauges on the outside of the stasis chamber, beyond whose thick crystal portholes he could see the body of James T. Kirk, sheet drawn up to his naked chest and arms, face relaxed in sleep. He had still been breathing when Spock had lifted him off the control console of the phaser banks; it had been only a matter of a minute or two before Uhura had contacted him over the comm link to let him know sickbay—and in fact most of Deck 7—had been cleared of the contaminant gas. Spock had carried him back up through the illegally pressurized—and crazily junk-filled —hull compartments, to the hole Scotty had made in the floor of Deck 7 directly over the uppermost of the three—a hole, coincidentally enough, in the floor of Mr. Spock's own office.

Though Spock was not a medical doctor, the gauges on the stasis chamber all looked normal.

He turned to Mr. Scott, who was leaning in the doorway. The chief engineer was still smeared head to foot with brown CHON residue, his hands further blackened with oil, and his red sleeves blotched with assorted other colors from pressure fluids, lubricants, and burns.

"We got the turbolifts going again," Scotty added, brushing back his short black hair and leaving a long greenish streak on his forehead. "And Deck Eight is about cleared. Lieutenant Uhura tells me there's a log entry of Transporter Room Four operating, though that was when that part of Deck Seven was still flooded with gas . . ."

"Indeed?" Spock said, raising an eyebrow, and nodded to himself.

"You mean to say you *expected* that?"

"Of course. It was only logical." He considered the captain's unconscious face once more, hollow-cheeked and lined with exhaustion, then stepped over to the comm link switch on the wall. "Lieutenant Uhura, can you patch me through to Dr. Gordon on the surface of the planet?"

"Dr. Gordon?" Scott whispered unbelievingly. "Last I heard, the poor lass was in intensive care and not expected to get over it! You mean to say—"

"Yes, Mr. Spock?" came the scarred, gritted voice over the comm link.

"Did you succeed in getting in touch with the patriarch Arxoras?"

There was a long pause. Then Helen replied, "Er, yes. Yes, I'm here with him now. The thing is—"

"I think it is necessary that you convince him to return to the ship with you as quickly as possible. Please reassure him of the safety of the shuttlecraft, and of our good intentions toward him and his people . . . but I have reason to believe that the Ghost Walker has returned to the planet . . ."

"Yes," Helen said. "Yes, I know he has."

Spock paused, hearing the flat note in her voice.

After a moment she went on, "How is the captain?"

"I think that is the reason," Spock said, "that Arxoras should be here."

There was another silence. Then she said, "I'll see what I can do."

Spock sighed as the channel closed out, and rubbed the bridge of his nose with tired fingers. His head ached in spite of the pain suppressants in the small medi-patch that the second-shift nurse had placed over the gash in his temple—a patch that stood out startlingly rosy against the greenish cast of his skin—and he felt weary to his bones. Before they had closed the captain in the stasis chamber, he had entered, hesitantly and cautiously, into a mind meld with him, and had been disturbed by what he had sensed. Perhaps one of the great Adepts, one of the ancient masters of the *kolihnar*, could have understood that frantic flickering of impulses, could have reordered it, straightened it, eased it. But he was a scientist, understanding only what every Vulcan school-child learned of the spiritual disciplines—he did not know if, as things now stood, his friend could even be saved.

The weight of that lay on him like a shroud of lead.

He turned back, to see Mr. Scott regarding him with worried eyes.

"An explanation of all things." Spock said slowly, "will be . . . forthcoming."

"I certainly hope so." Scott looked relieved to see him emerge from whatever dark reverie held him. "Including an explanation of why— All right, all right!" he added, as the second-shift nurse, a soft-footed young black woman, disapprovingly held out to him a handwipe. "I know this is a sterile environment I'm muckin' up! Including an explanation," he went on, turning back to Spock, "of why this alien intruder, after damn near drivin' the captain out of his mind and doing his best to murder you and Dr. Gordon, should have done all this just to blast a forty-hectare hole in the middle of the most uninhabited desert on the planet?"

Spock paused, considering how much of the events of the past week should—or could—be reasonably explained. At length he said, "That was . . . an error on his part."

"How could he make an error?" the chief engineer asked curiously. "It's not like he was shootin' off a hand phaser, you know. He had the best guidance program in the galaxy to aim with."

Spock shook his head. "His error," he said, "was to leave me alone with his targeting computer."

Helen folded up her communicator and turned back to the group assembled around the cold ashes of the fire between the two huts of the Research Institute, their faces grave and weary and, for a large part, dust-covered in the tawny citrine light. To Kailin Arxoras, squatting on one of the log sections with his long white hair knotted back and tangled with the grime of travel, she said simply in the tongue of the Midgwins, "He needs your help."

The patriarch, though he had been days upon the road and had not yet even returned so far as the main warren, nodded and said, "He shall have it."

And on the other side of the circle Yarblis Geshkerroth the Ghost Walker, destroyer of the Hungries and guard of his planet, hissed. "It is a trap! They will . . ."

"They will what, Yarblis?" asked Arxoras softly, and those who could understand the speech of the Midgwins —Helen, Thetas, Doctors Chu and Nomias and the two Vulcans—felt beneath the sweet, high chirping of the simple words all the colorings of tone and pacing that made up the language's delicate nuances, and sensed the telepathic component of the language that flowed still further beneath. "Will they destroy me who hold out my hand to them as a friend, if it is friendship with us that they seek?"

Yarblis hesitated, looking from face to face, groping for what he would say next. When he had entered the group around the Research Institute—the group that had itself been a gabbling reunion of Dr. McCoy's party and the small caravan that had only minutes earlier come threading its way out of the thorn jungle from the plague warrens of the south—Helen had thought Yarblis looked thoroughly taken aback, shocked and disoriented, staring around him at the dark-stemmed thickets, the wind-hissing gold sea of grass, the tall, pale rocks of the warren beyond them, as if he could not believe his senses. Helen had taken Arxoras aside and had been in the midst of explaining to him what she thought Yarblis had done, while, in front of the huts, McCoy and Nurse Chapel had listened to Dr. L'jian's account of the battle against plague—and the famine that had caused it—in the Walpuk country. Thetas, Chu, Shorak, and Nomias, exhausted from days and nights of travel, of inoculations, of tests and nursing, had only slumped quietly against the side of the Research Institute and numbly accepted the fructose-dripping rations handed to them by the two Klingons, while DeSalle and his myrmidons had looked on.

Then, angry, the Ghost Walker burst out, "They will twist you! As they have begun to twist you already, Arxoras my father, my friend! They will make you their friend with lies!"

"Is this worse than making me their enemy with lies?" the patriarch asked quietly, his wide silver eyes fixing themselves on Yarblis's immense yellow ones. Helen, seeing the small uneasy shifts in the musculature of the Ghost Walker's lined, sunken face, shivered, recognizing every fleet, delicate expression, every habitual twitch. For a moment she thought she was going to throw up, and turned away, cold and sickened with the depth of the recognition.

"They are . . . our enemies," Yarblis said. "They are

. . . the enemies of life. They will make us the enemies of life."

"What is life?" Arxoras asked slowly. "And why is life? Will they be greater enemies of life than one who would destroy life so that his opinion might triumph?"

"Only . . . only some life. Not all life . . ." Yarblis whispered desperately. "It was necessary . . ."

"These aliens . . ." The long, skeletal arm gestured with a beautiful sweeping motion toward the dust-coated forms of the two Vulcans, the emaciated little Argellian, the tiny old Chinese, and the Andorian half asleep with exhaustion between the two Klingons who carried him gently toward his hut. "These aliens have worked with us in the saving of lives of our families at Walpuk, searching far out into the distant ends of the warren where the licats had begun to hunt when the protection of the Consciousness Web failed, risking the illness itself, which could have killed them as surely as it was killing all those others."

"The Consciousness Web . . ."

"The Consciousness Web was not strong enough to combat this illness," Arxoras went on. "The Consciousness Web had held for days, and yet they died, and more and more died, and the vermin and the licats had begun to hunt through the warrens and take the sick and the dying." On the end of his round-sectioned neck, his head was tilted to one side, his eyes compassionate with pain as he looked upon the hunter, the friend, the brother/son he had loved. In the dusty stillness of the late afternoon, only the skreeking of the scarlet lizards could be heard in the thorn jungle around them—the soft humming of the web that had filled the air had ceased a short time before.

"Yarblis, what were you going to bring back to the Consciousness Web with you? You are *memmietieff* enough to have hidden the things you did, yes, so not to have polluted the web . . . so as not to have anyone know that what you told them of the destruction of this warren was a lie. But you would have brought lying into the web. And what you would not have hidden, because it did not occur to you that it was something that should be hidden, would have been your conviction that it was right to lie to us all for what you yourself considered good. That it was right to deceive us all, for what you yourself considered good. That it was right to kill, for what you yourself considered good. That it was right to make your concept of good—which might indeed *be* good, or might not, but you cannot know that—the rule by which we must all live, will we so or not.

"You did evil, that great good might come. And the evil that you wanted to do among us, to us, was greater still, and greater than you know, for these Hungries"— he nodded toward the door of the hut through which the Klingons had taken Nomias—"are dangerous, and would have taken fearful steps against us . . . Though perhaps you would have come to want that too."

And Yarblis looked away.

"You thought you had the right," Arxoras went on softly. *"That* is the seed of all evil. And so it is . . ." The deep folds of the patriarch's face, each lined with pale dust, contracted, and his great eyes filled with tears. "So it is, Yarblis my son, that I cast you out of the Consciousness Web. No one in the warren will turn against you, you will never lack for food, nor for a place to live, nor for a place of protection, for that is not something that we can do. But you are dirty with a dirtiness that would spread throughout the web, even as you feared that the dirtiness of wanting the life of one another more than the life of Rhea would spread among us. And for that, no more will the web have you. No more will you be our sibling. No more will any of us speak to you, or let you touch our minds, or our dreams, ever again."

For a moment Yarblis Geshkerroth stood in the midst of them—the aliens, and the several other patriarchs who had gone with the aliens down to Walpuk when the strength of the web had proved insufficient to the strength of the famine and the plague. "I did it for you," he whispered.

And Helen, looking back at him, saw him for the first time clearly in the sunlight, saw the huge extent of the disruptor scars that covered his chest and arms, that had blotched his scalp and caused the long hair that lay braided down over his ridgy back to be streaked with ashy gray; saw the passion and the weariness in his yellow eyes, the fierce strength of his lined face down which tears tracked like a river, glinting in the molten light. Arxoras held out a hand to touch him, but the Ghost Walker stepped back and turned away, waddling slowly past the tall aliens around him and out of the clearing, passing without sound or stirring of branches into the thorn forest beyond.

Kailin Arxoras turned back to Helen and, reaching up, took her soft, baby hand in his strong one. "Come," he said, and she saw that tears, too, streaked the dust on all his many facefolds as if he had stood in rain. "We must go now and heal your friend."

Dr. McCoy grumbled surprisingly little about shutting down the lights in the convalescent ward where they took Kirk after removing him from the stasis chamber—evidently, Helen thought, he had been thinking over what had taken place in the machine room and its relationship to the needs of the less-known side of the human organism. Gunner's Assistant Barrows's cache of candles was raided again—their soft glow gently illuminated the room where Kailin Arxoras, surprisingly calm for one who had never seen so much as a wheel before in his life, sat beside the bed, holding the captain's icy hand and singing softly in his high-pitched, birdlike voice. Now and then voices would pass in the hall, the muted murmur of the ship returning to normal.

"We can take him to a soundproof room," McCoy

offered to the little alien, but Arxoras had shaken his head.

"He needs to hear the sounds of his beloved as she breathes in her sleep," the old Midgwin replied, tilting his flat head a little to peer up into the doctor's face. "Among my people we would have flowers, and grasses, and grains in the room to help with the healing, that the dreamer may smell them and so be encouraged to return. But the smells of such things are less to him than the smells of . . ." The brow ridges folded a little deeper as he tried to identify what the ship *did* smell like. Metal and thin green vilfadge carpeting and recycled oxygen, McCoy picked out, when he thought about them . . . and, in this place, disinfectant and alcohol. But at length the old Midgwin only shook his head and concluded, ". . . the smells of this place. But have his friends here with him, that he may know them, and come back."

And so it was that Helen, and Mr. Spock, and Uhura, and Scotty were in the room when James Kirk opened his eyes and blinked uncertainly up at the ceiling in the semidark. For a moment he only lay, a slight frown of puzzlement creasing his brow, as if trying to remember. Then he turned his head a little, first to one side, where Arxoras sat on one of the tall-legged chairs designed to bring short aliens up to the height of things on a human-crewed starship, then to the other, where McCoy sat, holding his other hand.

"Bones?" he said softly, wondering why the physical touch, the warmth of flesh and the solidity of bone, was so deeply reassuring. The transporter . . .

But the thought eluded him.

McCoy nodded. "You'll be all right, Jim."

Carefully he disengaged his hand and reached out. "Helen?"

She took his fingers, warm now and strong in hers. Her face was expressionless and very white, but in the dimness, in his exhaustion, he only saw that she was with him. He smiled, profoundly relieved. His memories of what had happened to him were dim and chaotic, a confusion of images—a blurred recollection that something had happened to Helen, something terrible . . . something from which he had tried desperately to save her. An image, fragmentary but very clear, of Spock lying unconscious before the sealed doors of the shuttlecraft deck with the red warning lights blinking wildly across his body. A vague curiosity about whether he really had crawled through the food conveyor from Deck 8, and if so, why in the galaxy he'd done it . . . A nagging sense of wondering something about a secret room on Deck 23.

He had a dreamlike sense that reminded him of his old Academy acquaintance Finnegan's descriptions of having been extremely drunk—only Kirk had never been so drunk in his life that he couldn't remember what he'd done. Already it was fading, losing its reality . . .

"Spock?"

"Present, Captain," the Vulcan replied formally. After a moment's hesitation, Spock stepped forward and took his hand. "I am . . ." Spock hesitated again, not quite sure what it would be proper form to say, then concluded, "I am gratified to see you well."

Kirk's laugh was no more than a whisper and a lightening of his eyes. "I am overwhelmed, Mr. Spock." And then, as suddenly as the extinguishing of a candle flame, he dropped into sleep again.

"He will sleep for a long time now," Arxoras said, climbing carefully, with Chapel's help, down from the chair. "Half a day, perhaps. Good sleep. I feel within his mind that this body of his has had little. It was cruelly used, and his spirit also. You will find there are things he does not remember from his time of wandering, for such memories will have no place in the flesh to lodge, and will have been lost. Some only may come back to him later. Then you must help him deal with them as best you may. You are his siblings, his nest brothers. His healing is with you."

"You speak as if this were something you've dealt with before," McCoy said doubtfully, and the Midgwin cocked his head again, his long, dusty white braids tangling across his shoulders, to look up at him.

"I have," he said simply, and thereby opened a new chapter to Federation studies, not only of the Midgwins, but of the structure and composition of the mind.

In the corner of the room Mr. Scott was questioning Spock in a low voice about the ultimate fate of his assistant Ensign Miller—now in the next ward recovering, along with his opprobrious partner, from the throes of their peculiar virus. "Well, you've got to admit that when all's said, all they were doin' was trying to make decent chocolate—for which God knows there's enough people on board who'd thank them."

"The fact remains that they appropriated Starfleet property for their own use, for whatever purpose. Neither of them was authorized to operate an experimental laboratory, much less to—"

"And no worse than what Dr. McCoy did, puttin' the pair of 'em under hatches wi'out so much as a by-your-leave . . . You're no' going to clap that poor laddie Gilden in irons, are you? You'd be dead yoursel' if it wasn't for his book collection."

Silently, Lieutenant Uhura slipped out the door into the bright lights of the corridor. None saw her go, any more than they had seen Helen leave a moment before.

"Helen?"

She was leaning against the wall of the main corridor of sickbay. Her face was chalky and she looked almost worse than she had after she'd been gassed.

"What is it?" Uhura asked.

And Helen shook her head and smiled. "Nothing," she said. She started to turn away, then paused, and looked back at her friend—tall and coffee-dark and beautiful in her crimson uniform, one of the closest of the first group of close friends she had made in her life. After a moment she came back and took her hands.

"Uhura," she said softly, "will you tell Jim something for me when he wakes up?"

Uhura was silent, looking into the other woman's face. An older face than she'd had when she came on board the *Enterprise* a month ago; ravaged, as her voice had been ravaged. According to McCoy, the scarring on the vocal cords would heal in a few weeks. From her own experience, Uhura guessed that the look in the back of those hazel eyes never would.

"Anything you want," she replied.

"Tell him . . ." Helen paused, and shook her head, as if trying to clear away something—a dream, maybe, or a nightmare. "Tell him I understand that it . . . it wasn't him. That it was an alien that had taken over his body, that it wasn't his fault . . . that he has nothing to do with what happened. And maybe in six months, when the *Enterprise* is back—if it doesn't get rerouted elsewhere —or maybe in a year, I'll . . . my stomach, my guts, my skin will believe it, if I should happen to see his face, or hear his voice, or feel his hand touch me. Tell him I know it wasn't him. But right now . . ." She forced her voice steady. "I can't look at him anymore."

"I'll tell him," Uhura said.

Helen embraced her quickly, then turned and walked away, heading for the turbolift that would take her down to the hangar deck to wait for Arxoras, and thence, by shuttlecraft, back to the world that would become her own. Uhura stood for a long time beside the sickbay door, listening as the click of boot heels died away along the corridor.

After that the patriarchs of the many warrens united in Web to speak among themselves of the question of healing that the physicians of the Hungries had raised; and whether they should be asked to go away and never return. The Hungries themselves, both the dark-bearded Hungries and the pale Hungries with smooth faces, swore that if they were permitted to remain, they would only live among themselves and learn the stories of the Real People and talk to them about the way of Rhea.

As for Yarblis Geshkerroth the Ghost Walker, on the second night after the ending of the plague, he went to the hut of the woman Helen and asked her pardon for having hurt her, both in her body, and in her voice, and in her mind. This pardon being given, he went out of the Bindigo Warren, and away from the places where people dwelled, and casting himself in the river, was drowned.

From *Songs of the Midgwins,* translated and introduced by Dr. H. H. Gordon, Oxford University Press.

THE STAR TREK PHENOMENON

___ ABODE OF LIFE 70596/$4.50
___ BATTLESTATIONS! 70183/$4.50
___ BLACK FIRE 70548/$4.50
___ BLOODTHIRST 70876/$4.50
___ CORONA 70798/$4.50
___ CHAIN OF ATTACK 66658/$3.95
___ THE COVENANT OF THE CROWN 70078/$4.50
___ CRISIS ON CENTAURUS 70799/$4.50
___ CRY OF THE ONLIES 740789/$4.95
___ DEEP DOMAIN 70549/$4.50
___ DEMONS 70877/$4.50
___ DOCTOR'S ORDERS 66189/$4.50
___ DOUBLE, DOUBLE 66130/$3.95
___ DREADNOUGHT 72567/$4.50
___ DREAMS OF THE RAVEN 70281/$4.50
___ DWELLERS IN THE CRUCIBLE 74147/$4.95
___ ENEMY UNSEEN 68403/$4.50
___ ENTERPRISE 73032/$4.95
___ ENTROPY EFFECT 72416/$4.50
___ FINAL FRONTIER 69655/$4.95
___ THE FINAL NEXUS 74148/$4.95
___ THE FINAL REFLECTION 70764/$4.50
___ A FLAG FULL OF STARS 64398/$4.95
___ HOME IS THE HUNTER 66662/$4.50
___ HOW MUCH FOR JUST THE PLANET? 72214/$4.50
___ IDIC EPIDEMIC 70768/$4.50
___ ISHMAEL 73587/$4.50
___ KILLING TIME 70597/$4.50
___ KLINGON GAMBIT 70767/$4.50
___ THE KOBAYASHI MARU 65817/$4.50
___ LOST YEARS 70795/$4.95
___ MEMORY PRIME 70550/$4.50
___ MINDSHADOW 70420/$4.50
___ MUTINY ON THE ENTERPRISE 70800/$4.50
___ MY ENEMY, MY ALLY 70421/$4.50
___ PAWNS AND SYMBOLS 66497/$3.95
___ PROMETHEUS DESIGN 72366/$4.50
___ ROMULAN WAY 70169/$4.50
___ RULES OF ENGAGEMENT 66129/$4.50
___ SHADOW LORD 73746/$4.95
___ SPOCK'S WORLD 66773/$4.95

more on next page...

THE

STAR TREK

PHENOMENON

____	**STRANGERS FROM THE SKY**	65913/$4.50
____	**THE TEARS OF THE SINGERS**	69654/$4.50
____	**TIME FOR YESTERDAY**	70094/$4.50
____	**THE TRELLISANE CONFRONTATION**	70095/$4.50
____	**TRIANGLE**	66251/$3.95
____	**UHURA'S SONG**	65227/$3.95
____	**VULCAN ACADEMY MURDERS**	72367/$4.50
____	**VULCAN'S GLORY**	74291/$4.95
____	**WEB OF THE ROMULANS**	70093/$4.50
____	**WOUNDED SKY**	66735/$3.95
____	**YESTERDAY'S SON**	72449/$4.50

● ● ● ● ● ● ● ● ● ● ● ● ● ● ● ● ● ● ●

____	**STAR TREK– THE MOTION PICTURE**	72300/$4.50
____	**STAR TREK II– THE WRATH OF KHAN**	74149/$4.95
____	**STAR TREK III–THE SEARCH FOR SPOCK**	67198/$3.95
____	**STAR TREK IV– THE VOYAGE HOME**	70283/$4.50
____	**STAR TREK V– THE FINAL FRONTIER**	68008/$4.50
____	**STAR TREK: THE KLINGON DICTIONARY**	66648/$4.95
____	**STAR TREK COMPENDIUM REVISED** 68440/$10.95	
____	**MR. SCOTT'S GUIDE TO THE ENTERPRISE** 70498/$12.95	
____	**THE STAR TREK INTERVIEW BOOK** 61794/$7.95	

POCKET BOOKS

Simon & Schuster Mail Order Dept. STP
200 Old Tappan Rd., Old Tappan, N.J. 07675

Please send me the books I have checked above. I am enclosing $_____ (please add 75¢ to cover postage and handling for each order. Please add appropriate local sales tax). Send check or money order—no cash or C.O.D.'s please. Allow up to six weeks for delivery. For purchases over $10.00 you may use VISA: card number, expiration date and customer signature must be included.

Name _____

Address _____

City _____ State/Zip _____

VISA Card No. _____ Exp. Date _____

Signature _____ 113-33

Follow the adventures of the Starship *Enterprise* by beaming aboard Paramount Pictures' Official *STAR TREK* Fan Club. When you join, you receive a one year subscription to the full-color Official *STAR TREK* Fan Club Magazine filled with exclusive interviews, articles, and photos on both the original *STAR TREK* and *STAR TREK: THE NEXT GENERATION.* Plus special columns on *STAR TREK* collecting, novels and special events as well as a convention listing and readers' comments. Members also receive with each issue our special merchandise insert filled with all the latest *STAR TREK* memorabilia.

Join now and receive an exclusive membership kit including an 8 x 10 full-color photo, embroidered jacket patch, membership card and more!

Don't miss out on another issue of The Official *STAR TREK* Fan Club Magazine. Join now! It's the logical thing to do.

Membership for one year — $9.95-US, $12.00-Canada, $21.95-Foreign for one year (US dollars only!)

Send check, money order or MasterCard/Visa order to:

STAR TREK: THE OFFICIAL FAN CLUB
P.O. Box 111000
Aurora, Colorado 80011 USA

©1989 Paramount Pictures. All Rights Reserved. *STAR TREK* is a Registered Trademark of Paramount Pictures.